AGE

of

CONSENT

AGE

of

CONSENT

· · · · · · · · · · ·

Amanda Brainerd

VIKING

VIKING

An imprint of Penguin Random House LLC
penguinrandomhouse.com

LIBRARY OF CONGRESS CATALOGING-IN-PUBLICATION DATA
Names: Brainerd, Amanda, author.
Title: Age of consent: a novel / Amanda Brainerd.
Description: New York: Viking, 2020. |
Identifiers: LCCN 2019042729 (print) | LCCN 2019042730 (ebook) |
ISBN 9781984879523 (hardcover) | ISBN 9781984879530 (ebook)
Subjects: CYAC: Coming of age—Fiction. | Friendship—Fiction. |
Sex—Fiction. | Boarding schools—Fiction. | Schools—Fiction. |
New York (N.Y.)—History—20th century—Fiction.
Classification: LCC PZ7.1.B745 Ag 2020 (print) | LCC PZ7.1.B745 (ebook) |
DDC [Fic]—dc23
LC record available at https://lccn.loc.gov/2019042729
LC ebook record available at https://lccn.loc.gov/2019042730

Printed in the United States of America
1 3 5 7 9 10 8 6 4 2

BOOK DESIGN BY LUCIA BERNARD

For Chip

PART

one

ONE

"LET ME OUT," JUSTINE SAID.

"It's only a hundred yards to the dorm," her father replied.

"Stop the car!"

Miles pulled the wheezing orange Volvo onto the shoulder, and Justine surveyed the Griswold campus through the bug-spewn windshield. Manicured lawns with a mix of brick and clapboard clustered around a quad they called "the Green."

"Lugging that heavy suitcase is a lot more embarrassing than showing up in the rust mobile," he said.

"Oxygen," she said, opening the door and hauling her suitcase out of the back seat.

"Honey?"

He needed a shave and his eyes were moist with tears. "Don't forget . . ." he trailed off.

"I won't!" She shut the door and began walking across the lawn.

Don't forget what? Now the suitcase was making ugly divots in the perfect grass. She glanced around to see whether anyone noticed, but nobody was there.

Justine arrived in front of the dorm, sweating. She blew a wave of hair out of her face. A few weeks ago, sitting at their kitchen table in New Haven, her mother had pushed aside the toast crumbs and dirty teacups to read the letter describing Justine's new roommate, pausing here and there for dramatic emphasis.

"Tierney Worthington, 234 Victory Gardens, Moodus, Connecticut," Cressida had mused. "Moodus, how unusual. Not the predicted Greenwich or Darien?"

Justine fought the urge to snatch the letter back.

"Maybe Griswold isn't so homogenous after all," Cressida continued. "More than just heiresses and tennis champions."

"Don't count on it," Miles grunted, frowning over his glasses.

The dorm was a small colonial house with a columned porch. Justine saw several similar quaint houses around the Green with harried parents unpacking trunks in front of them.

As she hauled her suitcase up the steps, a silver car pulled in, a chrome panther leaping from its hood. A man in Bermuda shorts opened the trunk and heaved a suitcase onto the gravel.

"Tierney, exactly what did you pack? Rocks?"

A Tretorn sneaker appeared from the back seat, followed by a pretty, freckled girl with a ponytail.

Justine trudged up the steps and opened the door.

A living room off the stair hall had two sofas, a framed impressionist poster, and aggressively floral wallpaper. The carpet was hunter green, worn down from years of Tretorns, Justine thought, looking down at her pointy hot pink flats. She'd bought them at a thrift shop in New Haven, and until seconds ago they had seemed so cool. Now she realized they were trashy and cheap.

She climbed the stairs and found her room. It was cramped, with wooden bunk beds and matching dressers. At some point it must have been a real bedroom, Justine realized, as she noticed the wainscoting and the paneled doors. A dormer window framed the lawn. It could be charming, if only her mother were here to work her magic.

Tierney and her father were arguing in the hall.

Would she and Tierney undress in front of each other? Despite the features she hated, short legs and big nose, Justine had perfect breasts, and anyone who had ever seen them (five boys and one full-grown man) agreed. She unpacked her teddy bear, Henry, and set him down on the bottom bunk. The view from the top would make her dizzy.

Her roommate appeared, narrowing her eyes as her father struggled through the door with a suitcase. An errant piece of iron-gray hair was hanging down his sweaty forehead. He stuck out his hand. "Whit Worthington. You must be Justine." His grip mashed her knuckle joints together. "Where are your parents?"

"My dad had to take off."

"And miss Family Orientation Day?" He set the suitcase down and looked around.

"They have to work."

"Don't we all," he said, smoothing his hair back into place.

"This room is disgusting," Tierney said.

The pictures had been deceiving, Justine had to admit. Hadn't there been a photo somewhere of white bedspreads and flowers in a vase?

"And I have two more suitcases."

"Couldn't you have brought less?" Mr. Worthington said, rubbing his elbow.

Tierney stared her father down like a snake until he left the room. The same lime-green eyes now assessed Justine. "I'm Tierney. Nice shoes," she said. "Where'd you get them?"

"New Haven."

Tierney opened her clutch, pulled out a lip gloss, and applied it. "Does your father teach at Yale? What's his name?" She dropped the tube in the purse and closed the bamboo clasp.

"Miles. He runs a theater."

It took Tierney a moment to process this information. "Oh! Maybe I'll check it out when I'm enrolled. Loads of Worthingtons went to Yale," she added.

Tierney spotted Justine's stuffed bear. "No, wait, I have to have the bottom bunk."

"I'll barf if I have to sleep up there," Justine pleaded.

"I have acrophobia. You know, fear of heights." Tierney threw her clutch on the lower mattress.

Justine moved Henry to the top bunk. His button eyes stared down at her forlornly.

"Is that all you have?" Tierney asked, pointing to Justine's suitcase.

Justine nodded, suddenly anxious to get outside. "See you in a bit, I'm going for a butt."

"A what?"

"Um, a cigarette."

Tierney looked aghast. "What kind of parents would give their kid permission to smoke?"

Justine's parents, that's who.

Justine had filled out the permission forms herself, checking off "yes" for everything. Her father had signed without reading them. *Yes, you can smoke, yes, you can stay home alone while we go to England, yes, you can stay out all night drinking and puke on our front steps, yes, you can lose your virginity in our bed.*

"I'd never, ever, ever smoke," Tierney continued. "Daddy's a plastic surgeon. He says when you cut people open you can tell if they smoke by how their blood congeals."

Justine walked across the sloping avenue that bisected the campus. It was a cloudless day, and a breeze rustled through the maples. Her parents were firm believers in public education, and in theory, she was too. But the day after her friend Raoul overdosed on heroin in the boy's bathroom, she'd called Griswold and requested an application. An envelope arrived a week later, enclosing a glossy brochure. The cover bore a coat of arms with the school's motto, "Incipit Vita Nova," which Cressida proudly translated as "Here Begins New Life." Reading the course catalog, Justine felt a thrill of possibility—an entire semester on Faulkner, another on Emily Dickinson.

She was accepted with a full scholarship. At home, heated discussion ensued. Justine worried about keeping up with the wealthy kids. She wasn't concerned about the boys; boys were something she did well. But the money. She barely had enough to buy a soda. But all her parents could fret about was their daughter being corrupted by privilege. In the end, despite her parents' misgivings and her own, Justine enrolled.

An old friend from New Haven who had gone to Griswold had described townies roaring through in Camaros, chucking flaming beer cans and screaming, "Gas the Geeks!" The pristine campus was indeed a sharp contrast with Wormley, the sorrowful town that surrounded it. Justine didn't blame the townies for resenting this idyllic world.

She walked along lush playing fields, the white goalposts gleaming against the cerulean sky. Around the back of a brick athletic building were trash cans and discarded athletic gear. Next to this was a sandy patch with a few wooden benches and airport-style ashtrays. She saw a boy in a long trench coat, boom box on his shoulder, swaying like a cobra. Another boy, a jock, balanced a girl on his lap who was blowing smoke rings.

Down the bench sat a girl with lanky legs stretched out in the dirt. Calculatedly sloppy, Justine thought, but everything she wore, from the soft leather of her jacket to the polished toe of her combat boots, looked expensive.

Was Justine the only scholarship student here?

"Do you have a light?" Justine asked her.

The girl looked up from under a tangle of dark hair and chucked matches at Justine, who just managed to catch them.

"What's the Cat Club?" Justine asked, looking at the matchbook.

"Nightclub in the city. A.k.a. the Litter Box." The girl pulled a package of tobacco from her motorcycle jacket. Placing a pinch in the crease of a rolling paper, she fashioned a cigarette that looked like a joint.

Her fingernails were painted cobalt blue.

Justine glanced back at the blond jock, admiring the sharp arc of his cheekbone and the curve of his lats, visible through his T-shirt in all their masculine glory.

The girl leaned toward Justine. "Bruce Underwood," she whispered, "and yeah, he's a hunk of burning love."

Clearly, she needed to be much less obvious when interested in a boy. "I'm Justine Rubin."

"Ah ha! Fellow member of the tribe. I'm Eve Straus." Eve made quote marks with her fingers. "Diversity."

"Yeah, I'm rooming with Miss Country Club."

Eve smiled. "Lot of those around here. I got Tabitha the Texan. She's already put up tacky animal posters. You know that one with the kitten dangling from a branch that says 'Hang in there, baby'?"

"Please say you're making that up."

"I wish!" Eve flicked her cigarette in the dust.

The boy in the trench spun in a circle, ear to the boom box.

Bruce was braiding the girl's hair.

"How do you know that guy?"

Eve started rolling another cigarette. "I got into that special art studio that started Tuesday, so I've figured a few things out, like who the hot guys are."

Art studio? Justine hadn't seen that in the brochures. Maybe they didn't offer it to the scholarship students.

"I should have stayed in Paris." Eve sighed, and Justine could just imagine her at a café table behind dark sunglasses, cigarette smoke curling over the boulevard.

"The only place I've been in Europe is England," Justine said.

One summer her parents had traveled to London, her father looking for new plays for his theater. They rented a National Trust cottage in the Cotswolds and brought Justine along. She loved that time—the AGA stove, the rain streaking down the leaded-glass windows, the narrow streets of the stony village. There was no television and no radio, and they had spent hours on a picture puzzle of a unicorn under a waterfall.

"I hate England," Eve said. "Rains nonstop. The food sucks."

"Yeah," Justine agreed, even though her parents had cooked at the house to save money. "I could barely eat a thing. I was so skinny when I came back."

"You're so frigging skinny now!"

"I think she's a fox." The blond god materialized in front of them, cocking his head at Justine. She felt her face flush.

He sat on the bench between them.

"I'm Bruce."

Justine fought to find her voice. "Justine."

"Sophomore?"

She nodded.

"You spoken for?"

She shook her head. Boys did not usually fluster her.

"Cool. I'll drop by sometime," Bruce said, with a confident nod. Justine watched him go.

"Like how he just assumed we knew who he was, and where you live." Suddenly Eve jumped up. "Oh fuck." She dropped her cigarette and dashed around the other side of the building.

A bearded teacher with a clipboard headed over with long strides. "Name?"

"Justine Rubin."

He looked down at her with cool gray eyes, then checked his clipboard.

"Would I be correct in assuming we have a signed smoking form?"

"Yes."

He checked the clipboard again, running his finger up and down, flipping through the pages. Justine began to fear that the permission slip had gotten lost in the mail.

"Ah, yes, Rubin," he finally said, a tinge of disappointment in his voice. "Sophomore. See you first thing tomorrow in class. English, as in the language." He strode off.

Justine sank down on the bench and pulled out another cigarette, but realized that Eve had taken the matches. The Litter Box? A *nightclub*? How divine. Justine tried to imagine growing up in the city like Eve—the museums and restaurants and clubs. Someday she would live there, she thought, digging into her schoolbag for another pack of matches. She found some tucked into her copy of Baudelaire. The book was a treasure, clothbound in black with faded gold lettering. She read "Spleen" for the umpteenth time. Justine loved the line about the hearses passing by, slowly, in his soul. How many times had she fallen prey to the same ennui?

When Justine looked up at the playing field, she realized that the teacher must have frightened everyone away except for that strange boy, still twirling with his boom box. She watched him sway. He was tall and lanky, with fair, fine hair. With the speaker pressed to his ear his eyes slipped closed in ecstasy—no wonder, she thought, recognizing Bowie's "Rock 'n' Roll Suicide." *Oh no, love, you're not alone!*

"Hey!" she called, standing up and walking over.

His eyes opened, bulging and pale. He stared at her, without focus, and tilted his head closer to the speaker. *I'll help you with the paaaaain!*

She tugged at his sleeve.

"Are you tripping?"

He turned his back, shimmying out into the field.

She followed him.

The song ended with an abrupt stroke of strings. He whipped around. "Bowie's my drug."

"I'm Justine." She stuck out her hand.

"I don't touch people. Your parents fans of Sade?"

"Who?"

"The Marquis de Sade. He wrote a book called *Justine*. About S and M."

She shook her head, wondering if Miles and Cressida had named her that on purpose. It would be just like them.

"I have it in my room. You can borrow it."

His stare was as intense as a religious zealot's. She could see the backs of his eyeballs.

"What's your name?"

"Stanley." There was a slight twang in his voice. He looked down at the grass under his tattered sneaker, held together by duct tape.

"Where're you from?"

"Oklahoma. I'm a stranger from a strange land."

TWO

EVE STRAUS HURRIED FROM THE SMOKER TOWARD THE Bradley Arts Center. *Justine Rubin.* Maybe they could be friends. She looked like a fairy-tale version of Virginia Woolf. A rarefied kind of beauty, and maybe too particular for high school boys to observe. But then again, Bruce had pounced in two seconds.

Griswold. Eve recalled the fateful conversation she'd had with her parents, driving to the beach just a few blissful months ago.

"I'm not going back to Beaverton!" Eve had blurted out as her mother steered the car onto Montauk Highway. Her father turned around to stare at her in surprise. Her brother, Sandy, was blasting music on his Walkman, oblivious, gazing at the passing pines.

"What are you talking about?"

Eve tried to breathe. "Sorry, that came out wrong," she stammered. "I can't go back there, it's . . ." She began to cry. Her father looked at her in confusion, while her mother stared stonily at the highway. Eve had been miserable at her all-girls school, but once she had realized it, the truth seemed obvious. She managed to calm herself enough to talk. "I hate Beaverton, they've got me in a corner . . ." Eve glanced out the window at a passing Winnebago, and back into her father's bewildered face. "You try staying in a tiny all-girls school for your whole life!"

Frederick turned to Eve's mother. "What about Griswold?"

Deirdre pursed her lips.

Boarding school? Frederick had gone to Griswold, and Eve had visited once. She recalled an imposing modern-arts complex, green fields, athletes. It was idyllic, terrifying, and perfect. Why had she not thought of it herself?

"I'm not sure we have the pull," her mother said sotto voce.

Eve rolled her eyes. Of course her parents had the pull. Eve suddenly remembered that her childhood friend Clayton Bradley's family had donated that arts center to the school. She also recalled that Clayton's mother was a well-known painter—Eve's mother talked about her work with reverence.

"I'll make a call in the a.m.," Frederick growled. Go, Dad, Eve had thought. Nobody was going to tell him he couldn't get his kid into Griswold in September, certainly not his wife. Not even if it was already the middle of June.

Now here she was.

Eve mentally listed the reasons she had wanted to leave New York. Yes, she had felt trapped at Beaverton. The teachers were practically nuns and she had to wear an itchy wool kilt and a white blouse with puffy sleeves. It was like a fancy jail—the twenty-seven girls in her class even got their periods at the same time, like a stable of mares. And nobody could deny that Griswold was beautiful, with elegant Georgian buildings, big maple trees, and boys. Still, Eve had not expected the campus to be overrun with New England preppies wielding lacrosse sticks. Sweats were for sports, she felt like pointing out, not dinner. People frowned at Eve in her combat boots like she was a specimen in a jar.

In the city you were cool if you wore black and went to films with subtitles. Here you were a weirdo.

Eve spotted a familiar face heading toward her, Clayton Bradley himself.

"Hey! When did you get here?"

"A week ago," Eve said, gesturing at the arts center. "Painting studio."

"Oh great," he frowned, "next you'll turn out like my mother."

"You grow up to be my parents, I'll grow up to be yours."

"Grass is always greener," Clayton said, heading off with a wave. "Welcome to Griswold!"

Eve's parents were art collectors, but Eve had decided long ago that she would be different. She wouldn't buy art; she would make it. She would be a painter, and although perhaps not as famous as Clay's mother, Barbara, at least she'd create rather than just acquire.

Eve's boots squeaked on the concrete floor. She could see her canvas from the door. She had not dreamed it; her perspective was off.

She dropped her schoolbag beside the easel and stared at her painting. Leaning her head to one side she squinted at it, picked up her brush, and took a step back.

"Hi, cookie."

David McClurken was right behind her in his motorcycle jacket.

"Want to borrow my burnt umber?"

Damn. He could tell she was botching the painting.

But his expression was earnest.

"I should just start over."

"Not at all, it's really close." David pointed at the huge insect on the canvas. "The cockroach's shell is tilted. Painting ovals in perspective is really hard. Mind if I give you a tip?"

Eve handed him her brush. David made a few quick strokes on

the huge bug. Within moments it looked much better. He pointed at the spine of the painted book. "Don't worry about getting the lettering just right, leave a little to mystery." He grinned and handed back the brush.

"Thank you." She wanted to touch his dark curls.

"You're really improving."

Eve resisted the urge to disagree. It wasn't David's fault he was so talented.

"For you," he said, handing her an index card and a small brown paper bag. Before she could thank him again he moved to his easel.

David, in his black jeans and Joy Division T-shirt, didn't blend in here either—side by side she and David would look like a pair of bats.

Eve turned the index card over. A spidery, elegant handwritten poem, in what looked like German. David took German? She'd known him only a few days, but already he struck her as a hopeless romantic. Eve put the card in her schoolbag and walked over to him. His canvas was abstract, with muted smeary black shapes on a gray background. It was good, really good.

"Thanks for your help," Eve said. "See you at dinner?"

· · · · · · · · ·

Tierney was in the Claverly common room, giggling with a few friends. None of them looked up as Justine walked past.

She went upstairs and opened the closet. Every hanger was full of Tierney's clothes. Cotton shirtdresses, tailored button-downs, and cable-knit sweaters.

Justine remembered reading the Griswold packing list in horror. So many items, so few of which she had.

Even now, her face burned remembering shopping with her

mother. It had been a steaming hot day and the air-conditioning in the Volvo had been broken for years, but Justine fiddled with the controls in hope, the way she always did. Cressida ignored her. Finally, Justine gave up and rolled down the window, hot air sweeping through the car like a sirocco.

When they arrived at Goodwill, Cressida threw open the door, and they were greeted with an arctic blast. Her mother immediately strode toward the women's section.

Normally Justine loved a thrift shop, but unlike her favorite, Time Turns, Goodwill had the smell of decay and sadness. Justine headed to the men's section. She chose a few vintagey-looking plaid shirts and a camel overcoat that had retained some of its genteel style. Then she went to find her mother.

Cressida had several dresses over one arm.

"The packing list doesn't say I need a dress," Justine said, as Cressida pulled out a flowery ankle-length piece and held it aloft. It looked like the kind of thing a folk singer would wear while strumming a guitar.

"Isn't this divine? It would have been wonderful with your long hair." Her mother gazed wistfully at the garment.

Last week Justine had chopped off her lovely blond tresses in favor of a trendy short do that was long on one side and short on the other. "Mom, it's *my* hair."

"As you have taken pains to demonstrate."

Tierney had jammed her several suitcases of clothes into both bureaus, leaving only two drawers empty. Still, they were enough for Justine's pathetic secondhand wardrobe.

Getting to her feet she spotted Tierney's striped makeup kit. She poked her head out the door of their room and shot a furtive glance down the hall. Deserted.

Just a quick peek. The bag was on her side of the bureau anyway. She unzipped it to find a regular pharmacy of orange bottles: diazepam, ranitidine, and acyclovir. Three roller-ball lip glosses in glass tubes, a palette of sky-blue eye shadow, and a bottle of Lauren perfume. Justine had always longed for that fragrance. She spritzed her wrists, and again behind her ears. At the sound of giggles in the hall, she quickly closed the bag.

At suppertime, Justine walked across the footbridge that spanned the gorge separating Lower and Upper campus. Ferns waved from below, tall birches clustered next to the railing. She heard footsteps behind her and turned to see Stanley, wearing a jacket covered in black ostrich feathers. Moth-eaten, it was like something from the costume closet of her father's theater. Maybe Cressida hadn't been completely mistaken, Stanley was about as far from a tennis champion as Justine could imagine.

He handed her a book. *Justine, or the Misfortunes of Virtue.*

She thanked him, and stuffed it quickly in her bag. They walked in silence, Stanley's feathers billowing in the breeze.

In contrast to the classic Georgian architecture of Lower, the buildings in this part of the school were asymmetrical concrete lumps from the seventies. "Pods for living and learning," the brochure had read. Now they had cracks in the walls, and on the side of one someone had graffitied "MORGAN LIVES."

Stanley pushed open the glass doors of the dining hall. "Be there in a sec," Justine said, pausing in the cinder-block vestibule, pretending to tie her shoelace. She spent a moment examining the flyers tacked to a bulletin board: "Bassist Wanted," "Typing by Tina," "Join the Pep Squad!" Once Stanley was gone, Justine walked in.

Scanning the sea of students, she spotted Eve with a group of kids by the massive windows.

Justine got into the line and realized she was behind Stanley.

"Should we sit with the maggots?" he asked, as their trays were filled with bowls of gooey spiral pasta.

"Who?"

"Those kids from New York."

"Maggots?" Justine asked, glancing back into the dining room where she could see Eve speaking to a dark-haired boy, gesticulating.

"From the Big Apple?"

"Stan the Man!" the dark-haired boy called out, as they approached the table. "What's with the getup?"

"Like it?" Stanley asked.

"You look like my grandmother." He held out a hand to Justine. "Clayton Bradley. I go by Clay." His handshake struck her as both oddly formal and charming. "These losers are Christina, Kitty, and Peter. I believe you know Eve. The guy with the headphones is Damon, but don't bother talking to him. He isn't listening."

"Justine," she said. She glanced at Christina, realizing she was the girl on Bruce's lap at the smoker.

"Avoiding the sausage?" Clay pointed at her tray.

"I'm a vegetarian."

"So's my mom. Have you been one long?"

"Ever since I saw the sausage."

Stanley giggled and covered his mouth. He reminded Justine of a boy in her class in public school; an eccentric outcast, he'd been beaten up by a bunch of thugs at school. He returned stitched up like Frankenstein. And the school had done nothing about it. Justine glanced around the room. With its high ceiling and wooden trusses, it reminded her of the barn her parents had renovated in Woodstock. It was impossible to imagine violence in a place like this.

Then Justine saw Bruce, sitting with some beefy jocks. He caught her eye and winked.

She quickly returned to her food but the pasta was barely edible. Next to her, Eve was doodling in a small notebook, sketching something like a spaceship.

Clay stood up. "Anybody want anything? I'm getting milk."

"Some sausage for your girlfriend," Peter said.

Clay ignored him and walked off.

"What's his name again?" she whispered to Eve.

"Who?" Eve looked up from her sketchbook.

"Milk guy."

"Clay Bradley. We grew up together."

Justine asked, "Bradley, as in the Arts Center?" The modern centerpiece of the campus, featured in the brochure.

Eve nodded. "Yep. And it spells FUCK."

"What does?"

"If you look at the building from the smoker, the parts spell FUCK." Eve drew the letters in the air.

Justine decided she needed a closer look.

Clay came back and when he sat down Justine noticed his dark lashes matted against his ivory skin.

"Jesus, did you see Winkler? He's on the warpath," Christina said.

"I did," Stanley said. "He tried to bust me at the smoker."

"Me too," Eve said, shaking the ink in her pen toward the tip.

"Was he the one with the clipboard?" Justine asked.

"He's a god around here. Every sophomore gets him for English," Stanley explained. "He teaches five sections, like an orchestra. He could have taught anywhere; he's brilliant."

"And hot," Christina said.

"Even if he does look like a penis," Eve said, looking up from her drawing.

They all stared at her.

"Here," Eve said, and did a quick sketch. It looked like a mushroom, and then a head began to emerge. "See? The wispy hair, the scrunchy beard."

"Winkler the Wanker," Stanley said.

"I hear he's a tough grader," Clay said.

Justine watched him wipe the milk off his mouth. His lower lip was like a piece of pink candy. He looked up at her.

"I hope I'm in your section."

He was a delicate and lovely creature.

"Hope we all are," Eve agreed.

Just then she saw Tierney passing Bruce's table. Tierney stopped and bent down to talk to him, her wheaty hair brushing his shoulder. Tierney giggled, and rested her hand on Bruce's arm.

Eve nudged Justine, holding out her sketchbook. The mushroom Wanker now had a speech bubble that said "Eat Me."

Justine laughed and glanced back in Bruce's direction, but he was gone.

• • • • • • • •

That evening Eve lay on her bed trying to decipher David's poem. But the German revealed no clues. Who could she ask? Her mother spoke French, her friend India Clarkson was fluent in Italian.

Eve wondered what India was doing tonight in New York. Getting stoned, certainly, but then what?

She turned on her side and stared at Tabitha's side of the dorm room. Tabitha's mother had decorated it, and Eve had to admire the fully tricked-out Texan vibe. There was a lacy beige tablecloth tacked to the wall in loopy folds. Above, Mrs. Sparkman had hung gold-framed posters. The kitten holding on to a branch. Another, a view of a ranch with split-rail fences before a setting sun. The bed was piled high with blankets.

Eve recalled the letter Tabitha had written her over the summer, on scented paper. "Can't wait to meet ya!!! We're gonna be such good friends!!!" Each exclamation mark terminated in a bubble heart. The letter announced her most important details—cheerleader, only child, rodeo fan. And a boyfriend at Griswold, already. A junior. Impressive. Eyeing the twin beds, Eve wondered if she'd have to listen to them fooling around.

· · · · · · · ·

Justine squeezed Close-Up on her toothbrush and looked in the mirror. Being told she was beautiful all of her life still hadn't convinced her. She knew better; she had sex appeal, not beauty. Other girls made boys fall in love with them. Not Justine; boys didn't want her to be their girlfriend, they just wanted to fuck her.

Tierney's reading lamp was on, and she was kneeling next to the bed in a plaid nightgown. What on earth was she doing, Justine wondered, as she climbed up the ladder and got under the covers with her teddy bear. She thought of mentioning the hangers and the bureau drawers, but why bother? She could hear Tierney muttering under her breath, and the bunk bed creak.

"Were you praying?" Justine asked.

"Why do you want to know?"

"Curious."

"Don't you say yours?"

"I'm Jewish."

"That sucks," Tierney said, and clicked off the light.

Justine lay staring at the ceiling, not remotely sleepy. It was only eleven and Justine was used to staying up until two or three. After theater openings, her parents threw big parties. One evening when she was nine she danced with Frank Langella. In the morning Cressida found her sleeping in a ball under the dining room table with lipstick smeared across her face.

"Do you always breathe so loudly?" Tierney asked.

"I have a deviated septum."

"What's that?"

"It's where the bone in the middle of your nose slants. It makes it hard to breathe."

"Is that why you have a bump?"

"No. But if you look at my nose from below, you can see how crooked my nostrils are."

"Let's see," Tierney said, clicking the light back on.

Justine leaned over the edge of the bed.

"Whoa! How do you even breathe?"

Justine slumped back on her pillow. "One day I'll get my nose fixed."

Tierney turned the light off again. "Good, then maybe you won't sound like Amtrak."

THREE

THE CEILING OF MR. WINKLER'S CLASSROOM WAS A HONEY-comb of concrete, with recessed lights set in the squares. Desks were arranged in rows, and by 8:25 Eve was already slouched in the front, legs out, combat boots crossed.

"Aren't you the early bird," Justine said, sliding into a chair.

"Sucking the big slimy worm."

Justine opened the backpack she'd owned since seventh grade. Although it had sentimental value, she couldn't help but gaze longingly at Eve's brand-new one.

People were starting to file in. Clay headed for the back. Even with his hair a mess, he was still cute.

Mr. Winkler arrived and slapped a leather briefcase on the desk. As he turned to the chalkboard Justine looked at his tight corduroy ass.

He wrote, "Robert Winkler, PhD. English 10."

Eve pointed to her notebook where she'd scribbled "Humbert Humbert" just as the teacher turned around.

"Something amusing, Miss . . ."

"Rubin."

"Laugh now, suffer later." He handed Eve a stack of papers. "Take one and pass it."

Justine looked down at the mimeographed page. *Catcher in the Rye*, snooze, she'd read it twice. *Cat's Cradle* by Kurt Vonnegut. Didn't they sell his books in airports? Reading the course catalog, Justine's mother had gloated over how many of the teachers had PhDs. One, Mrs. Tibbets, the editor of the *Griswold Quarterly*, had even published a well-regarded feminist novel and a story in *The New Yorker*. She flipped the page over, searching for the revered classics of English literature. *The Scarlet Letter* and *Romeo and Juliet*. Okay, acceptable.

Eve threw a note in her lap.

In my mind I'm probably the biggest sex maniac you ever met—Holden Caulfield (Just like the Wanker!!!)

"Strike two." Mr. Winkler was over her, holding out a hand.

Justine dropped the paper onto his palm. He read it.

"Who wrote this?" His voice was dangerous.

"I did," Eve admitted, looking up at him.

"Miss . . ." He smirked at her.

"Straus."

"Please share this brilliance with the class."

"In my mi—"

"Stand up!"

Eve got to her feet and met his gaze. "In my mind I'm the biggest sex maniac you ever met—Holden Caulfield."

The class tittered.

"Oh, do read on." Justine caught a twinkle in his eye.

"Just like the Wanker."

The class burst into laughter. Eve began to sink into her chair.

"Silence!" Mr. Winkler said. "Did I tell you to sit down?"

He crossed his arms, radiating power. Eve stared right back. "I see you are familiar with Salinger. But remember, it's better to quote accurately or not to quote at all. Holden says, 'In my mind I'm the biggest sex maniac you ever *saw*.'"

The class laughed again.

"The Wanker?" he continued. "How *clever*. Why don't you tell us all what that means?"

"It means he who wanks," Eve replied. Justine saw the edge of her jaw twitch.

The class roared.

Justine gazed at Eve with admiration. She was as unassailable as a figurehead on a ship.

"Your command of British slang is an improvement over your Salinger," the teacher said, stepping closer.

Eve held his eye.

"Writing notes in my class is not only bad manners, it's forbidden." He entwined his fingers and flexed them. "See me after class." His knuckles gave a sharp crack.

Justine waited for Eve on the bridge.

"You were a goddess in there!"

"Oh please, he doesn't scare me," Eve said, not breaking her stride. "The motherfucker wants me to go to his house for tea on Thursday."

Justine tried to walk faster, but Eve's legs were much longer.

"Miss Straus," Eve mimicked, "how do you take your tea? Foreskin or no foreskin?"

She swayed her hips and strode ahead. "One testicle or two?"

"Wait up!" Justine panted.

"Catch me!" Eve said, and took off, weaving and dodging around the students hurrying to class. Justine could barely keep sight of her. Suddenly Eve leapt onto the railing and several students stopped and gasped. The ground was terrifyingly far below, and Eve began a tightrope walk along the narrow wooden rail. A crowd was starting to gather, people murmuring in amazement. Suddenly Eve teetered, wobbled, yet by some miracle regained equilibrium. She took a few steps forward and grabbed one of the slender birch trunks, swinging her body around it and sliding to the ground below. Several students cheered and clapped. Justine saw her take off down the path next to the gorge.

Justine ran after Eve, pounding down the bridge, onto the path, and into the limestone courtyard of the arts center. She skidded to a halt just in time to see Eve disappear through one of the doors. She stood there, alone, trying to catch her breath. The art center's walls mirrored and reflected the campus like massive postcards. Eve had disappeared through the looking glass.

Glancing at her watch, Justine saw there was an hour left before French. She walked to the smoker hoping someone else was there, but the place was deserted. And she was out of cigarettes.

She hurried down the hill toward Wormley. The campus faded away and the maples dissolved into cracked sidewalks, broken bottles in the gutters, and vinyl siding. Jethro's Deli was on the corner of Elm and Ridge. Beyond a storefront with neon beer signs was a counter of worn Formica, a few shelves of canned food, and the aroma of burned coffee and dead mouse. A stringy-looking man sat behind the counter, wielding a toothpick on his gums like a tiny crowbar. An ice hockey game fuzzed on a black-and-white TV.

Justine walked down the candy aisle, suddenly craving strawberry Twizzlers. She passed Bit-O-Honey, Good & Plenty, Sky Bars. The red box was empty.

"Excuse me," she said, "do you have any more of these?"

The man grumbled something, stood up, and shuffled into the back while Justine watched a commercial for Mount Airy Lodge. He came back with a box under his armpit and set it down on the counter. He stabbed the toothpick into the cellophane wrapper, vivisecting it from top to bottom.

"How many?"

"Uh, just one, please, and a pack of Benson & Hedges."

He stopped and cocked his head.

"Figured a hot chick like you'd smoke Luckys." He was missing several front teeth, and the remaining were sharp and stained. "How old are you?"

She decided to tell the truth. "Fifteen."

"How long you been a smoker?"

"A year."

"I started when I was eleven. Nasty habit. Lookee," he croaked, holding out his left hand, which had a tattoo of an angel. Four fingers were shiny stumps. "Lost 'em cause o' smokin'. Nasty habit." He slapped a pack of Benson & Hedges down on the counter, and the Twizzlers. "Two fifty. Sweets for a sweet." Gummer grin.

Two blocks later Justine was back in the clean and leafy world. The campus was quiet, most kids were in class.

Stanley was at the smoker, sitting with his eyes closed. He did not open them when she sat on the bench. His long plaid scarf was hanging in the dirt.

"You okay?" she asked.

"My boom box is out of batteries. I'm listening to music in my head."

They sat in silence, Stanley still with his eyes closed.

She reached into her bag for her Baudelaire. She found the poem called "Music" and read aloud.

> *"Oft Music possesses me like the seas!*
> *To my planet pale,*
> *'Neath a ceiling of mist, in the lofty breeze,*
> *I set my sail."*

Stanley let out a deep sigh. Even if Justine had to quit smoking altogether, she would scrounge up enough money to buy him new batteries.

FOUR

EVE WALKED TO MR. WINKLER'S ROOMS IN THWAITE, A colonial house converted into a dorm. The chirping of crickets droned on, the sky was inky, the night moonless. It was only the first week of school and Eve was in trouble. And to think, her parents' rules had seemed draconian just a few weeks earlier.

On fall afternoons in the city, Eve would come in from school and the sun would slant through the apartment windows, glazing the walls amber. In the kitchen, Patsy would make her hot chocolate and toast with cherry preserves, and Eve would eat while Patsy watched *General Hospital*. She wasn't allowed to take food into her room—every New Yorker was waging war on roaches and losing. After the snack, Eve would go to her room, lie in a sunny spot on her carpet, and draw. She might read, lulled by the muted hum of traffic outside, or talk on the phone with her best friend, India Clarkson. God, she missed India. Eve shivered in the damp New England air. It was still September but already she could feel the chill.

Her old life felt so cozy and safe from here.

The only good thing about this place so far was Justine.

Mr. Winkler's door was ajar and she hesitated on the threshold.

"Enter ye who dare!"

His apartment had a small vestibule painted navy blue, with an Oriental carpet and a brass umbrella stand. Eve walked into the living room, where a fire blazed in the hearth. It was how she imagined professors' apartments at English boarding schools.

The teacher was lounging on a faded pink velvet sofa. Light from the fire flickered over piles of books, and a low lamp was lit. A blue-and-white tea service steamed on a low table. He patted the cushion beside him.

"How do you take your tea?"

"Black."

Eve perched on the edge of the sofa.

"Please. Make yourself comfortable," he said, patting the seat beside him again. She eased herself back into the cushions. His jacket had those brown leather buttons on the sleeves, like little bonbons.

"So, Miss Straus, you're a fan of Salinger?" he asked, handing her a cup.

"I've read *Catcher in the Rye* a bunch of times, but I'm not that into it." She took a sip of tea, it was Earl Grey, her favorite.

"What are you 'into'?"

She looked up and saw a smirk on his face. David Bowie and surrealist painters suddenly seemed like childish pleasures. "I like reading all sorts of things. No offense, but isn't *Catcher in the Rye* kind of easy for tenth grade?"

"What would you suggest, Miss Straus?" His tone was ironic, but his expression was curious, smiling.

Eve thought about it. "Something we might not read on our own, like *Anna Karenina*." The steam rose from her tea in a cloud of bergamot.

"Wonderful novel. Did you like it?"

"I haven't actually read it," Eve admitted. She added, "But I've always wanted to. You should challenge us more."

"Should I?" Mr. Winkler glanced down at the hole in her jeans. He lifted his eyes back to her face. "*Anna Karenina* is considered one of the greatest novels ever written," he said. "However, in English class we read works written in English, not translated from Russian."

"Oh, right," she said, blushing.

"I'm sure you'll find a reread of Salinger enlightening."

"Are you going to give us new insights?"

"I plan to. How old were you when you first read it?"

She thought for a moment. "Twelve?" It seemed awfully young to her now, although she hadn't felt too young at the time.

"What makes you think your classmates are as precocious as you are?"

She held a sugar cube to her lips and sucked on it. *Precocious.* She had been called that before and wasn't sure it was a compliment.

"Can I ask you something?" she said, wiping her hand on her jeans.

"May you?"

"Why do grown-ups think Holden is a realistic teenager?"

"You mean grown-ups like me?"

Eve felt herself blushing again.

Mr. Winkler watched her, motionless.

"He's a total loser," she managed. "He fails out of school and has no friends. The fact that we're supposed to relate is insulting."

"So is passing notes in my class, Miss Straus." He stroked his beard.

Eve felt a prickle of sweat on her upper lip.

"I'm really sorry, Mr. Winkler."

"It was a pretty bold move on the first day," he chuckled, leaning back on the cushions.

Yeah, Eve thought, a precocious move. She gazed at the fire, which had died down to red embers. The room was radiant and warm, the sofa soft, the tea fragrant. When Eve was an artist, she would have a big studio with a huge stone fireplace and a fire going all the time.

"You have a lovely profile," Mr. Winkler said.

Eve froze.

"Almost like a Picasso."

Trying to steady her hand, she took a sip of tea. She could imagine telling her friends in New York, playing out the conversation in her head: "There was this teacher, and he was so into me, so one night I let him . . ."

"But I'm sure you've heard that before." He shifted a bit closer. It could have been accidental. "You're obviously an advanced reader. Tell me your favorite books."

"Um . . ." Eve tried to relax. "You first."

He gestured at the piles on the floor.

"I have so many. I love *Lord Jim*, *In Cold Blood*, of course Updike."

"Those are such guy books!"

He laughed and leaned closer. "Miss Straus, I'm a guy." She had never touched a beard before and wondered if it was soft or scratchy. "Your turn."

"*Wuthering Heights*, *A Moveable Feast*, and . . ." She glanced at his expectant face. He would think she was showing off. "*Sentimental Education*."

Mr. Winkler set his cup down, stood up, and walked to the fireplace. He picked up a log and tossed it on the embers, where it crackled and sizzled into flame.

"I'm also an admirer of Flaubert," he said, picking up the poker and leaning back on the mantel.

She swallowed, heart thumping.

He laughed. "Tell me . . ." The poker landed with a *thwap* in his hand. "What in particular do you like about *Sentimental Education*?"

Eve took a breath. "For one, the writing's incredible. And it's a real love story."

"A *love story*?" He looked genuinely surprised.

"He loved Madame Arnoux so much!"

"He was silly. A fool."

"Because he was in love with an older woman?"

They regarded each other in silence.

"But once he got her he didn't want her anymore," Mr. Winkler said.

The mantel clock chimed. It was almost curfew.

Eve stood up.

Mr. Winkler walked toward her, holding the poker like a sabre. "You're a very smart girl, and a sophisticated reader, but the themes are more complex than just love. I look forward to discussing this further. And"—*thwap*, he struck his palm—"if you keep writing notes in my class, I'll be forced to take disciplinary action."

Eve nodded mutely.

"Good night," he said.

Face burning, Eve slipped out his door and into the night.

FIVE

INDIA CLARKSON LEFT HER APARTMENT ON FIFTY-FIFTH Street and walked west toward the Hudson River. She passed a gas station and averted her eyes as a cab driver tucked his dick back into his pants. She crossed the bridge over the sunken tracks where trains traveled from New York City toward Eve Straus at Griswold. India's life had always been lonely, but now Eve was gone and India had dropped out of public school after just a few weeks. Her father spent most of his time high on cocaine when he wasn't trying to steal money from India to buy more. He had run through what Kiki had left him, letting the family house in Bedford fall into disrepair. India had just managed to rescue her father's horse, Mr. Ed, from the filthy stable.

She could hear the horses stomping their hooves in the low city stable, she could smell the manure. A hansom cab was parked on the sidewalk, a driver in a top hat was replacing dead red carnations with new ones. Those flowers always reminded her of death.

She walked up the ramp to Mr. Ed's stall. He was staring into the corner, swishing his tail against flies.

"Hey, you," she said softly.

The horse moved to her and nuzzled her face with his thick

velvet nostrils. His nose hairs were graying. India closed her eyes, resting her face on his neck, inhaling his delicious odor. This was life, warm and pulsing under her cheekbone. He whinnied.

"I know." She looked around. Concrete, steel, urine. It was brutally urban. "I have to get you out of here." India put her arms around his neck. His large dewy eyes gazed down without reproach. He was a pure creature. She felt his hot breath on her face. "This weekend," she promised, thinking of the money she'd withdrawn from her account. The money had been given to India in her mother's will, but that didn't stop her father from trying to get access.

India would send Mr. Ed on a horse van to Long Island. Toppings was a clean stable, and she would see Mr. Ed on weekends. She kissed his jowl and headed out of the stable.

India walked farther west, toward the river. A white ocean liner was berthed at a pier. The thing was huge, it blotted out the sun. *Southampton Princess*, she was called. Southampton, England, not Long Island. India sat on a bench, the damp, rank breeze from the water lifting her hair.

India's grandfather had had a yacht, *Mata Hari*, named for her grandmother's favorite lipstick shade. India and her mother, Kiki, had sailed around Italy before ending in Rome, starting in Venice and making their way around the boot to Civitavecchia. India had been terribly seasick at first, and recalled her nurse, Mademoiselle, doling out small sips of ginger tea. It helped, and by the time they reached Ancona, India was eating gelato every day, the best at Giolitti in Rome. *Riso*, that was her favorite flavor. Like frozen rice pudding.

Kiki would lie on the deck for hours, her palms turned up to the sky, her eyes shaded under a massive cloth hat. She didn't read, hardly ate, barely spoke.

India had been too young to understand, helplessly watching her mother retreat further into herself. And then that day at the Hotel de Russie . . . India would never go back to Rome.

. . . .

J ustine was alone at the smoker, reading Rilke. She had hoped to run into Bruce again but had had no luck. Maybe he ate in the dining hall at Hill House, where only juniors and seniors could go? She hadn't seen him on Upper campus since that first night. Had he gone there only once, to scope out the new girls? He had found Tierney, that was for certain, although she probably already knew him. Tierney seemed to know everyone.

The sky was turning indigo. Floodlights illuminated the playing fields in a chemical green, and Justine felt crampy. She had run out of tampons and was almost out of money. To top it off, she was down to her last cigarette.

It infuriated Justine how irresponsible her parents were with "the evil green stuff." It wasn't as if Miles didn't have a job, as if Cressida hadn't just finished the living room of her friend Gretchen's town house. Yes, the Cassandra Theater was small and regional, but it was highly respected, with a reputation for premiering plays before they went to New York. It even gave them health insurance.

What were her parents doing with their cash? Justine suspected them of nothing but a childlike inability to hold on to it. It was depressing. Cressida was always hunting for things in the house she could sell, and had even tried to pawn one of Justine's prized possessions, a first edition of *The Wind in the Willows*. When her grandfather died, he'd left the family a sum adequate to pay off their debts. What did Cressida decide to do with it? She bought a barn. Justine knew they could not afford two houses. All through elementary school she remembered the phone ringing and Cressida ordering her not to answer it, usually toward the middle of the month. It was a miracle that the Rubins had gotten their act together to fill out the paperwork for Justine's scholarship at all.

Nobody here would understand. Well, maybe Stanley, but she had a feeling his story was so grim that peering into it would be like staring into the abyss. What would it be like to be Clay, and have your parents donate a whole building? Then there was Eve, rolling Parisian cigarettes in a leather jacket. Justine pulled her ragged flannel shirt around her ribs. She wasn't like any of them. Tierney had sniffed her out in a heartbeat, judging Justine as several castes below and not giving her a second thought. Justine didn't think Eve judged her, but then Justine had been careful not to let Eve know the reality of her family situation. Eve would never understand what it meant to worry about money. After a few more drags, Justine stood up, ground out her last cigarette, and headed back to Claverly.

Tierney and her friends were sitting on the bed eating Doritos. That Kitty girl from dinner was there, and a stout, dark-haired girl with a jaw so massive, Justine thought, it could be put on display in the Museum of Natural History.

Cat Stevens sang on the turntable.

"Kitty, Jackie, my roommate."

"We've met," Kitty said through a mouthful.

"Justine Rubin," she said to the other.

"Jackie Borden."

Were those actually whales on her turtleneck?

"Rubin"—Jackie paused—"like the sandwich?"

For a fleeting moment, Justine thought of making something up but didn't have the energy. "It's Polish." She threw her bag on her desk with a thud. "Can I borrow a tampon?"

"You didn't bring any?" Tierney asked, the green eyes sweeping across Justine like searchlights.

"I use pads," Jackie said. "But I'm a virgin and you're probably not."

"I can always tell who isn't," Kitty said.

"Makeup bag." Tierney pointed to her desk. Justine picked up the floral bag and started to unzip it.

Tierney leapt up and yanked it out of her hand. "Rule numero uno, don't touch my stuff." She turned away and rummaged through it, then handed Justine a tampon. "You owe me."

When Justine went back to the room, the three girls were heading out.

"Where are you guys going?"

"Where are we *going*?"

Justine looked at them blankly.

"Pep rally, as in football kickoff?" Jackie flared her nostrils like a bull.

"I'll pass."

"Is that a Polish joke?" Giggling, they headed down the hall.

She stood there for a moment, wondering if she should let herself eat the rest of their precious Doritos.

Something hit the window.

Then again; the faint clink of a pebble.

She pushed open the sash and saw Bruce standing below under a streetlamp. His handsome face shone in the lamplight. He gestured that he was coming up and headed to the door.

She ran to the mirror, sniffed her underarms, fluffed her hair, and pulled off her dirty flannel shirt. She had on a tank top underneath.

Bruce opened the door.

"Don't you knock?" she asked, turning around.

"You look so hot," he said, staring. So did he, but he probably knew it.

"Dorito?"

"I brought something better," he said, opening his hand to reveal a plastic bag bulging with green buds. "Where's your bong?"

He knew she had one! "It's hidden," she said, pulling it from behind a *Webster's* dictionary on the shelf. It was long, and pink. She'd bought it in a head shop in Woodstock.

"Bruce, meet Shirley, Shirley, Bruce."

"Nice to meet you. Can you fill her up?"

She draped her flannel shirt over the bong and tiptoed into the bathroom. Nobody was around—they were all at the pep rally. She glanced in the mirror. Her tank was just slightly, perfectly, transparent, her eyes large and blue.

"Why aren't you down at the football field?" she asked as she set the bong on the desk.

"I wanted to see you."

"How'd you know I wouldn't go?"

"Psychic." He moved closer. His hair was like sunlight; he could ride a chariot across the sky.

"I need two towels," he said.

Justine grabbed one from the back of a chair, another from a pile on the bureau.

Bruce bundled one into a jelly roll and put it over the crack under the door, then rolled up the other and handed it to her.

"I'll handle the first toke," he said, lighting the bong and taking a deep drag, the smoke gargling up Shirley's throat. He blew the smoke into the towel.

"Don't geek," he warned. She inhaled as much smoke as she could, it seared her lungs. Her eyes teared up, and she exhaled into the towel as well.

Bruce lit another bowl, sucked it to ashes, and set the bong on the desk.

"It reeks in here," she whispered, already wasted.

"Paranoia, the destroyer." His eyes were slitty and bloodshot. Red, white, and blue.

"Shit," she said, grabbing the back of the chair so she didn't fall down the rabbit hole.

He pulled her toward him. "God, you're beautiful," he said, and kissed her. She could taste the pot on his tongue.

He had a hint of stubble on his chin, like a grown man. And he'd said she was beautiful. They swayed like palms, and tumbled onto Tierney's patchwork quilt, the bag of Doritos crunching beneath them. She felt a stuffed animal under her shoulder. They were going to shred Tierney's precious heirloom coverlet. Bruce moved on top of her, kissing her neck, her ear. He tugged at the button on her jeans.

"I have my period," she said, sitting up slightly.

"So?" He unzipped her fly. Little pink roses decorated her undies.

She thought she heard voices in the hallway. Maybe she didn't care. Bruce started pulling down her pants. His fingers pushed into her panties. Her hand went to undo his buckle.

The door opened and light spilled in from the hall.

"What's going on?" Tierney demanded.

Justine pulled on her jeans, jumped up too fast, and steadied herself on the bunk bed against the head rush.

"Get off Sally Rabbit!"

"Who's in there?" Jackie's voice rang out. She looked at Justine and then pointed at the bong. "Are you insane?"

"Get him out of here, and get that, that *thing* out of here before you get me kicked out of this school!" Tierney shrieked. Bruce stood up and smoothed his hair.

"Hi, Bruce." Jackie flushed. He stared at her, squinting. "Jackie Borden, first boat."

"Nice whales, Jackie. Worthington, impressive hostess skills. Next time I'm visiting your roommate, maybe you'll be polite." He patted Justine's ass on his way out the door.

Tierney's face was hot and twisted. "If you got bodily fluids on my quilt," she warned, "you're dead."

"What are you going to do about it?" Justine shot back. "Club me to death with your Barbie?" She pushed past Tierney and her friends and headed downstairs into the common room, leaving Shirley on the bureau in all her pink, plastic glory.

SIX

THE LEAVES ON THE MAPLES WERE TURNING A BRILLIANT yellow, fluttering like a hundred thousand goldfinches. Justine had to admit that autumn at Griswold was gorgeous, and a vast improvement over the sad gingkoes of New Haven. Under the canopy of leaves, she entered a surge of students on the path and fought her way upstream. She hadn't seen Bruce since Friday, now it was already Wednesday . . . and all of a sudden there he was, walking in her direction.

Bruce high-fived her as he passed, and Justine glanced around, hoping someone had noticed. But the robots marched on.

Bruce might end up her boyfriend, Justine told herself, for maybe the tenth time that morning.

She was dying to tell Eve about his visit, but what if nothing more ever happened? She'd look so pathetic.

That evening Justine ate supper quickly. There was a big test on the Battle of Hastings tomorrow. She scanned the dining hall. Bruce was nowhere to be seen. Neither was Eve. Justine rose and hurried back to her room through an icy drizzle.

Tierney and Jackie were on the lower bunk poring over the history book.

"Hi," she said.

They did not respond.

"What did you do with my bong?"

They ignored her.

Justine stared at them, but they continued to pretend she did not exist. She felt a desire to throw something. Instead, she picked up her schoolbag and headed back into the rain.

Bitches.

Anger coursed through her like fire, despite the freezing rivulets of water running down her neck. She trudged up the wet steps of the library, where a bronze statue of Eliot Haverlock stood at the top. The poor sucker had been sculpted wearing a toga and holding a scroll, and now some student had put a baseball cap on his head. So much for his million-dollar donation. His legacy was a half-naked statue, used for silly jokes.

The vaulted reading room was quiet. Low lamps with green shades glowed along oak tables, and rows of bookshelves receded into the darkness. Justine sat down, quietly unpacking her textbook. She caught a sudden movement in her peripheral vision. Down an aisle, she saw Bruce. He was talking to Clay, Clay resting his hand on Bruce's shoulder and leaning in. Bruce gave Clay a soft punch in the shoulder. They looked up, noticed her, and approached her table.

"What are you doing here?" Bruce asked. A girl across the table stared at him. But, then, everybody stared at him.

"Homework," she said, keeping her voice low and tossing her hair out of her face.

Bruce's smile was like light in the dim library. "You know Clay?"

She nodded.

"We were discussing crew," Clay said, twirling a pencil in his delicate fingers. Justine racked her brain for something to say but she didn't know the first thing about the sport.

"Rowing is incredible," Clay added, the pencil flying out of his hand and skittering under a bookshelf. Was he nervous too?

"How's Jackie?"

"Which one's she again?" Bruce asked.

"Cap'n Crunch," Clay reminded him.

"Right, the big girl. We also call her the jaws of death."

Justine giggled. She couldn't help it, she felt like she was floating up toward the brass chandeliers.

"Sssh!" the girl across from them hissed.

"Follow me," Bruce said.

"Since when do you tell me what to do?" Justine asked.

His expression was that of a wolf assessing a bunny.

"Ask her about fall break," Clay said, hitching his book bag higher on his shoulder and heading off.

"He's throwing a major party at his mom's in the city," Bruce explained. "You're invited."

"Jesus!" the girl said and snapped her books closed.

"Stay put, sugar puss, we're leaving," Bruce said.

Justine started shoving her things in her bag. A party in the city? Justine imagined girls in short dresses and boys in ties. Gin and tonics, cut-glass ashtrays, antique tables. Please God, find a way for me to go, she prayed.

Bruce was leafing through the copy of the Marquis de Sade.

"A little light reading?" he asked, sauntering away with the book.

"Give it back!"

"*Justine*,'" Bruce stopped and read, "or a tale of virtue justly punished?" He handed it to her.

"It's by the guy who invented S and M," she said, trying to look him straight in the eye. His cheekbones glowed in the light. He truly was the most beautiful boy ever. "St-Stanley lent it to me."

"Who's that?" They walked to the end of the room.

"Glasgow, the tall guy with the boom box?"

"The homo?"

She winced at the word, but Bruce's tone was more matter-of-fact than cruel. She followed him down the hall, past doors to darkened offices.

Justine imagined going to the party in New York with Bruce, his arm around her as they stepped off an elevator into an apartment with black-and-white marble floors and doors to a terrace overlooking the skyline. Eve would have lent her a dress and she'd have done her hair and . . . Justine imagined Tierney's expression of envious surprise.

Bruce stopped at a door labeled JANITORIAL, opened it, and pulled her inside.

Orange light filtered through the transom, the room smelled of disinfectant and damp mop. Bruce kicked a bucket out of the way and kissed her. He slipped a hand under her shirt. Justine felt her stomach flip over. She wrapped her arms around his broad shoulders and pulled him closer.

"You have such great tits," he murmured. "Anyone ever tell you they're perfect handfuls?"

They had, but she didn't tell him that. Bruce took her hand and pressed it on his jeans. She pressed back.

Footsteps in the hall and a light knock.

"Guys, ten minutes." It was Clay.

They were quiet until the footsteps receded.

"How'd he know we were in here?" she whispered.

"He knows how much I like you."

She unbuckled his belt, unzipped his fly, and began to move her hand up and down. His hand closed around hers, squeezing her fingers. Bruce was breathing hard. He had stopped kissing her.

Bruce groaned and ejaculated. He wiped his palm on a towel hanging from a mop.

"Not bad, Rubin."

"I didn't need your help," she replied, trying to keep the bitterness from her voice.

"Of course you didn't," he said. He tucked his hand under her chin and looked at her. "I know you have all sorts of skills. Next time I'll take my sweet time with you."

He opened the door as she pulled down her shirt.

"Ladies first."

Next time. Justine smiled to herself. Bruce Underwood wanted a next time.

As she lay in bed listening to Tierney's soft breathing, Justine wanted to think about Bruce but instead her mind filled with memories of Gerald Sweeney. Gerald had been the artistic director of her father's theater. Thirty-three years old, a charismatic man with a sweep of reddish hair, golden brown eyes, and strong hands. She used to love the ginger hairs on the backs of his fingers. He wore an ascot, in an ironic sexy sixties way, and read Tennessee Williams.

Gerald's pursuit of Justine had started off innocently enough when she was thirteen. He gave her that first edition of *Wind in the Willows*; root-beer candy sticks (somehow, he knew they were her favorite); a black velvet box with a bear that danced to "Fly Me to the Moon" when you opened it. In the beginning, Gerald would take her out in the afternoons to a hotel in New Haven that served British tea and scones. Justine felt wonderfully grown-up, ordering jasmine tea, swirling the floral liquid with a silver teaspoon. Her mother had done an elaborate braid in Justine's hair, fussed over her outfit, and even allowed Justine to wear her grandmother's heart locket and silk scarf. It still smelled of French perfume.

Gerald described plays she had never seen. The sets and back-stage dramas, the funny snafus. He cracked open the world for her like a candy egg. Justine knew he was flirting, and she liked it. She felt like a girl in a foreign film. When he kissed her for the first time, his tongue in her mouth had been a surprise, like a large hunk of steak. At fourteen, he deflowered her on the stage of her father's theater, in Desdemona's bed. It hurt, but Gerald took it slowly. After all, he had waited so long. She bled, which frightened her, but Gerald laughed and said Desdemona would be stabbed on those satin sheets anyway. It all felt like it was happening to some-one else, as if Justine were floating under the canopy watching him make love to her from above.

But a few weeks later Gerald showed up an hour late for their movie date. Justine stood in front of the theater, the cold of the damp April Sunday seeping through her clothes. When she saw Gerald hurrying down the street, she felt a wave of relief. He apologized, an appointment had run late. But his eyes refused to meet hers.

Gerald drove her home and took her clothes off. It was only after sex that he told her it was over. At least he had wanted her, that one last time.

She rolled over and faced the wall, hugging Henry close.

And now, Bruce in the janitor's closet. *I know you have all sorts of skills*, he had said. Indeed, she did, and Clay's party was where they'd have another chance, unencumbered by Griswold's rules.

If she could just get her mother to send her the train fare, she could go.

In the city, anything was possible.

SEVEN

A WEEK BEFORE FALL BREAK, EVE SAT IN HER DORM ROOM in Londry watching Tabitha comb her long hair. The strands were so fair they seemed almost white. Every now and then, several would be borne into the air on gravity-defying static. Tabitha had a childlike face and large, surprised eyes. But her body was full-figured, and the contrast made her look like a Playboy cartoon. Eve imagined walking into Clay's party with her, a girl who looked like she'd stepped out of a brothel in a Hollywood Western.

"Where are you guys going tonight?" Eve asked.

"The Mee-ill," said Tabitha. The Mill was the only decent restaurant for miles. "Stefan had to make reservations a week ago!"

What a backwater Wormley was, thought Eve. At Lutèce in the city people had to get reservations months ahead. It was never worth it, and Eve would bet that The Mill would not be either.

"Think he would translate this?" Eve held out the index card. Tabitha squinted at it. She rarely wore her glasses, which had lenses as thick as soda bottles.

"It's in German," Eve explained.

"We're kind of in a hurry, but you can ay-ask."

Eve looked at the note again; David's beautiful handwriting had smudged in her bag.

The door opened. "Steffie!" Tabitha cried, throwing her arms around the solid mass of her boyfriend. Stefan was wearing leather shorts, woolly knee socks, and a Loden coat with hammered silver buttons. He looked like a Christmas tree ornament.

"What's the occasion?" Eve asked, trying to keep a straight face.

"As if we need one." Tabitha blushed, stroking Stefan's arm.

"We must go, Schatzie."

"Could you tell me what this says?" Eve held out the card.

Stefan studied it, furrowing his soft pink brow.

"He iss very in love with you."

Eve felt herself blush.

"Who's it from?" Tabitha asked, peering at it.

"David McClurken."

Tabitha gave a small squeak. "That punk guy?"

Explaining that David was new wave, not punk, would be a waste of breath, so Eve just nodded.

Tabitha looked worried. Boys in Texas probably never wore black unless they were going to their grandmother's funeral.

Stefan translated:

> *"If only you knew, what I alone know,*
> *If only I knew, what you alone know,*
> *If you only knew what you wanted,*
> *Would you know what I want?"*

"Excellent German," he said. "He must be a native speaker."

Eve shook her head.

Stefan looked at her dubiously, as if such language skills were beyond Americans.

"Come, Tabbilein." Stefan reached for Tabitha, who gave Eve a quick, apologetic shrug as they hurried off to supper.

What an exquisite poem.

Eve wondered how on earth Tabitha had a boyfriend and she didn't. Maybe she was too picky. Being discerning was not the road to happiness, that was for sure. Stefan was handsome and all, but who wore traditional Bavarian garb to a restaurant in Connecticut? None of it seemed to bother Tabitha, who continued to think he was the best ornament on the tree.

Eve looked in the mirror. She wasn't pretty, but her narrow face and sharp cheekbones did make her dark eyes larger and more striking. An interesting face, but with few soft edges. Everything about Eve's features telegraphed "complicated." Boys like David liked to believe they could see through her tough exterior. Black turtleneck, Nietzsche, repetitive industrial music—he was the type that always went for Eve's particular bouquet of Sturm und Drang.

Eve pulled out her sketchbook and started to draw his portrait.

She put down her pencil. "You have a beautiful profile," Mr. Winkler had said, "like a Picasso." Coming from him that had been a compliment. So why had she been so nervous? She wasn't a baby. And what an idiot she was for bringing up Flaubert and showing how little she had understood. He was probably still laughing about it. What would it be like to kiss him? What if he did it and she didn't know how to kiss him back? That would be far worse than misquoting Salinger. Maybe she could practice on David.

There was a knock. "Phone!"

Eve threw her sketchbook in the desk drawer and ran down the hall to pick up the receiver. God, she hoped it was India. Her friend would dispense sage advice, one way or the other.

"Hello?"

"Darling."

"Hi, Mom!" Eve slumped on the stool in the tiny phone booth.

"How are you, pumpkin?"

She thought about making something up, but David and Mr. Winkler were rattling around her brain.

"So-so," she admitted.

"Why just so-so?"

"It's Saturday night. There's nothing to do. I'm bored." Eve could hear her mother pause, having always said that only boring people got bored. Tonight Deirdre let it go. Eve tilted the stool backward, reading the graffiti left by students through the ages. *Graham my darling, "in absentia."* What did that even mean?

"I saw in the newsletter that they have an excellent selection of films at the Bradley." Eve imagined her mother running a red nail over the film schedule pinned to the corkboard in the kitchen. She could almost smell Chanel No. 5 wafting through the phone.

"Yeah, *La Dolce Vita*," Eve said. "They played that last Saturday too."

"Can't complain about that! Your father says hello. He just got in the shower." Eve couldn't help imagining Frederick's hairy ass. Her parents had read some child psychology book from the 1970s about not hiding your body from your children. She tolerated it until she was thirteen, when she asked her naked father not to walk around naked anymore. Eve would never forget his look of hurt. Now she had to cleave the image of her father and the Wanker in half, stuffing them into opposite sides of her cortex.

"Mom, I think I'm homesick."

There was a silence, but Eve knew what her mother was thinking. Eve had begged to come here. She had no right to complain. Eve felt tears come to her eyes and was glad for the privacy of the tiny phone booth.

"You'll be home soon for fall break." Her mother's voice was chirpy with cheer.

Eve was counting the days. "Can I bring my friend Justine? She's really cool and smart, you'll love her, she reads poetry and her parents—"

"There's a fabulous book called *Justine*," Deirdre interrupted.

"Really? I've heard it's total porn!"

"Not at all! It's romantic and beautiful—I read the whole *Quartet* one summer in college. I'll find my copy and send it to you."

A sadomasochist book in a care package from her mother? Nothing made any sense. Eve traced a heart with *Tina loves Greg*. She wondered how long ago it had been etched into the wall. Did Greg love Tina back? Bet he didn't write poems in German.

"How's English?"

"*Catcher in the Rye*."

"In *tenth* grade?"

"Couldn't agree more."

"I'm sure your teacher has her reasons."

"*His*." Eve heard her voice jump several decibels. "I should go, I have a paper on the Bayeux Tapestry."

"Ooh, what fun! We miss you terribly, darling."

She missed her mother too. In fact, she ached to be home.

"Mom?"

"Mmm?"

"Love you." Eve hung up.

· · · · · · · ·

Justine was leaning against the wall blowing smoke rings into the wind when Eve rounded the corner.

"Great news, the mother figure said you could stay with us for fall break weekend!"

"Yay!" Justine said, throwing her arms around Eve. "Does that mean we can go to Clay's?" Cressida had not sent her a dime.

"Of course! Jesus, it's freezing." Eve said, pulling her coat around her.

"I need to tell you about Bruce," Justine said. She blew another smoke ring, and Eve watched it wiggle away. "He came to my room the other night and we fooled around and Thursday we had a tryst in the library."

Eve felt a stab of admiration. "Wow, good work." It wasn't only Tabitha who was getting somewhere. She squinted at the illuminated limestone flanks of the arts center, wondering if the Wanker knew it spelled FUCK.

"David wrote me an amazing poem."

"David's sexy," Justine replied. "I saw him at soccer today. He does have that Michelangelo body."

He did, it was true. Eve closed her eyes. "I'm thinking of losing it to him. Just out of sheer ennui."

"It's a constant struggle."

"That was a confession," Eve said, waiting for Justine to look horrified.

But Justine just shrugged. "I knew anyway."

Eve pulled out a cigarette, Justine lit a match. Eve leaned toward the flame. It blew out instantly.

"Gimme." Justine lit it under her down jacket. She exhaled and handed it to Eve.

Eve smoked in silence, wondering how Justine had known. She hadn't realized it was so obvious. Screaming "I'm a virgin, I'm a virgin" was not good, maybe worse than being "complicated." She'd never throw off the yoke at this rate. Eve wanted to ask Justine how many guys she had slept with, but she didn't want to pry, or appear more naïve. She sucked on her cigarette and hoped her silence implied complicity and mutual knowledge.

"Whatcha gals doing?" Stanley said, setting his boom box on the bench.

"Our nails," Eve said. "Why aren't you at Fellini?"

"Seen it."

"Which one?" Justine asked.

"*Dolce Vita*," Eve told her.

"What does Justine need with film?" Stanley asked. "She's been living it, in the janitor's closet with Bruce."

Even in the dim light Eve could see Justine redden.

"How'd you hear?" Justine asked.

"Word travels," Stanley replied.

The film must have ended; kids were streaming out of the arts center. Even from this far away, they could hear them belting out a song.

"How can someone see a Fellini film and then sing 'American Pie'?" Eve laughed, flicking her cigarette into the night.

"Top forty is the opiate of the masses," Stanley said. "Speaking of, I found out we can do our own show, ten to midnight is free at the radio station, Fridays. *I am a DJ, I am what I play*," he sang. Eve and Stanley started chatting excitedly about having their own radio program, but Justine couldn't listen.

What had Bruce said about her? When boys bragged it was often embellished, and not in a good way.

Eve was lighting up again. "Anyway, it means asking Tibbets for permission." She tried, unsuccessfully, to blow a smoke ring.

Stanley shrugged and pressed a button, and "Young Americans" began to play. *Took him minutes, took her nowhere, heaven knows she'd have taken anything . . .*

That song had always depressed her.

"Miss Straus?" The Wanker appeared like a genie. Justine saw Eve drop her cigarette in the dirt—too late. He beckoned Eve with his finger. Silently, she followed the teacher up the hill.

Justine glanced at Stanley. His eyes bulged. They both were thinking the same thing; Eve was screwed.

....

E ve followed the Wanker's corduroy ass up Elm. Her stomach was in a foul knot, the taste of tobacco souring in her mouth. All was lost. What was he going to do to her?

When they reached his apartment, the teacher held open the door. Eve shuffled in. The portrait above the mantel frowned down. There was no tea service on the coffee table this time, and the hearth was cold. Eve didn't remove her coat.

She stood trembling.

"What on earth were you doing smoking?" he was saying. "You don't have parental permission, and anyone could have seen you!" He gestured around the room.

"I . . ." She'd never make him understand what it was like to be in that phone booth, tracing the heart, hearing her mother, reading David's poem, watching Tabitha flounce off with Stefan.

"It's just that I'm . . . I'm so depressed!" It was the excuse she could think of, but now, for some reason, she burst into hot tears. "I hate Griswold!" Eve slumped onto the sofa and buried her head in her hands.

The teacher sat beside her. "Come on, it can't be that bad." Eve couldn't speak, sobs racking her chest. She couldn't believe she was crying in front of him, but she couldn't stop. He held out a box of tissues.

"Breathe." He gave her a gentle smile.

Eve took one and wiped her face. "I'm so sorry."

"Hush. It took me time to adjust to Griswold too."

She wondered how long he had been at the school.

"Tell me what you hate so much."

Everything. She missed her bed. She hated sharing a dorm room. She couldn't stand the food. She couldn't bear to read *Catcher in the Rye* again. She didn't have a clue how to talk to David. She was a shitty painter. Though she really liked Justine, they had only known one another a few weeks. And Clay was an old buddy, but Clay was a guy. She missed India. She missed home. And now she was going to get suspended.

Eve turned her teary face toward him. "Everything's so different from what I expected, and the kids are just . . ." She trailed off, not knowing how to define feeling like a black crow in a dovecote.

"I understand, it's a big change," he said. "You just arrived, and it takes time to find your place. But"—he sighed and shook his head—"breaking rules won't help anything. You've put me in a terrible position."

"Please don't tell! My parents will kill me. Please, Mr. Winkler, I'll do anything!" Her voice was ragged with desperation.

She fell to her knees before him. "Please!"

"Get up."

She flushed and sat back on the sofa, face burning with shame.

"It would have been easier for me to let you off if you'd been alone . . ." He threw the tissue box on the coffee table. "What if I overlook it this one time but then one of those friends of yours says something?" He thought for a moment, stroking his beard. "Eve . . . you deserve another chance."

She felt dizzy with relief.

"How about I take you to supper and give you a strong talking to?"

"That's it?" she asked, trying to keep her voice steady. "Just supper?"

"What do you mean, *that's it*?" he said. "I'm offering you a punishment. Take it or leave it."

"That's amazing but . . . can that solve this?"

"Oh, Eve . . ." He stood up and walked over to the mantel, propping an elbow on the stone. "I think it can. I do."

She didn't believe it would be that easy, but she didn't trust her judgment at all anymore. Eve tried to smile. "Thank you so much, Mr. Winkler. Which dining hall should we go to?"

He laughed. "Dining hall? We'll eat at an actual restaurant!"

Eating out with her teacher. Dressing up, using real table linens—Eve hadn't realized how much she missed evenings out with her parents.

"Consider it detention. Extracurricular detention." He sat back down beside her and touched her knee reassuringly. Then he left his hand there.

Eve could feel her leg trembling. He took his hand away.

"So," Eve said, "you won't bust me?"

Mr. Winkler held out his little finger. "Pinkie swear." They shook.

Eve stood up and wondered if kissing a man with a beard would be like going down on a girl. She hated the fact that her brain went to those places. He was right, it was not always a gift.

"It's a plan. Next Saturday. I'll reserve a table at The Mill," he said, standing up.

Eve wondered what her mother would say if she knew she'd been invited to dinner with her teacher. She'd probably be relieved.

EIGHT

Fall Break

JUSTINE AND EVE SLOUCHED IN THEIR SEATS AS THE TRAIN lurched toward the city. Outside it was drizzling, that almost-freezing rain that made Eve think of England. Next to her, Justine was looking out the window—she was so beautiful, the slope of her nose like that of a countess, the pouty mouth rouged hot pink. Eve wondered what kind of mark Justine would leave on a boy.

She turned to look at the man across the aisle. He was asleep, his pants smeared with stains. A hairy strip of belly rose and fell between his shirt and belt as he breathed. Eve stared, mesmerized. What if she crept across the floor, knelt between his knees, and unbuckled his belt? She might be able to unzip his fly before he woke up. She shuddered at the thought of his expression. How big would he be? How would it taste? Other than her father, she had never seen a grown man naked. If only she knew what to expect. No matter how bad it was, the unknowing was worse.

"Is Bruce going to the party?" Eve asked.

Justine looked up from her copy of *Pale Fire* and nodded.

Eve wanted to ask Justine about Bruce. But she didn't want to pry.

"It's so great to get away," Justine said. "I feel like all I do is study."

"Really? Griswold is so much easier than Beaverton. It's like summer camp in comparison."

Not for the public-school kid on the scholarship, Justine thought, fingering a tear in her pants. Justine knew Eve would never understand. In her soft world, money was never a factor. What would Eve do when she found out that Justine only had the small change in her pocket? She would probably think she was trying to be hip.

Justine had waited for her mother to mail her some money, but then, in typical fashion, Cressida had forgotten. Did her mother imagine that things would magically work themselves out? She'd borrow the money from Eve and find a way to pay her back. *I have always depended on the kindness of strangers.* Somehow that wasn't how it went in real life.

When the conductor came by, Eve paid for both their tickets without word or ceremony, and Justine felt a wave of gratitude and affection for her friend. Maybe Eve understood more than she let on.

Justine loved New York—she and her mother visited every year or so, staying with her mom's friend Gretchen on Bleecker. Justine recalled one weekend in particular. After a day of hunting for fabric on the Lower East Side and a supper of Cressida's famous roast chicken, Cressida and Gretchen had gone to bed early. Around midnight Justine had snuck out to CBGB. The club was just down the block. But when she came back a police car was parked in front of the house. A street fight had awoken her mother, who, finding Justine's bed empty, had called the police. And there in Gretchen's parlor was a cop taking notes while Gretchen and Cressida slugged vodka straight from the bottle.

———

The view outside finally changed from a smear of ochre into a tangle of brick buildings, billboards, and power lines. The train plunged into the tunnel under the station. When it finally came to a stop the girls grabbed their bags and made their way up the escalator into Grand Central.

Crowds crisscrossed the massive vaulted space and rays of light streamed through the wide, arched windows, making patterns on the floor. Justine admired the golden zodiac signs etched on the sea-green ceiling.

"What sign are you again?" Eve asked.

"Capricorn."

"Oh, right. We're totally incompatible." She took Justine's hand and pulled her through the hordes of commuters.

"Wait! I don't have a token!" Justine panted.

Eve stopped, whipped around, and held Justine's shoulders.

"Let's get one thing straight. When you're with me, you do not take the subway. You take taxis. You eat out. You shop. And I pay for it and you don't get all weird, because you're my date. Got it?" Eve glanced at her watch. "Fuck, it's almost five."

The cab drove up Park Avenue. Justine accepted Eve's offer of a cigarette and rolled down the window to smoke. The city air had the tannic scent of wet asphalt, which she inhaled like an elixir.

Park Avenue was cleaner than Bleecker Street but, in Justine's opinion, much less interesting to look at. The brick buildings stood with their jutting cornices, stalwart as soldiers, their backs against

the sky. They seemed to regard her with disapproval, their unifor-
mity like some luxurious version of a Stalinist regime.

Justine thought of meeting Eve's parents and suddenly felt carsick.

Eve said, "Mom said she'd read, um, the book. *Justine.*"

"Big deal." Justine shrugged. "My mom's read Erica Jong. That's
much worse."

"I almost barfed when she told me," Eve continued.

"It's not like she's never had sex. She had you, didn't she?" If
Justine could keep up this sassy banter, pretending not to care,
she just might survive the Strauses.

Eve fiddled with the button on her coat, then put her hand in
Justine's. "Do you love me?"

"Of course!" Justine said, squeezing Eve's hand in response.
"What the . . ."

"Say it!"

"I love you. Silly dope."

Eve removed her hand and glanced out the window.

Justine stared at the back of Eve's head, wondering why she had
become silent. After a moment she poked her in the shoulder.

"What's wrong?"

Eve turned and shrugged. "Dunno. I've been so excited to come
home. Now I'm feeling kind of pukey." She glanced back at the
passing avenue, tapping her fingers repeatedly on her leg.

Me too, Justine thought. It really was going to be that bad.

They pulled up in front of an awning, where a doorman in a navy-
blue cap bustled out to meet them. A tattoo peeked out from beneath his white collar. This incongruity did not alleviate Justine's
sense of impending doom.

The whole weekend seemed like a terrible mistake.

"Hi, Tony, can you send that stuff up the back?" Eve asked, stepping out of the cab. The doorman knocked on the trunk and their stuff was loaded onto a luggage cart without their having to lift a finger.

The lobby was an intimidating expanse of polished marble floors and mirrors. Justine wiped her sweaty palms on her ripped jeans.

The elevator opened directly into a square room with pale beige stone floors, empty except for an enormous gash along one wall, which disgorged plaster and wires.

Justine wanted to ask what had happened—it looked like a crime scene, but she stopped herself. It was probably one of those things she should know.

Eve saw her staring.

"That's art. By Horace Anders. Mom!"

Justine looked around, amazed at the huge room with nothing in it. She had known that Eve was rich, but this apartment was so much cooler than she had expected. Instead of gilded antiques and old master paintings, they had modern art and a pink neon tube running across the ceiling. Justine had pegged her own family as the people who at least had taste, if not money. But the Strauses were not only loaded, they had style.

"On the phone!" Eve's mother's voice sounded muffled, as if it were ensconced in a distant, upholstered chamber.

"Shoes off," Eve said, kicking off her combat boots. She headed down a hallway lined with photos, Eve and her parents in front of the Parthenon, Eve in a bathing suit holding a swimming trophy. Justine paused before a picture of a beautiful young boy with light curls, dressed in an old-fashioned sailor suit.

"Who's that?" Justine asked.

"My brother, Sandy."

"You have a brother?"

"There's a reason I never mention him."

"He's not . . ." Justine was suddenly worried.

"Dead? I wish! Sandy's coming home later, you'll have the pleasure."

"He's really beautiful," Justine commented.

"He's fourteen, you perv."

Just the age I was, Justine thought. "He looks like . . ."

"Yeah, I know, the boy from *Death in Venice*, you don't have to say it. Blah blah, I hear it all the time."

How had she known?

They walked down the hallway to Eve's room, which, of course, had the softest powder-blue carpet and tufted velvet window seat. A poster of Bowie hung on the wall, in all his glory and glamour. Flame-red hair, sky-blue suit, holding a sax.

Justine wandered to the window and looked outside. Taxis honked angrily. Justine couldn't help wonder where Tierney was tonight. In Moodus, her father sipping his gin and her mother roasting a ham? No matter how uncomfortable Justine felt here, it gave her pleasure to imagine Tierney somewhere sequestered and provincial.

When she turned she found Eve hugging a woman in a fuchsia dress with treacherous shoulder pads. She had black hair with a white skunk streak in it—just like Cruella de Vil.

"This is Justine," Eve said, gesturing toward her friend.

Justine hopped down from the window seat and shook Mrs. Straus's cool and bony hand.

"Lovely to meet you, Justine. Eve has raved about you."

Justine tried to come up with an appreciative response but Mrs. Straus had already turned to face her daughter. "As soon as your father gets home, darling, we have to leave." She straightened her gold watch and glanced at it. "There's some chicken and salad in the fridge. And save some for your brother."

"Let me guess," Eve said, "Lutèce?"

"Yes, in fact. But we'll be home long before you. Remember to mind the curfew. Whose house?"

Eve did not reply.

"That poor, sweet Clayton Bradley?" Mrs. Straus persisted.

Justine couldn't help it, she giggled.

Mrs. Straus gazed at her like something in an aquarium. "Eve, lend your friend something to wear, her pants are shredded."

"It's called fashion, Mom!"

Justine blushed. "Sorry, the hole started on the train."

"Justine, don't mind me, I'm just being a mother," Mrs. Straus said. "It's unsafe to go down to SoHo showing all that lovely skin. Eve, twelve o'clock, don't forget."

"Justine doesn't even have a curfew!" Eve protested. Justine wished she could hide under the bed. Why had she worn these ratty pants? Now Mrs. Straus would think she had been raised like a wild animal.

"Well, there must be fewer temptations in Greenwich."

"She's from New Haven!"

Mrs. Straus looked at Justine with interest. "Does your father teach at Yale?"

"He runs a theater," she said, feeling ashamed. She had always been proud of it, but now it sounded like he was in a traveling circus.

"He must have unpredictable hours. That would make a curfew impractical." Mrs. Straus massaged her taut forehead. "Unfortunately, our lives are very humdrum and Eve has to be in by midnight or she turns into a pumpkin." She rested a hand on her fuchsia hip. "Sorry to cramp your style. Eve, about tomorrow . . ."

"What?" Eve asked.

Mrs. Straus gave her a pointed stare.

"What?"

Mrs. Straus looked at Justine. "Our family has had reservations at the Quilted Giraffe for months. It's a table for four, and they weren't able to change it. We tried, but, Justine dear, I'm afraid you'll have to stay here."

NINE

EVE LET THE HOT WATER OF THE SHOWER CASCADE DOWN her back. She squeezed some shampoo onto her palm and considered simply ignoring her mother's ridiculous curfew. At least her mother couldn't impose the same arbitrary laws on Justine. Justine could roll in whenever she damn well pleased—she might even stay out all night and watch the sun rise over the East River. It enraged Eve. In the Griswold Rulebook Eve had learned the term "in loco parentis." As far as she was concerned, her mom was adhering perfectly; being a parent, and loco too.

Anyway, it wasn't kind of Deirdre to begrudge Justine her freedom. Speaking of kindness, leaving her home while they went out to dinner without her—it was like they were punishing her for nothing. Eve could imagine Justine staring out the window onto Park Avenue, wishing she were staying with someone else, anyone else.

The Quilted Giraffe served these incredible little crepes filled with caviar. Maybe Eve could bring one home in a doggie bag.

Once Eve had disappeared into the pink bathroom off her room, Justine tried to tell herself if didn't matter, that she had no interest in sitting at some fancy restaurant with Eve's family. But it wasn't working. She got up and explored Eve's room. Anyone could tell that some housekeeper was in Eve's room regularly cleaning and straightening. The beds were made, the sheets ironed. A lamp of pale-yellow porcelain sat on a wicker nightstand, with a carafe of water and a glass. Her own room in New Haven was so different, with its wall of exposed brick and window onto the overgrown garden, the wind chime tinkling in the crab apple.

But there were similarities. Eve had ceramics she'd made on her shelves, like Justine, and Justine was gratified to see that Eve's skill level was as low as her own. The head of a man with an enormous nose struck her in particular. Justine reflexively touched her own nose, the hated thing.

Eve's selection of books was more varied than hers, and many of the editions were hardcovers. There was far more poetry: Dylan Thomas, Keats, Plath. This was something she loved about Eve; she read and read everything. There was even a copy of *Les Fleurs du mal*, but a different translation, with a gray cover. She pulled it off the shelf, sat on the soft window seat, and started to read. Since when did "dungeon" rhyme with "grunge on"? She put the book aside and went back to staring out the window.

Eve turned off the water. Wrapping herself in a robe, she stepped from the steaming bathroom back into her room.

"What are you wearing?" Justine asked.

"The robe I stole from the Hotel du Cap."

Justine didn't know what that was, but she wasn't about to admit it. "I meant tonight."

"Red mini and white go-go boots. You?"

Justine sifted through a mental inventory of her weekend bag. It didn't take long.

"Can I borrow something? I kind of hate everything I brought."

"Of course!" Eve made a grandiose gesture in the direction of her closet. Justine jumped off the window seat and opened the door. "Most of my best stuff's at school," Eve apologized.

Still, Justine thought, looking at the rows of dresses and skirts, this was a treasure trove.

"How about this?" Justine fingered a brown suede dress with fringe. It looked vintage, but it was soft and buttery. "Think I could pull it off?"

Eve didn't tell her friend she had never worn it because she found it a tad too Pocahontas. It had been her mother's eons ago, and it was hard to imagine she had ever worn it either. But on a blonde?

"Try it."

Justine tore off her clothes.

Eve quickly turned around. Even now, seeing people naked embarrassed her.

"Well, what do you think?" Justine said.

The dress seemed to have been custom made for her, the chocolate brown perfect with her skin tone, enhancing its golden burnish.

Eve clapped. "Amazing! Shoes?"

"I have my pink flats," Justine replied, not telling Eve about the tear in the sole. "Got stockings?"

"Crappy selection. Navy cable tights or control-top nudes." Eve pulled open a drawer. Justine noticed it was an antique dresser on which rested a silver-framed photograph of a woman, maybe Eve's grandmother, in a long dress and pearls.

"Why do you wear control top?" Justine asked. She had never

even seen a pair of control tops and had always pictured those thick elastic stockings for varicose veins.

"I stole them from Mom."

"She needs them less than you do! A skinnier woman I never saw!"

Eve laughed and handed her the package. Justine's outfit would blow her red mini out of the water. She knew it wasn't a competition, but she had imagined herself as the sophisticated city girl, showing her ingenue friend around her glittering hometown. Now there was a crazy curfew and Justine was exquisite. But she always was. Eve needed to get used to being a Picasso next to a Botticelli.

TEN

JUSTINE ROLLED DOWN THE WINDOW OF THE TAXI AS THEY careened down the FDR. The cold air swept across her face. Rushing past her were the glossy black of the East River, the silver Queensboro Bridge, and the cherry-red Pepsi-Cola sign. The New York skyline twinkled and glistened, reflected in the shimmering surface of the water.

The driver got off at Houston Street and drove past boarded-up tenements, twenty-four-hour bodegas, and a take-out joint called Cuchifritos. Justine had no idea what that meant, but she loved how it felt on her tongue. *Cuchifritos.* It sizzled like Pop Rocks.

"No, *straight* on Houston, then down Wooster!" Eve hollered through the Plexi divider, then slumped back in her seat. "These drivers don't know their way around. Like, what if I just landed from Tokyo, or . . . Wait, no! Left on Wooster! Oh my God!"

The taxi bumped over the cobblestones and stopped. Justine stepped onto the curb over a grimy puddle. She looked around. One of the streetlights was out, another blinking like a strobe. Columned buildings with darkened windows leaned over the deserted street.

This was nothing like Bleecker Street, with its bohemian cafés and worn brownstones. It reminded Justine of the waterfront near the theater in New Haven, lined with warehouses instead of apartments. Clay lived in this industrial neighborhood? Her respect for him increased.

"Is my hair trashed?" Eve asked, slamming the door in frustration.

"Complete disaster. First aid required."

Eve pulled a can of Aqua Net from her bag. She aimed it at her coiffure, sprayed, then threw it back in her purse. She squinted at the buzzers. "Do you see Bradley?" There was no door, just an elevator that opened onto the street.

Justine pointed to a label. "What's the Earth Room?"

"A whole loft full of dirt. It's really cool," Eve said, eyes running up and down the buzzers' labels. She pressed one hard, and the elevator opened, spilling fluorescent light onto the sidewalk.

The elevator was so clanking and rickety that Justine could hardly believe it was functional. As it heaved reluctantly upward, Justine heard the pounding bass of a Human League song. After a couple of unpromising groans, the door opened to reveal a huge loft with Corinthian columns illuminated by hundreds of votive candles. Dancing kids were everywhere, and beyond them were brick walls hung with paintings of nude figures, the light flickering across their pale bodies. A claw-foot tub stood in the middle of it all, full of ice and beer.

It reminded Justine of the parties her parents threw, smoky and crowded, with a mix of grown-ups and kids, and an air of endless possibility—if the adults could get fucked up, so could the teenagers.

"Hey, you made it," Clay said, appearing from around a column, a beer in his hand. His hair was sticking up and his shirt was untucked. He looked great.

"Did you just wake up?" Eve joked.

"Disco nap. Now I'm on my second wind. Make yourselves comfortable."

Justine scanned the crowd. Through a haze of smoke, she could see a bunch of kids lounging on a mustard velvet sectional—but no sign of Bruce.

"Hey!" Clay high-fived Damon.

"Hey, Justine!" Damon yelled over the music. "Señor Broom Closet's in the bedroom with Christina." He gestured toward the back of the loft.

Justine stiffened.

Eve pulled Justine toward the bathtub. "Ignore him," she urged, handing her a Schlitz. "He's a fucking idiot. He'll say anything for a reaction," Eve added, popping the top off her beer.

Justine took a long sip. She didn't love the sour yeasty taste of it, but if it anesthetized her, who cared?

"Can we get high?" she asked.

"Maybe Damon's got blow."

Justine gaped. She had meant pot, but she should have guessed. Cocaine. Coke was something only millionaires could afford.

"Let's be polite before it gets crazy," Eve said. Turning to Clay she asked, "Where's your mom?"

"This way," he said, and Justine thought she detected reluctance in his voice. They headed to a candlelit corner where four adults sat around a hookah. They were talking and nodding like bobbleheads on a dashboard. A bearded man, a small woman with a flat-top haircut and massive hoop earrings, and the third an androgynous model Justine thought she had seen in *Interview* or somewhere. She was too tall and angular not to have been in a magazine.

One of the women was reclining on a Victorian chaise, wearing a black dress embroidered with floppy clocks. Her gray hair hung to the floor. She held one of the hookah tubes in a heavily ringed hand, like the caterpillar in *Alice in Wonderland*.

"Barbara," Clay said, touching her arm. She stared at him without recognition. "Barbara!" he raised his voice. "Eve is here. And this is Justine Rubin, a friend from Griswold."

His mother moved her vague blue eyes over them, like searchlights through fog. She nodded.

"Mrs. Bradley," Justine started.

"Mrs. Bradley is dead." Her voice rattled like pebbles under water. "It's Barbara."

"Barbara, I love this loft!" Justine said, and looking at the clocks on Barbara's dress, "Are you a Dalí fan?"

Barbara smiled, and Justine saw the flash of a gold tooth. "Not really, but our time is running out. What did you say your name was?"

"Justine Rubin," she replied. Eve noticed Clay gazing at Justine with admiration.

"And your dress is wonderful too!" Barbara said to Justine. "I had one like it years ago. Where do you hail from?"

"New Haven."

"Her parents run a theater," Eve said.

"The Cassandra?" Barbara pushed herself a bit higher on the chaise.

"You've heard of it?" Justine asked.

"Heard of it? I've been there." Barbara waved her hand in the air, rings glinting in the candlelight. "I saw Liv Ullmann's *Ghosts*. Fabulous!"

"She came over for dinner during that," Justine said, recalling the actress's cascade of coppery hair, the light freckles on her apple cheeks.

"I adore Liv. I must meet your parents. So few people are truly in the arts these days. All the rest just grinding away. Money, money, money . . ."

Justine imagined Barbara and Cressida sipping coffee in the Rubins' kitchen.

"Eve, I assume you're showing your friend Manhattan's earthly delights tomorrow?"

"We're going to the Quilted Giraffe for dinner and my mother won't let Justine come."

Barbara laughed. "Who wants to go there anyway? Justine can hang out with us! It's just Clayton and I, we might see a film."

Clayton and me, Justine could hear her mother say.

"That sounds great, Mrs. Bradley," Justine nodded uncertainly.

"Barbara!" A waft of patchouli hit Justine's nostrils. "I thought *Fanny and Alexander* or maybe . . ." Barbara sighed, her eyes slipping further out of focus. "Have you tried the MaryJane?" She gestured toward the sofa. "It's the best homegrown Jamaican in the uncivilized world."

"I'd love to," Justine said as if she were accepting an invitation to tea. "Thanks so much."

"If you like it I can get more for tomorrow night. We seem to be kindred spirits." Barbara lowered her voice. "Clayton won't approve." She winked.

"Honey," Barbara said to her son, "why don't you show the girls the new work? Paint's still wet." She let out a throaty chuckle, put the hookah tube in her mouth, and closed her eyes. They'd been dismissed.

········

Y our mom's amazing," Justine said excitedly as they walked toward the canvases.

"Yeah," Clay shrugged.

"No, really. She's so authentic!"

Eve turned back to see Barbara exhale a cloud of smoke. The floor was out of balance, with all the marbles sliding toward Justine. Eve felt a wave of possessiveness, about Clay, about this loft . . . this was her world. She had wanted to show it to Justine, not have her settle in right away. Was her friend really coming back here tomorrow night?

Clay walked them past the windows, the candlelight reflected in the glass making them look like altars. The paintings still smelled of paint and linseed oil. The first canvas was of a woman holding a tray with a man's severed head on it. His eyes stared, milky and blank, his blood pooled on the pewter around the ragged stump. The woman was beautiful and young, likely just her age. Eve felt goose bumps spread across her skin.

Clay noticed Eve's stunned expression and said, "I know, so violent. It's gotten worse since she split with Dad. It's all revenge, all the time, twenty-four hours a day. Wait until you see this one."

They moved down the wall past a St. Sebastian pierced with arrows, but at the next painting Eve drew in her breath. It was a David and Goliath, the young man a perfect portrait of Clay.

"Jesus," Eve said.

"That's Philip before he lost his hair." Clay pointed to the dead giant. Eve recognized Clay's father's crooked nose, his gray eyes.

Eve leaned closer to the canvas. The tiny brushstrokes were practically invisible. "Revenge sure has been good for your mom's work."

Eve headed into the kitchen, where she spied India Clarkson. Her dear friend was sitting on the concrete counter, cross-legged, her eyes shut. Eve's sadness faded, she hadn't seen India since August. The girl was like an exotic princess, every part of her delicate and fragile. Her lashes lay on walnut cheeks, her lips were parted, her teeth ivory. But her most magnificent feature was the lustrous brown hair that cascaded halfway down her back.

India sat, her spine perfectly straight, her hands folded in her lap. She wore a cropped military jacket with shoulder lapels and slim black trousers. The girl had always exuded elegance and refinement without moving a muscle.

India's mother had drowned herself in a bathtub in Rome five years ago. India's father spent most of his time drugged out in Palm Beach. So now, at the age of sixteen, India lived on her own.

"Yo!" Eve poked her knee. India slowly opened her eyes and gave her a sweet smile as if returning from a long journey.

"Eve, darling!" she sighed, touching her hands together as if in prayer. "Seeing you is pure joy."

India hopped off the counter. "I've missed you so much." She gave Eve a soft peck on the cheek, shy as usual about physical contact.

"Me too," Eve said.

"Let's celebrate." A bottle of red wine sat on the counter, next to a few drinking glasses. India poured them each a glass.

"Cincin!" she said, and they clinked glasses. Eve slugged half of it.

Eve lit a Marlboro and exhaled. Alcohol and nicotine coursed through her veins. India smiled at her dreamily.

"How's Griswold?" India asked softly. She had spent last year at Miss Grey's, a boarding school with stables, but had gotten expelled. Now she was in public school in the city.

"Still adjusting. The kids are really different from my old friends." India smiled. "Friends like me?"

"No comparison! Classes are decent, but it's also weird having boys in them. Girls are so much smarter, except for one or two." Eve realized Clay had never spoken a word in English class. At Beaverton they gave you a better grade if you participated.

"Teachers at boarding school are also an odd bunch," India commented.

Eve threw her cigarette into an empty beer can in the sink. "One of them's taking me to supper."

"Who's the Casanova?"

Eve blushed. "It's fine. I can handle him."

India looked dubious, and took a sip of wine, a gold bangle glinting on her wrist. "There was one of those at Miss Grey's who had dinner parties with a group of carefully chosen girls. As if each of them could advance him in some way. He was an excellent cook. Does this man know about your family?"

Eve shook her head, unsure if Mr. Winkler would be impressed by Deirdre and Frederick. There were kids from much fancier families than hers at Griswold.

"It's never just a meal," India replied. She wrinkled her nose. "Mmmm, something smells delicious!"

Pungent pot smoke was wafting in their direction from the sofa. India headed toward it. Admiring India's elegant saunter, Eve wished her oldest girlfriend was with her at Griswold.

. . . .

"Your mom's such an amazing painter," Justine said.

Clay nodded, still staring at his mother's painting, but then Justine saw his expression go dark.

Justine didn't understand; if her mother were a famous artist she'd have been thrilled—just being here was a dream—the hippest loft, the coolest party, the best city on the planet. She could stay forever.

Suddenly she spotted Bruce on the sectional. Her heart jumped. "I need another beer," she told Clay and hurried off. She grabbed a can from the tub and forced herself to slow down and walk casually toward the sofa.

Bruce and Damon were draped on the cushions, Damon holding a small plastic bag of white powder.

"Hi, gorgeous," Bruce said, slurring slightly, patting the sofa beside him. His eyes were bloodshot. "I was hoping you'd be here," he whispered, leaning toward her, his breath beery. "But I gotta piss, be right back, save my seat," he said, as he rose unsteadily to his feet. Justine watched as he walked toward the back of the loft. Clay slid onto the sofa and Eve arrived, holding a glass of wine that she set down on the table amid ashtrays overflowing with cigarette butts, empty beer cans, and crushed potato chips.

Damon started cutting lines on a mirror with a playing card. He bent over and snorted one through a rolled-up bill, then another, before he offered Clay the bill. Clay shook his head. Damon showed Clay the card.

"Don't say no to the suicide king."

Before Clay could respond, a beautiful girl walked toward them.

"Hey!" Eve saluted, waving her over. "Justine, this is India Clarkson." India perched on the sofa and crossed her legs, as if she were at a ladies' luncheon. She held a glass of wine and wore one of those bracelets with little circles you could unlock.

"Nice to meet you," India said, holding out a hand.

"You too," Justine replied, as India's hand barely made contact before it slipped from hers.

"Are you at Griswold as well?"

"Yes."

"Doesn't it totally suck?" Eve asked.

"I tried to warn her," India said.

Eve shrugged. "I was going batshit at home. Sharing?" she asked Damon.

He handed her the bill.

"I went to Miss Grey's," India explained to Justine, waving her fingers, the bones of which were like those of a small bird. "Past tense."

Had India gotten kicked out? The girl was so elegant and poised it was hard to imagine her doing anything wrong.

Eve was holding the hair out of her face with one hand and snorting half a line into one nostril. She offered Justine the bill, wiping her nose with the back of her sleeve. Justine shook her head.

"Why did you leave?" Justine asked India.

"Poor academic performance," India said solemnly.

Justine wondered how badly you'd have to do to get booted for bad grades. She'd heard Damon had all Ds.

"That's not the story," Eve said, sniffing. "India got kicked out for trying to ride her horse back into the city. How is Mr. Ed anyway?"

"Much better, thank you."

"Who's Mr. Ed?" Justine asked.

"My father's horse," India replied. "I rescued him. He was half starved."

"He lives with her," Eve explained.

"In her house?"

They all laughed.

"No," India said. "He's finally in a good stable on Long Island."

India opened a hinged box and took out a cigarette rolled in black paper.

"Allow me," said Clay, flicking open his Zippo.

"I can't believe you still have your father's lighter," India said, blowing out a stream of smoke. "It's so debonair."

"Dad *was* debonair," Clay said bitterly.

Justine wondered for a second if Mr. Bradley was dead. But surely someone would have told her that. "Can I have some of that?" She indicated a metal bowl with a pile of tangled weed. Even through the cigarette smoke and booze, she could pick up its sickly sweet scent. Barbara had excellent taste.

Clay pulled a wooden pipe from a box on the table, took a pinch of weed, and stuffed it in the bowl. He lit it for Justine. His dark head leaned close to hers as she inhaled.

For the first time since she'd started smoking pot, Justine didn't immediately feel like she was going to choke or cough. It must be really good quality. Barbara was right, it was strong. Really strong.

The room began to recede, and people's voices grew further away. Justine leaned back on the sofa and closed her eyes. The room started to spin.

Justine had gotten drunk for the first time when she was eight or nine, maybe the same night she had danced with Frank Langella. She couldn't remember; the parties all merged into one. She had finished off the abandoned glasses of champagne, even though she knew it was like eating chewing gum off the sidewalk. The stuff was absolutely delicious and the bubbles tickled her tongue. Within a few minutes she was wasted.

She felt a jab on the arm.

"Wha?"

"Are you deaf?" Eve was saying. "I said let's dance!"

"Too stoned . . ." Her tongue was fat and blocking everything.

"Oh great! You're going to sleep and I'll be up till five!" Eve jumped up and started dancing with Clay and India. Eve was bopping from foot to foot. Jesus, she was making Justine dizzy. India was swaying. Clay was jerky, a white boy with no rhythm. She had never been this stoned. She didn't know how to get off the sofa.

By the time Justine woke up, she had no idea how much time had passed. Clay was beside her, eyes closed, mouth slightly open. She was aware of desperately needing something to drink, and stood up, steadying herself on the arm of the sofa. The party was still raging, the bass and her head throbbing in unison. She headed toward the back of the loft, weaving down a long hallway, balancing with her hand on the wall. A floorboard creaked and sagged beneath her foot. So many doors. First one, king-size canopy bed. Next, storage with canvases and paint supplies. Finally, a bathroom.

Justine leaned over the sink and gulped handfuls of water. Then she lurched to the toilet where she puked up chicken, lettuce leaves, and beer. Hanging over the bowl, she panted, still stoned. In the mirror her eyeliner was runny, blackened, and ghoulish. *Nosferatu.* A medicine cabinet held a bottle of Scope. Justine breathed, feeling a little better. Had Eve left? She didn't have cab fare to get home.

She opened the bathroom door.

Bruce emerged from a bedroom across the hall.

"There you are," he said, and pulled her into the room with the huge bed. He kissed her, and she held on, clutching his shoulders for balance. They moved toward the bed and stumbled onto it, landing hard on the satin covers.

Bruce leaned on one arm, putting his hand between her legs.

"I've been wanting you so much," he murmured. His eyeballs burned red in the candlelight. *"Justine."* He pinched her inner thigh, then moved his hand up, touching her through the stockings, then unbuckling his belt. Justine took the belt and pulled it free.

"Lie down." She pushed Bruce onto his back, climbed on top, and straddled him. Then she drew the belt slowly through her fingers, looking down at him pinned beneath her. "What was *Justine* into?" She stretched the belt across his chest with both hands, leaned down, and kissed Bruce slowly, enjoying his impatience.

He gripped her hips and flipped her over, grabbing the belt and pulling her arms over her head. Kneeling on top of her, Bruce strapped her wrists to the bedpost. She watched his face, intent and determined. He tore her stockings to her ankles. One of her flats fell to the floor with a thud.

Bruce's eyes were glassy as he fumbled to unzip his pants. He pulled them to his knees, his T-shirt still on as he spread her legs and tried to thrust into her. It didn't work.

He leaned down and licked her sweaty neck. He tried again. She was too dry, it chafed.

Justine struggled to move. She would help him.

But Bruce was pushing over and over at her, without success. She was tied up so tightly. She needed her hands free. She tried to spread her legs farther.

"Fuck!" Bruce came all over her stomach. He collapsed on top of her, panting. Then he stood up, disappeared, and came back seconds later, wiping the semen off himself, then sponging some of it off her stomach.

He threw the soiled paper on the floor and started out the door.

"Hey!"

He reappeared in the doorway.

"Untie me!"

He hesitated, looking at her splayed body. She pulled her legs closed.

"I was thinking we'd have another go." Bruce blew her a kiss before closing the door behind him.

The air from the window was congealing the liquid on her stomach. She prayed it wasn't on Eve's dress. Her wrists ached from the belt. Justine heard a soft cooing and turned to see a pigeon squatting on the sill. Its beady eye met hers. Had the bird watched everything? The pigeon cocked its head to the side, as if sympathetic, but then took off in a flutter.

She closed her eyes and passed out.

"Justine?"

She opened her eyes a crack. A blurry, dark-haired figure was approaching the bed.

"Jesus Christ! What happened?" Clay came into focus, looking furious.

He grabbed a paisley shawl off a chair and threw it over her sprawled nakedness.

"Don't look," she said, but it was too late. He had seen.

Clay unbuckled her and she rubbed her sore shoulders. Sitting up, Justine pulled the shawl around her. The cum was cold and sticky on her stomach. "Where's Eve?"

"She left; she couldn't find you."

"What time is it?"

"Past two. Shit, are you okay? Was this Bruce?"

Justine nodded, then shook her head. Suddenly she was about to cry.

"Hang on!" He ran out the door.

Tears ran down her face. How was she going to get back to Eve's?

The door opened, but instead of Clay, Tierney's friend Jackie stared at her.

"Get out," Justine said, failing to hide her tears.

Jackie crossed her arms over her boiled-wool jacket. "Glad to see you're paying the rent." Her face was bright red from alcohol.

"Eat me."

"You're not my type. Anyway, all the other bathrooms are full," she said, lumbering across the room.

The sound of the toilet lid being lifted was followed by vigorous peeing.

Jackie came out, stuffing her turtleneck into her skirt.

"Did you even flush?" Justine asked.

Jackie snorted and slammed the bedroom door.

Clay reappeared with a can of Coke. It was the best thing she'd ever tasted. He sat next to her on the slippery satin.

"Thanks." She wiped her eyes and looked into his.

Green, full of pity.

"Don't look at me, I look like shit."

"You're incredibly beautiful."

She eyed him suspiciously, but saw he meant it.

He leaned over and picked up her shoe. "I'll wait outside for you to get dressed. I can take you home."

"You don't have to," she said.

"I want to."

As they rode up Park, Justine stared bleakly at the hookers on every corner. It was bizarre that such a fancy street was lined with prostitutes at night, and she couldn't help staring at their sequined dresses, their thigh-high boots. How many men did they blow a night? How much did they charge?

The silence in the cab was laden with things unsaid. She needed to talk, anything to dispel the awkwardness. "Can I ask you something?"

"Sure." Clay ran his fingers through his hair.

"Why'd Barbara say you wouldn't approve?"

His smile was rueful. "She thinks I'm square. I'm the only semi-responsible one in my family." The cab hit a bump and caught air. "Slow down! Here, put your seat belt on." He leaned over and buckled it for her. "My family's nuts. Sister's in a cult in Hawaii, and you've met my mom."

"Is your dad dead?"

"No, why?"

"Sorry, when you and India were talking about his Zippo . . ."

"He might as well be." Clay gazed out the window. "He left us."

"How old were you?"

"Unfortunately, it was only a few months ago."

The cab pulled up in front of 1122.

"I'll watch you get inside," Clay said.

"Thanks." She moved away, wishing they had more time. She wanted to know about his family. Sister in a cult? How was that possible? The only cults she had heard of were like that one with the purple Kool-Aid. Still, at least she wasn't the only one with a kooky family. Maybe she and Clay had more in common than she had thought.

"Anytime," he replied, staying on his side of the cab. Of course he wouldn't get near her, she thought bitterly; she was covered in sperm and puke.

She climbed out. The door was locked and so she rang the bell.

A gaunt man opened it.

"May I help you?"

"Hey, Jakey!" Clay leaned out the window. "She's staying at the Strauses'!"

"Ten-four, Bradley."

Clay gave Justine a small smile, then she watched his cab disappear into the night.

Justine hung the stained dress over Eve's shower curtain rod. Naked, she crawled under the soft covers and fell into a dreamless sleep.

ELEVEN

INDIA CLARKSON LAY ON THE CUSHIONS EXHALING POT smoke. Was it her imagination or did she need more to flip the switch these days? Maybe Jimmy had sold her an inferior batch.

The phone rang. India let it. Nobody she wanted to talk to called before ten.

Had her father found her number? She'd made sure it was unlisted, but she knew she wouldn't be able to hide from him forever.

Two men argued on the street below; a dog barked. It was called Hell's Kitchen for a reason, inhabited by drug dealers, prostitutes, and people on the edge. But here India had been able to hide from anyone who had known her before. She had become another person. And in ways she had not anticipated. After moving in, India had gone out to buy votive candles from the store and several strangers had nodded at her on the street. It was mysterious, but then in the bodega on the corner of Tenth Avenue the clerk addressed her in Spanish. India answered him in his own tongue; she was fluent in Spanish, French, and Italian, the gift of Mademoiselle and several governesses. India realized that with her dark hair and olive skin, they all took her for a local Latina.

India thought about what Eve had said about her English teacher taking her to supper, and how her warning signals had flashed. All men wanted the same thing.

The phone rang again. India regarded the plastic thing, imagining who might be on the other end.

"Hello?"

"Is this Miss Clarkson? Thomas Lentmore, curator at the Metropolitan Museum of Art. Can you speak a moment?"

India imagined the Greek vase her grandmother had donated smashed in shards on the museum floor.

"Yes?"

"I'm a curator at the Costume Institute, and we're putting together the Yves Saint Laurent show."

Was this a joke?

"I'm sure you know all about it."

"No," India replied, "I'm afraid I don't." She twirled the phone cord around her wrist until it left a white spiral indentation on her skin.

The curator cleared his throat. "I know it may sound unusual. It's the first time a museum has done a major retrospective of a living couturier," he said. "It's a bit late in the game, but we know Kiki was a muse of his. A board member suggested you might still have some pieces."

India glanced back into the living room, at the garment rack. "I'm not sure I do." Cupping the receiver with her cheek, she rubbed the curly marks on her wrist.

"Would it help if I described the pieces she had in mind? Or perhaps I could pay you a visit? The show is terribly soon, I could come this afternoon."

India went rigid. "I don't have much anymore. You're wasting your time. I'm sorry. Goodbye."

India walked back into the living room. The garment rack held many floor-length gowns, tailored cocktail dresses, colorful silk blouses. Touching a purple tulle and black velvet piece, India checked the label, even though she knew what it said. There were many Saint Laurents, but India recalled this particular dress being created for Kiki by Yves himself. She remembered sitting on the carpet of his studio in Paris, looking out the window into the court-yard garden, listening to the metal rasp of scissors, gathering up small pieces of black lace as they fell to the floor. Her mother had been the perfect size 2.

India hadn't understood the designer at the time, the frightened look on his face, his darting glance, his pinched posture. He had made her uncomfortable with his restless unease in his own body, a discomfort that she now understood so well.

India looked in the mirror. Everyone said she resembled her mother, the same small bones, high cheekbones, dark eyes, black hair, olive complexion. It was hard to believe that half of her genes were her father's.

That Greek vase of her grandmother's had been on a pedestal at home, spotlit, a centerpiece with agile black figures prancing across a terra-cotta surface. Now in the Metropolitan, its beauty was dimmed by its proximity to so many others, just a bunch of pottery lined up in a dusty storage facility.

India imagined these dresses hung on lifeless plastic manne-quins lined up in similar fashion.

This fabric had touched Kiki's skin, had absorbed her perspira-tion and perfume, and India would be damned before letting some covetous curator touch any of it.

E ve yanked the boiling sweater dress away from her chest and fanned herself with her hand. "Where is my brother? Just watch my mother take it all out on me."

"What time was the game supposed to be over?" Justine asked.

"No idea. Give me a fag," Eve demanded.

"I thought you couldn't smoke in here," Justine said, chucking a gold box of Benson & Hedges at her.

"If Mom comes, I'll just blame you." Eve exhaled in the general direction of the window.

Thank God none of them knew about last night, Justine thought. She had expected Eve to beg her for details about the party, but the whole day, Eve hadn't asked her a thing. Suddenly Justine wondered if Eve sensed that something was wrong. Justine felt an all-too-familiar stab of shame. On one hand, Eve's discretion was a relief, but on the other hand, it implied that Eve suspected the worst.

But the worst wasn't even Bruce. It was that Clay had seen her naked and covered in semen. Despite being wasted, Justine remembered every detail. And even after that, he had taken her all the way home.

"Where the hell is Sandy?" Eve said. She whirled on a heel toward Justine. "When are you leaving? What movie are you seeing?"

"Something foreign," Justine replied.

If Eve thought she was still going to Clay's, then she obviously had no idea what had happened last night. Justine should have known that Eve was way too innocent to imagine such things. And she was glad Eve didn't know, but still, how much she longed to lay her head down on Eve's lap, for Eve to stroke her hair and tell her it hadn't been her fault.

"Barbara will probably go for a silent film with no subtitles." Eve threw the sweater dress in the direction of her closet. "She'll mime along."

Deirdre stormed in. "Have you stuffed your brother in a trunk?"

Just then they heard Sandy in the front hall. "Mom? I'm starving!"

. . . .

In the cab to the restaurant Eve stared out the window. Was Justine actually going to Clay's? She had been awfully vague about her plans. Maybe it was because Barbara and Clay had been vague themselves.

Eve had pretended to be asleep last night when Justine came home. She had seen the stained suede dress hanging in the bathroom in the morning. She didn't dare ask what had happened. It must have been with Bruce, and it must have been bad. Justine had been uncharacteristically quiet all day, losing track of conversations midsentence. Eve didn't want to pester her for details.

The Quilted Giraffe was nestled in a discreet town house on Second Avenue.

"Straus, table for four."

The maître d' consulted his list. Deirdre was staring at two people by the bar.

"Look, Frederick. It's Margot and Keith!" Deirdre waved to them and headed in their direction.

"Darling!" Keith Wilson kissed Eve's mother on both cheeks. He was always so stylish, with his salt-and-pepper hair and double-breasted blazers. "Margot, you remember the Strauses?"

Margot Moore, SoHo gallerist, fierce-faced with blazing red lipstick. "I've known Deirdre and Frederick since before I knew *you*."

"These are our children, Eve and Sandy," Frederick said, nudging Sandy forward.

"Eve aspires to work in the art world," Deirdre said. "You're her role model, Margot."

Eve wished she could submerge herself in someone's cocktail, but Margot was busy scanning the room to see if she knew anyone else.

Frederick signaled the bartender.

"Margot's doing a new Massimo Sforza show," Keith said. Margot turned back to them, taking a sip of her kir royale.

Deirdre clasped her hands. "Oh please! Let me have one!"

Her mother had been dying for a Sforza painting for as long as Eve could remember. It was unclear why they were so difficult to acquire.

"Is he still having his moment?" Frederick asked, handing Deirdre a martini.

"Frederick," Margot said, looking at Eve's father with pity, "Massimo is a legend. We're fortunate to witness history in the making. And, Deirdre, I'm sorry," she said, "I know how eager you are for a Sforza but I'm afraid all the good pieces are already spoken for. I know your taste. I wouldn't sell you one of the inferior works."

Deirdre sloshed some martini on her dress and began dabbing a spot on her chest with a bar napkin. The paper started to disintegrate, leaving white dandruff on the magenta fabric.

"When's the show?" Frederick asked.

"Right after Labor Day," Margot said.

Almost a year away, and all the best pieces were spoken for? Margot must be lying.

"Eve was at a party at the Bradleys' last night," Deirdre said.

Eve looked at her mother in surprise.

"Bradley?" Margot asked. "As in *Barbara Bradley?*"

Eve nodded.

"Barbara's new work is on display in her loft," her mother continued, "for an intimate few. Eve and Clayton have always been so close."

"Barbara is one of the few true artists left in SoHo, and I mean in a real *1968* way," Margot said.

"They're practically cousins." Deirdre flashed Margot her most convincing smile.

"I just love Clayton," Keith said. "Isn't he the most delectable thing?"

Frederick grunted something unintelligible.

"Loosen up, Freddy," Deirdre said.

"It's okay, sweetheart," Keith said. "Freddy hasn't been comfortable around me since I came out. No, really! I'm used to it. A lot of my old friends are so distant now."

The maître d' appeared. "Mr. Straus," he said, "your table is ready."

The maître d' led them through the hushed restaurant to a table in the center of which was a bird of paradise in a black vase.

"Your father likes to face out," Deirdre said, pointing Frederick to the chair by the wall. Eve sat and picked up her peach jacquard napkin, which had been carefully folded into a giraffe on the plate. The apricot-and-gold plates were set on a soft brocade tablecloth, flanked by silverware with black porcelain handles.

"Welcome," the waiter said, staring at Sandy. "My name's Darius. May I offer you a cocktail?"

"I need a moment with the wine list," Frederick said. "Is Barry available?"

Barry was the owner and chef.

"No, he's in France," the waiter said.

"He said he'd be here." Her father's voice was edgy.

"He'll be back Sunday," Darius reassured him.

Eve's parents exchanged a sour look.

"Can I have a Shirley Temple?" Sandy asked.

"I suppose," Frederick said. "Eve?"

Eve just shook her head. Her parents never let her have wine, and she was too old for silly kid drinks.

"One Shirley Temple," Deirdre said, and the waiter moved away.

Frederick gazed glumly at the wine list. After a moment he snapped it shut and looked up at Eve. "Honey, I've been meaning to tell you that you look great. Griswold agrees with you."

"It must be all that fresh air," Deirdre said.

Eve tried to smile, then stared down at her plate. How could she begin to explain all that had happened in just a few weeks?

"They've raised the price of the beggar's purses," Deirdre mused, examining the menu, which was bound in peach suede. Those were the little crepe bundles that Eve had wanted to bring home for Justine.

"Have whatever you want," Frederick said, peering around the restaurant.

"Eve, what are you reading in French?" Deirdre asked.

"*Huis Clos.*"

"God, I hated that book," Frederick said.

"And in English class we just read *Catcher in the Rye*. And now *Cat's Cradle*." Eve had already heard her mother's protestations on the phone, but this time neither parent reacted.

"Interesting syllabus," Deirdre said. "What on earth does she have in mind?"

"It's *Mister* Winkler, I told you that. And *he's* taking me out. To The Mill."

"Really?"

Eve nodded.

Deirdre digested this for a moment then put her hand on Eve's. "Sweetheart, that sounds very flattering. They always talk about how much more involved the teachers are with the students at boarding school. I do wish he didn't have you reading Vonnegut. That's not even literature!"

"Griswold sucks," Eve agreed.

"Please don't say 'sucks.'"

Sandy leaned toward Eve. "Is he giving you an A for ass kisser?"

Eve tried to give him a swift kick under the table, but her foot collided painfully with the metal post in the center instead. Glasses rattled and the bird of paradise wobbled treacherously.

Deirdre steadied the vase with her hand.

"What's Steak Diane?" Sandy asked.

Eve aimed another jab at her brother under the table with her finger.

"Beef," Frederick replied. "Try it. I might order the Veal Oscar."

"I had no idea they were revamping all those old classics!" Deirdre said. "How inventive."

"Maybe. Either way we'll need a good red."

Deirdre fiddled with her fork for a moment, then said in an unctuous tone, "I love it that you're getting so much attention from your English teacher. He must see how intellectual you are." She prodded her husband. "Frederick, did you hear, he's taking her to The Mill?"

Her father nodded distractedly.

"Don't you think I should be really flattered?" Eve asked her mother.

"Of course you should," her mother said, as the sommelier hurried toward them. "You're obviously making a very good impression."

While Frederick ordered a Burgundy, Eve gazed at the decor, the soft peach hue, the tall vases, the still lifes of fruit bowls on the walls. Soft lighting cast a warm glow on the tables. There was a low thrum of conversation, and the waiters and water bearers moved around the room like ballet dancers. She felt the well-being that always descended on her in a good restaurant. Was Justine cabbing it down to Clay's right now? Curled on the sectional in a tête-à-tête with Barbara?

"What's your hot friend doing tonight?" Sandy said.

Eve rolled her eyes.

Deirdre pursed her lips. "Probably out, prancing around half naked."

Eve was about to object, but Deirdre's tense expression kept her momentarily silent. Every one of Eve's friends couldn't be like India Clarkson, with whom Eve could play golf and ride horses. Was it Justine's freedom, her blithe spirit, or her beauty that made Deirdre squirm?

"She's the best thing about Griswold!" Eve blurted.

Frederick, unperturbed by this outburst, patted her arm and took a sip of his water. "I didn't make one friend the whole time I was there," he said. "Would have made it more bearable."

"What?" Eve snatched her arm away. "I thought you liked it!"

"Sssh! We're in a restaurant!" hissed Deirdre. "Please keep it down."

"I hated it," Frederick said quietly. "I was horribly homesick."

"Why didn't you tell me?"

"Darling, you had your heart set on going there, your father wouldn't have wanted to dampen your enthusiasm," Deirdre said.

"And it was thirty years ago," her father added. "And you're an utterly different person than I was, and we live in a different era. For one thing, it was all boys!"

"Isn't *parenting* kind of timeless?"

"Sometimes, sweetheart," her father said, "as a parent you have to take a back seat."

Why didn't they take the back seat when haranguing her about grades? Or when ordering her who not to be friends with?

"You'll make the best of it," said Frederick, with a firmness in his voice that Eve knew was final.

"Dinner with a professor? Looks like you already are," Deirdre said.

Sandy slurped his Shirley Temple. "Want to see me tie my cherry stem in a knot?"

· · · · · · · · ·

Except for the occasional horn floating up from the street, the Straus apartment was quiet. Justine lay on Eve's guest bed, watching the pattern of headlights kaleidoscope on the ceiling. *Bruce.* Was he angry at her or embarrassed? He hadn't acted sorry in the least. And sweet Clay, coming to find her, taking care of her. Seeing her like that.

Justine stared at the ceiling until her eyes started to water.

Finally, she got up and tiptoed down the carpeted hallway and across the stone foyer into the library, a lurid haven of lacquered plum, with a velvet sofa and ottomans. A bottle of Stoli sat on a wire shelf in the bar fridge, crystal tumblers on the counter. On a silver tray rested Bacardi, Averna, Campari. She picked up a bottle of Scotch with a name like the croak of a frog and took a whiff. It smelled like the sole of an old shoe. Justine poured herself a full glass of the vodka and padded back across the stone foyer and into the living room.

It was as muted as a museum. Backlit glass shelves lined a wall and displayed a collection of conch shells. A face was reflected in the glass. She whirled around, sloshing her vodka on the floor. It was just a photograph of a naked man, with bees crawling over him like cloves on a ham. It was creepy, and an odd choice for such an elegant living room. But then again Barbara Bradley was painting severed heads—the macabre seemed to be in fashion.

Down the hall, Justine crept into the Strauses' darkened bedroom and opened the closet door. A patchwork of color swam before her. She was getting drunk, and it felt good. She thrust her face toward the mirror as she fluffed up her hair, then turned to focus her blurred vision on the rows of dresses, gleaming bags, and hundreds of pairs of heels. Stepping farther in, Justine touched a cherry tulle, a black satin strapless, and a narrow floor-length silk jersey with a design of toucans. She slipped off her clothes and pulled the toucan dress over her head; it was perfect, clinging lovingly to her hips, pooling at her ankles. The dress reminded her of that book with the photo of Veruschka on her parents' coffee table.

Justine donned a pair of green sandals and tottered into Mr. Straus's bathroom. Black toilet, black marble counter. The man of the house. She opened the medicine cabinet and examined the orange prescription bottles, rich-person candy like Tierney had, Aramis cologne, Bel Ami deodorant.

The phone rang and Justine jumped. She downed the vodka, the icy liquid shuddering in her throat, then went back to the library and knelt by the fridge to pour another. The phone rang again. She answered it.

"Hello?"

"Justine? It's Barbara! Barbara Bradley."

"Oh . . . hi!"

"Clayton and I were just choosing a film. I thought you might want to weigh in."

"I don't think I can come."

"Why not?"

"The Strauses were pissed that I came home so late last night," she lied, "so I should stay put." *And your son saw me naked and strapped to your bed covered in semen.*

"Why would the Strauses care?" Barbara asked. "You aren't their child."

"True, but they seem very strict."

"Watch out, Eve will become a tattooed biker chick if they aren't careful."

Justine imagined showing up in this fabulous outfit. Too bad she couldn't face Clay, and, anyway, she didn't have cab fare.

"Raid their liquor cabinet," Barbara advised.

"Already on my second."

"Good girl. Nighty night."

"Night."

She hung up. The vodka was going down easily now.

Justine glanced at her watch. It was only ten. She dialed her parents' number in New Haven. It rang and rang. They could be in

Guam as far as she knew. Justine thought of her father's stubble, her mother's soft cheek when she kissed her good night. Although loath to admit it, she missed them. Justine longed for the familiar clutter of home: the potted plants on the sills, the mismatched mugs on the open wooden shelves in the kitchen, the long farm table piled with old copies of *The Paris Review*. This apartment, with its limestone floors and glossy walls, felt like an expensive mausoleum.

Justine downed the rest of the vodka, then staggered back to Eve's room and collapsed on the bed, still wearing Mrs. Straus's dress.

TWELVE

"UGH, YOU REEK OF CIGARETTES," TIERNEY SAID, BARELY looking up from her magazine.

Justine threw her mail on the desk.

"Hi, Tierney, how are *you*?"

"Fine," Tierney said, returning to her magazine.

Justine unzipped her duffel and started piling dirty clothes into a plastic laundry basket.

"I'm only responding because breeding demands it," Tierney added.

"Do you have any quarters?" Justine asked wearily. "I can give you some dollar bills in exchange." Her mother had finally sent her thirty dollars in singles.

"Why don't you just use the laundry service?"

"Too expensive."

"Life sucks, and then you die." Tierney turned the page. "Aren't you going to be polite and ask me about *my* weekend?"

No, she wasn't. She was going to gouge this girl's eyes out.

Tierney gave her a conspiratorial look. "I heard a rumor about Bruce."

Justine froze, heart pounding. Had Clay told anyone?

"He's going out with Christina. They just went public, but they've been seeing each other in secret all semester." Tierney gave Justine a smug smile, then thought for a moment. "He bagged his crew race to be with her this weekend. What an idiot. My father always says dating can't beat varsity." Although Tierney had sneered at her father when he was dropping her off, she enjoyed quoting his lame apothegms, always with an unconscious tilt of her head toward the Yale banner on the wall as if it were a family crest.

"What if you and Eve don't get into Yale?" Justine snarled.

"Eve who?"

"Straus?" How could her own roommate not know her best friend? Even if Tierney lived under a rock, ignoring Justine's life must have taken effort.

Tierney took a sip from her grape soda and looked at Justine blankly. "Do I know her?"

"She's in our English class?"

"That punk girl?"

Tierney had no idea what punk even looked like. Was she just goading her?

"Eve's dad went to Yale, and her grandfather, and great-grandfather!"

"Big deal"—Tierney waved a dismissive hand—"so did mine."

Miles and Cressida had met at Bard College, but Justine was sure her roommate had never heard of the place.

Tierney threw the magazine on the bed and stood up, stretching her arms over her head like a lazy cat in the sun. She strode to her desk, dug in her makeup kit, pulled out a prescription bottle, and shook a few pills into her palm. What Justine would have given for one to dull the pain. Tierney's eyes closed as she chewed.

"What are those?"

The lime-green eyes opened. "None of your beeswax. What's Eve's last name again?"

"Straus."

"Are they rich?"

Justine stared at Tierney. What did that have to do with anything?

"Eve Straus . . ." Tierney repeated, throwing the makeup kit back in the desk and locking the drawer. She stuck the key in her pocket. "Jewish."

Justine stood up, resting the laundry basket on her hip.

"What does being Jewish or rich have to do with anything?"

Tierney looked at her pityingly. "Jews have to buy their way in. And Jackie told me about you and Bruce at the party."

"She has no fucking idea what happened," Justine said, heading for the door. She'd had more than enough of Tierney's bile.

"I bet you feel pretty used."

Justine would never speak to Tierney again. The room would be like one of those monasteries where you weren't allowed to talk. The silence would have a presence. Justine tore open the door and hurried down the hall.

·········

Once Eve had dumped her bag on her bed, she walked down the hill to the mailroom, thinking about her father's confession. If he'd been miserable at Griswold, why hadn't he said anything? It just made her even more homesick, thinking about it.

Why wouldn't her parents talk to her about anything that had happened when they were her age? Did they think that sharing their own experiences would topple them from some pedestal? Eve wondered what they had done back then. She wondered if they had been really naughty.

But they wouldn't tell her a thing.

The narrow mailroom was empty. Sunlight slanted across the brass postboxes. She turned the combination lock of her mailbox and pulled out a postcard with an image of the *Mona Lisa* with a moustache.

Come to my room this evening, so we can discuss your paper.

It had today's date on it. Tonight. Only a few hours away.

"Hey, cookie." David McClurken was next to her. He was taller than she'd remembered.

"Hi," she said. David made her nervous.

He pointed to the postcard. "Your friend's a fan of Duchamp." His pronunciation was perfect.

Eve looked again. Under the *Mona Lisa* there was some block lettering. She turned it over, and on the reverse side it said "L.H.O.O.Q. Marcel Duchamp. 1919. Centre Pompidou."

David's leather jacket gave off a meaty smell.

"Come for a cig?" she said.

"I was going to take a walk up in the Skeets. I want to show you something. You can smoke up there."

The Skeets, formerly a skeet-shooting range when Frederick was at Griswold.

She wondered if David knew that kids went there to make out.

They strode across the footbridge in silence.

"You know that postcard?"

Eve nodded, grateful that he didn't know it was from Mr. Winkler.

"Know what those letters mean?"

She shook her head.

"In French, it means she's horny."

How sly of her teacher. The Wanker was such an evil genius, Eve thought, blushing.

"Oh. Do you really speak French and German?" she asked, trying to hide her embarrassment.

"You read my poem."

Eve nodded. She should have told him sooner and told him how much she liked it.

"I take German, but my mom's French. It's my first language," he explained.

Eve was impressed. "Where are you from?"

"Kalamazoo, Michigan."

She imagined ranch houses on a cul-de-sac and kids riding bikes. "How'd you end up there?"

"Dad's family is from Kalamazoo. He met my mom during the war and brought her back." They had reached the footpath and the birch leaves were a brilliant yellow. Sparrows flitted in and out of the branches, sending an occasional leaf fluttering down like a magic carpet.

"You're from New York, right?" His eyes were a soft brown. His mouth was nice and full, and he had a habit of pausing midsentence, pursing his lips, as if what he was about to say were of great importance. "And," he said, pushing a curl of dark hair off his forehead, "you went to an all-girls school." *And you're horny*, Eve imagined him saying. Did he want her to be? She looked at him, and tried to tune in. Static!

"How do you know all that?"

"I know a lot about you. Like your birthday."

Eve stopped, putting her hands on her hips in disbelief.

"August fourth," David said proudly.

Eve tried to hide her surprise.

"Tibbets is my adviser," he explained. "I asked her."

"Didn't she wonder why you wanted to know?"

They had reached the Skeets, a beautiful sloping meadow high above campus, surrounded by thick forest. The grass was long, dry, and waving in the breeze.

"She didn't have to. I told her that I have a crush on you." He looked down at her earnestly. She felt simultaneously queasy and excited. If she and David were on a desert island she'd fall madly in love with him. But at Griswold, somehow, she wasn't sure. And she was going to the Wanker's tonight. How she wished she were still at home.

Suddenly Eve felt like she was going to start crying.

"I have to go," she said.

"Run, run away." His voice was softer than the wind.

She strained to hold back her tears.

David rested his finger gently on her sternum. "You aren't as tough as you pretend to be." He leaned forward. Finally, he was going to kiss her. But all he did was whisper, "It takes one to know one."

Eve clenched her jaw, wishing David would just make the decision for both of them, kiss her, push her down, take her right there, the scratchy grass making fuck knots in her hair. But still he stood there, gazing at her, his brown eyes moist with emotion.

"What did you want to show me?" she asked, stepping back.

David held a finger aloft. "Listen."

The trees surrounded them in a colorful ring. A bird trilled somewhere in the forest, *peter peter peter.* Another answered it. A duet. Grass rustled around her legs like skirts. *Peter peter.*

"What is it?"

"Tufted titmouse. And look. Purple martin."

A bird swept past. Then another song, a rapid jumble of rising and falling notes.

"Doesn't it sound like 'If I sees you, I will seize you'?" David said.

Eve flung herself down on the ground, arms spread. The sky was growing dark, a single star shone above. She gripped a clump of grass and tore it like hair from a scalp. David lay down. There she was, she thought, ripe for the picking.

"So, are you going to seize me?"

David looked sideways. "If I could be sure that was what you really wanted."

> *If only I knew, what you alone know,*
> *If you only knew what you wanted.*

Eve chucked the grass into the night and gazed back at him. *I want him*, she thought, feeling the warmth of his breath on her cheek. David would take her right here, right now, not the Wanker, never the Wanker.

"I can wait," David said.

A martin arched over her head, forked tail dipping in and out of the tall grass. The birds would soon migrate, fighting wind and weather for warmth and sunshine. How Eve wished she could shrink herself down and, clinging to their bony shoulders, ride home on their beating wings.

"Kiss me," she whispered.

David leaned down and kissed her gently, but briefly. He sat back and stroked her hair.

Her stomach rumbled. He glanced at his watch. "Shoot. Dinner's over in twenty minutes." He jumped to his feet and held out a hand. Reluctantly, Eve let him pull her up and walked beside him across the footbridge toward the dining hall.

THIRTEEN

MR. WINKLER OPENED HIS DOOR, SWIRLING BRANDY IN A snifter. He was wearing jeans and a flannel shirt and looked casual and young. Which, it occurred to Eve, he actually was. He was barely out of college. Or graduate school, anyway.

"Greetings," he murmured. "How was your holiday?"

"Good, and yours?" Eve said, sick with nerves.

He did not answer, but beckoned her in and closed the door behind her. She followed him into the living room. "Drink?"

"What are you serving?"

"Anything you desire," he said, his eyes sweeping across her and resting, ultimately, on her face. "At my house you can relax."

"Luxe, calme et volupté?"

"Miss Straus, you amaze me . . ." he said.

Eve threw her jean jacket on the sofa.

"Seriously, what can I offer you?" He gestured to a rolling cart full of liquor bottles. So much for tea, she thought.

"Bourbon."

"Neat?"

"Okay," Eve replied, having no idea what that meant. She sat on the sofa and swung one leg over the other, hoping she looked confident, like a girl who knew what she wanted. She remembered the brush of David's lips on hers.

He poured the caramel liquid into a glass and handed it to her. It burned her tongue, like cotton candy gone wonderfully wrong.

"So . . ." he said, sitting beside her, "I have a poem I'd like to read you." He picked a book up from the coffee table and leafed through it. "It's called 'The Shark's Parlor' by James Dickey. He signed this collection for me. He spoke here last year and made a big impression on—"

"You're going to read me poetry instead of discussing my essay?" Eve interrupted, poking his thigh. "What would people say?"

"They might say I was educating you. But if you aren't interested in poetry . . ." Mr. Winkler tossed the book back onto the table.

She looked into his face, which was aglow with excitement. Excitement Eve had caused. Fuck poetry, she thought, he was going to kiss her.

"Shall I put on some music?" he asked. "Do you like Steely Dan?"

"Um, got any Bach?"

He pulled an album from the shelf and set the needle on the vinyl; lugubrious organ music filled the room. It was like being in a cathedral in Europe.

"Now, if that doesn't set a serious enough tone for you, Miss Straus, we're in big trouble." He sat next to her on the sofa and donned his tortoise reading glasses. They made him look very intellectual.

God, he was so unlike David, Eve thought. So at ease with girls. Chucking the essay aside, he would have his way with her. Bach would be their soundtrack. It would hurt as he ground her into the sofa, but she would want it to, she was ready. The reading glasses would be crushed beneath their bodies.

He picked up her essay and flipped open the cover page.

"Damn, where's my red pencil?" Mr. Winkler opened a drawer. "The beginning is strong."

"At least they taught me how to write a topic sentence at Beaverton."

"You never told me you went there. One of my girlfriends at Princeton was a Beaver. Amazing school. Here, this sentence needs some tweaking. . . . Vonnegut meant that ice-nine . . ."

Mr. Winkler had had a girlfriend? Of course he had. Probably many. It dawned on her that he might even have one now.

"Are we going to go over this sentence by sentence?" Eve poked his thigh again. He removed his glasses and looked at her. She swirled her drink, trying not to spill. Now she was in for it.

"I've been thinking about you," he said.

Should she admit she had been thinking of him too? Surely that would do it. He would pull her to him, his beard tickling her face as he slipped his hand under her shirt and unhooked her bra with an expert hand. It was as inevitable as the birds migrating. But she couldn't form the words.

Mr. Winkler picked up her paper and waved it at her. "I've been thinking this paper is a C plus."

"What?!" Eve exclaimed. Her teacher just looked at her.

"I've never gotten anything less than an A minus in my life!" she protested. "How could it be so bad? Please! Let me revise it, I'm sure I can make it better."

"I certainly hope so," he said. She felt like she was clutching on to the back of a moving train.

"Tell me what to do," she asked, her voice unsteady.

"With your paper?"

Eve blinked at him. "Could you give me comments and let me do another draft?"

"Don't you think I've made enough exceptions for you?" He touched her thigh slowly, deliberately.

She watched his finger, the hairs on his hand, the depression on her jeans that remained.

"Yes," she said, her heart thumping, "you have."

The clock chimed.

Eve gulped the bourbon. Her veins were on fire with the stuff.

"I'll give you one more chance on the draft."

"Thank you, I won't disappoint you, I promise."

"No, I don't imagine you will. Just don't look at me with that sad face. It kills me."

The mantel clock showed ten minutes until curfew. "I have to go," she said.

He nodded, handed her the jean jacket from the back of the sofa. "We're all set for Saturday. The Mill. Seven p.m." He smiled his cat grin as she pulled on her coat. "Nighty," he purred.

Outside it had started to drizzle, and Eve took off at a run across Elm Street as a car whizzed past, tires hissing on the wet asphalt. The air was cool with mist. Her footsteps echoed in the deserted stone courtyard of the arts center. She was a surrealist painting of a girl running with a wheel.

She would run forever and never come back.

Eve reached the footbridge, pounded across, then skidded to a stop, seeing the dorm mistress, Mrs. Tibbets, checking the clipboard behind the glass door.

"Thirty seconds, Miss Straus."

"Sorry! I was meeting with Mr. Winkler."

"Well, you barely made it. Were you stargazing on the way home?" Tibbets asked in a gentle voice as she fingered her turquoise necklace.

FOURTEEN

JUSTINE DREADED BUMPING INTO BRUCE WITH CHRISTINA. She decided to lie low for a few days, avoiding the smoker and eating on Upper campus. She would love to get revenge, but it was probably impossible. Did Bruce tie Christina up and come all over her stomach?

She also dreaded bumping into Clay.

On Friday afternoon, after slipping her *Cat's Cradle* essay through the mail slot at the Wanker's, she trudged toward the smoker. She had written the essay in a hurry and it was far from her finest effort.

It was just above freezing, and cold bit through Justine's coat. She had only a thin T-shirt on underneath and her cotton pants were far too light for the weather.

Stanley was there alone.

"Where've you been?"

"In the city." As if it happened every weekend, as if she were a maggot herself.

"I stayed here."

Oklahoma was pretty far away. Did Stanley stay for Thanksgiving and Christmas too?

"How'd you end up here anyway?"

"It's a long story, but basically one of my teachers found an ad in a paper for Griswold and encouraged me to apply. It was a miracle."

Stanley must also have a full scholarship.

"Bruce is going out with Christina."

"I heard," Stanley said. Of course, everyone had.

She had just been the girl he could drag into the janitor's room, or tie up at a drunken party.

"Asshole," she said.

"Hell hath no fury."

"*Fuck fury!* I'm going to chop his dick off."

They sat in silence. Justine watched the paper on her cigarette burn down, the ash tail growing dangerously long.

"How would you feel if I had a go with him?"

Justine stared at Stanley. He stared right back. The ash on her cigarette fell to the ground.

Suddenly it was all so ridiculous that Justine started to laugh, then choked on the smoke. She hacked and coughed until she finally regained her composure.

"My instincts have had years of fine-tuning," Stanley said, moving the dial on his boom box to another station. "He's such a horn-dog he'll do it."

Should she be offended? Did Stanley know what he did to her at Barbara's? Justine squinted at him, searching his face. He was absolutely serious.

Then maybe it hadn't been her fault after all. Maybe Bruce *was* just an organ with no brain. She clenched her jaw in disgust.

A lopsided moon had risen in the sky.

"He's such an asshole."

"Do I hear foul language?" Eve asked, coming around the corner.

"Stanley thinks Bruce will get it on with him."

"Oh, give me a break!" Eve snorted, pulling out a cigarette. "Talk about wishful thinking!"

"You're going to get busted again." Stanley wagged a long finger.

Justine suddenly had an image of Clay throwing the shawl over her. She put two fingers on her forehead, trying to press the thought away.

"I'm one hundred percent correct," Stanley said.

"Jesus H. Christ. Why do gay men think everyone else on the planet wants to try it? Bet you ten bucks," Eve said, holding out her pinkie finger.

"You know I don't have any money," Stanley said.

Eve offered Justine her pinkie.

"Broke," Justine said, holding out the lighter.

"Oh fine!" Eve said, grabbing it and lighting her cigarette. She inhaled deeply and let out a cloud of smoke, then waved her cigarette in the air. "How's this? If Stanley can screw Bruce by the end of the year, we each have to eat five of those gross dining-hall sausages."

"Nah. He can do better." Justine said, playing along. "How about, if he succeeds, we both have to dance in the Skeets naked and Stanley can invite anybody he wants to watch?"

Eve's jaw dropped open.

"How would he prove it?" Eve asked.

Justine thought for a second. "Pubic hair," she said.

"The tuft test . . ." Eve said, bursting into giggles.

It would never happen, but just imagining Bruce bent over and Stanley having his way with him made Justine feel there might be justice in the universe.

"You're on," Stanley was saying. "I've always wanted to score with one of the P.E. gods." He grinned happily. Justine eyed him. He must be bluffing. She couldn't imagine him scoring with anyone.

She stood up, tossed her hair, and said, "See you naked in the Skeets."

Eve was chewing a thumbnail. She didn't think Stanley was bluffing. "Will I see you at supper?"

Justine nodded and headed back to her dorm. The moon gazed down on her. The moon that had seen it all.

She turned up the Roxy Music on her Walkman and tried to disappear into Bryan Ferry's lament.

As she was crossing Elm Street, Justine felt a tap on her shoulder. Clay.

She removed her headphones.

"Hey," he panted. "I wanted to see how you were."

Had he been running after her?

"Why?"

"Uh, you know. The party?"

She stared at the pavement, crossing her arms over her chest.

"It's not like that kind of thing happens all the time," he said, almost apologetically.

"No, it just happens to me."

"I know how you feel," he said softly.

That was impossible. Justine knew it was. And she didn't want his pity. Or anyone else's.

Clay's breath made clouds in the cold air. He shifted from foot to foot, trying to stay warm. Rubbing his hands together, she noticed the tips of his fingers were blue. "What are you doing tomorrow night?" he asked.

Saturday night and no plans. Championship tiddlywinks.

"Come see *WarGames*."

"In town?"

"No, right there." He gestured to the arts center.

"Who with?"

Clay smiled, cocking his head. "Me! Who did you think?"

Was he asking her out? She blushed. "Uh no, NO! Yeah, sure. It's a date. I mean . . ."

God, she hated her fumbling idiot self.

"Excellent! I'll come get you around seven-thirty?"

"Yeah, great."

He touched her shoulder briefly then started to walk away. Justine watched him for a moment.

"Clay?"

He turned back.

"Thanks."

Clay shrugged, as if to say this is the way boys act. But they both knew it wasn't.

· · · · · · · · ·

Eve tore several blouses and dresses from her closet and threw them on the bed. Thank God Tabitha wasn't here to ask where she was going.

Blouse and skirt or dress? She was going to sweat right through anything she wore, she was such a wreck. Eve imagined her unsteady hand as she tried to sip her cocktail, imagined sloshing it down her front.

At last she chose the vintage teal and black dress with jet buttons. Her mother didn't let her wear heels, but maybe that was just as well, she'd probably trip. She put on black flats and then, at the last minute, a bit of mascara and lipstick.

The Mill was in an industrial brick building with steel casement windows overlooking the Wormley River. It must have been some kind of real mill at one point, Eve thought as she climbed out of the taxi. The interior was now a series of small wood-paneled rooms, with gold-framed paintings of fruits and flowers, and brass lamps on the tables.

"Reservation, mademoiselle?" asked a red-faced man with a roseate nose, behind a chipped oak lectern.

"Wanker? I mean, Winkler?" she said, her voice shaking.

The host led her into a warmly lit bar with a mural of a battle on the wall. There he was, sitting casually on a stool, sipping a martini. Only he had shaved off his beard. His denuded chin had a deep cleft, which his facial hair had previously concealed. Eve couldn't help but gape.

"Like it?" Mr. Winkler touched his face, stroking the bare skin.

She nodded mutely. He looked suddenly vulnerable, barely more than a boy.

"Wow," he said, eyeing her up and down, "you look beautiful."

"Oh, thanks."

Eve climbed onto a stool, crossing her ankles. Mr. Winkler's face was illuminated in the glow of the lamp, his transformation unsettling. Had he done it for her? She felt her cheeks redden. This felt like a date, a real date.

She glanced away, around the low-ceilinged room, looking to see if anyone she knew was here, anyone who might see her with the Wanker. But there was only one other couple in the bar, a woman with a meringue of white hair with a man in tomato-colored corduroys, sitting at a small table under the battle mural. They both had creamy-looking drinks with umbrellas and pineapple as garnish.

"What would you like?"

"Sloe gin fizz, please."

He called to the bartender, "Hank! Coke and grenadine for the lady."

The bartender glanced at them, then busied himself with the soda gun.

She gave Mr. Winkler a questioning look.

"Eve"—he lowered his voice—"at my house you can be any age you like. But in public, you're sixteen."

Fifteen, actually, but she decided not to enlighten him. "Fine by me. I hope he puts in extra cherries." Eve grabbed some bar nuts and started munching on them, wondering, with a twinge of nerves, if tonight she could—or should—call him Bob.

"When's your birthday?" she asked.

"April twelfth."

"Hmm, Aries, the ram."

"Anything wrong with that?"

"Hotheaded and impulsive."

The bartender set down her soda, several cherries submerged in it. She was positive he and the Wanker exchanged a knowing look. How many girls *had* Mr. Winkler brought here?

"Don't be fooled by astrology, Eve. I control my impulses."

"Oh, sure you do," she said, twirling the plastic stirrer in the glass.

"Speaking of, about that paper . . ."

That made her smile. He was just being pompous, puffing hot air. And, after all, she thought, looking around at the bar, they were far away from school.

"Can I have a sip of your cocktail?"

He pushed the martini toward her. She poked her own straw into the clear liquid, a drop of grenadine unfurling like a plume of blood.

Once the Wanker had finished the pink cocktail, the maître d' led them into a small room with a few tables with checkered tablecloths and oil lamps, all of them empty. Their table overlooked the water.

"Table ten, as requested," he said, placing menus on the table, bowing slightly, and walking away.

"Stiff competition at the old *moulin*," Eve joked, looking around at the vacant seats as she opened the menu. The names of the dishes were in French, followed by a fleur-de-lis. There were no prices— Eve had seen this before in restaurants. Her father explained that it was good manners. Right, thought Eve, so oblivious female diners could order the chateaubriand, unaware that it was the most expensive thing in the restaurant? Power struggle, even on a menu.

She was grateful for the translations into English. "What are you having?"

"The *brandade de morue* is delicious."

"So gloppy. My dad loves it, it's practically all he ate the whole time we were in Provence."

"How come you're so sophisticated?"

Eve looked up. Was he making fun of her? "Why, because I've been to France?"

"You continue to surprise me," Mr. Winkler said, leaning forward. "You quote Baudelaire, Salinger, you're well read, well traveled. Unusual for a girl of your age."

The flickering flame of the oil lamp danced on his chin. She watched it.

"You don't like me without a beard."

"No, I do! It's just that you look so much younger!" Almost appropriate for me, she thought. This made her even more anxious.

Mr. Winkler stroked his chin self-consciously. "I'm not that much older than you, you know." Had he grown the beard on purpose to make himself look more mature? And had he shaved it off tonight so that they would look less conspicuously like teacher and student?

"I think I'll have the steak frites."

"How do you like it?"

"Really rare."

The waiter appeared. The Wanker drained his martini and ordered another round.

"You actually drink vodka with food?"

"Gin. Why, is that déclassé?"

"*Totally.* You have *so* much to learn." She giggled, and sat more comfortably in her chair.

"We can teach each other." He put his hand briefly over hers. She felt goose bumps spread up her arm. "Tell me about yourself, Eve," he said.

"Let's see." She unfolded her napkin in her lap. "Born August fourth, that's Leo. German Jewish family." She wasn't sure why she had mentioned that, maybe because of her mother's endless digressions into their family's heritage, how long they had been in the States, how her great-great-grandfather had been in Taft's cabinet, how his brother had started this department store . . .

He gestured for her to continue.

"I went to Beaverton, as you know, and hated it from day one. Uptight maiden-aunt teachers trying to punish me because I was smart. Every time I'd raise my hand they'd ignore me on *purpose,* even if I was the only one who knew the answer." Eve paused, realizing that she was close to launching into an uncontrolled rant: how much she hated her brother, her mother and father's rules, her mother's obsession with art, her mother's social climbing, her father's hairy butt. How she missed them and the safety of home so terribly.

"This must be boring for you."

"I'm hanging on every word! Please."

"My parents are so strict that I might as well be from a family of Mormons." His eyes moved to her chest. Eve pretended not to notice. "None of it's done me any good."

"What do you mean?"

"What's the point of all that education if it makes you hate ninety-nine percent of the universe?"

"I'm not following."

Eve swept her hand in the air. "Who are these people at Griswold? They're profoundly boring, preppy, and bland. On Halloween they'll probably come to my room to borrow clothes."

He laughed. "Such drama! Eve, you're sophisticated, not a freak. Don't conflate them."

"It's a metaphor! Nobody's read a book over a hundred pages long or seen a foreign film. The only fun they have is getting totally wasted on whatever they can find."

"So you felt like a misfit at home because you were a late bloomer and you disliked the rigidity of your school. Then you leave your cosmopolitan existence for a new place, which disappoints you because the students are from less urbane backgrounds than your own. That is not exactly a tragedy."

"And they dress like they popped out of *Little House on the Prairie!*"

Mr. Winkler laughed out loud. "Can't you get beyond fashion?"

"Fashion and style are not the same thing."

"A lot of your fellow students are very intelligent. I grade their papers, I know. And a lot of them have faced difficulties at home that they take pains to conceal." He lowered his voice. "I admit none of them come close to you in terms of worldliness, looks, or, um, sex appeal."

Eve felt her cheeks grow warm.

Here was a real man, not a milquetoast like David. Mr. Winkler, no, *Bob*, admired Eve frankly and openly. He could teach her what to do. So what if she hadn't been past second base? She had sex appeal. Was it so shameful to admit inexperience? Her heart was pounding, she could almost hear it over the rush of the river.

"So," he said, after the waiter set down their food, "for a few years you have to suffer with Tierney and her crowd. Big deal. You have your whole life ahead of you! And like that river, life moves on."

She sawed into her steak, but suddenly she wasn't very hungry.

"You have nothing to be afraid of," Mr. Winkler said.

"The only person I'm afraid of is right here." Eve pointed to her chest and let her finger linger on her sternum, sensuously, she hoped.

She vowed to enjoy it when he took off her bra and not to be too self-conscious.

"Eat your *brandade*, Bob."

· · · · · · · ·

As Clay walked with Justine toward the arts center, she kept glancing around at the other students, wondering what they'd think seeing the two of them together. But nobody blinked an eye. Maybe everyone *didn't* know what Bruce had done?

WarGames had just opened. She had no clue how Griswold had gotten a copy.

"It's because of Bruce's father," Clay explained. "He's a Holly-wood hotshot. He gets the films while the movie is still in theaters."

Justine hadn't even known that Bruce was from the West Coast. Whatever. The last thing she wanted to do was discuss Bruce.

But Clay continued to describe the vicious divorce Bruce's parents were going through back in Los Angeles. "His father sawed the dining table in half. Then he changed the security code on their front gate and his mom retaliated by drowning their dog in the swimming pool. The usual awfulness."

Justine thought that this was exactly the type of sensational story Bruce would brag about. He had probably made it up. She wondered whether she should tell Clay about Stanley's theory, and then thought about their bet. She didn't know if it was a bet she wanted to win or lose.

They entered the art center's limestone lobby. On the wall was a plaque: "To Papa. *Pereunt et Imputantur.* Barbara and Philip Brad-ley, A.D. 1974."

"What does that mean?"

"The hours perish and are reckoned to our account."

"Speak English."

"No matter what, we have to pay for the passing of time. It was on a sundial at my grandparents' house. Cheerful, no?"

A horde of kids surged into the theater through the double doors, and she caught sight of Bruce, his arm around Christina, who was giggling.

"Fuck," Justine muttered.

"Ignore him."

As they passed, Bruce leaned over and whispered in Christina's ear. Justine didn't think it was possible, but against the pale lobby walls he looked more handsome than ever. The world was so unfair. Surely there was a portrait of him somewhere, in some attic, leering and covered in zits, getting uglier with every passing day.

Clay and Justine walked into the theater. There were almost no seats left, and they had to sit in the front row. When the lights went down, Justine sat perfectly still, not daring to brush Clay's arm.

They slipped out a side exit when it was over.

"Smoker?" she suggested.

Clay opened his jacket to reveal a bottle of gin. "Better. Skeets."

As they walked across the footbridge, images from the movie flitted across Justine's brain. She was terrified of nuclear war, and these days it was on every television. It seemed like a bunch of politicians were sitting behind desks in the government about to flip a switch and then the whole planet would be toast.

These dark trees, the waving ferns, the furry woodland creatures huddled in dens for warmth, all of the vibrant, pulsing rhythm of life. Annihilated in a stroke.

"Do you think that could actually happen," she asked Clay, "that someone could cause total world destruction in a few seconds?"

"With how nuts the Russians are? It could happen tomorrow." His voice was toneless, matter-of-fact.

All of this gone, she thought, imagining incineration, burned trunks, smoke rising into the sky.

They reached the path that led through the woods.

They walked for a minute. It was silent except for the crunch of twigs beneath their feet.

"Would you push the button if you could?" Clay asked.

"And kill everyone on the planet? Of course not!"

Clay was quiet. He stared at the path.

"Wait, you would?"

She could see him nodding through the darkness.

"The only thing wrong with the world is people," he explained. "Hit the button and *poof!* Detonate. A chance to start again."

"But what about your family, your friends?"

"That's a sacrifice I'm willing to make."

She wanted to laugh, but he sounded almost serious.

They emerged into the clearing. The field was empty, encircled by a fortress of trees. Wind whipped through the grass. The clouds had been blown aside and stars glittered above. They were alone here. Alone in the world.

"It's like a giant playpen," Justine said, and twirled around.

The trees watched from all sides.

"It is, kind of, but don't you ever feel trapped here sometimes?" Clay looked around. "Like, I feel as though any moment the circle will get tighter and tighter, closing in on us, till we can't breathe."

"Hand over the gin; you're freaking me out," she said.

They sat on the cold ground, and Clay handed her the bottle.

She took a big swig and shuddered as the liquid tumbled down her throat, fierce and pungent.

"Ugh, gross!"

"Beggars can't be choosers."

"Tell me about your sister."

"You mean about the cult?"

Justine nodded. She handed Clay the bottle of gin. He took a swig.

"It was a couple of years ago. We were in Hawaii with Barbara, and this guy walked up to us on the beach, playing some kind of flute. He was totally hot for Char." Clay tilted the gin into his mouth. "Barbara was thrilled, saying Char was having an awakening. It was fucking pathetic." Clay handed Justine the bottle. "After a few days Char followed the guy to some farm in the hills with no electricity. Bunch of freaks. Call themselves Children of Gaia. Barbara gets letters sometimes."

Clay fell silent.

Justine had never had a sibling and didn't know what the loss of one would feel like. But maybe it made pushing the button that much easier.

She took another gulp and lay down flat in the grass, staring up. "Look, Orion's belt," she said, pointing.

Clay propped himself on his arm. He was so close she could feel the warmth of his body. The stars shone above, and he pointed toward the horizon. "And that's my sign, Scorpio."

She handed him back the bottle.

"Barbara's obsessed with astrology." He took a deep swig and winced as he knocked it back.

She sat up slightly, the stars beginning to dance in front of her eyes. She really could not hold her liquor. But with Clay she could be drunk and not worry.

"Is Scorpio good with Capricorn?"

"Dunno." He wiped his mouth with the back of his hand and offered her the bottle again.

"I'm crazy drunk already, you?" she said.

"Me too." Clay laughed.

Justine took an unsteady sip and handed Clay the bottle, and flopped onto her back on the grass. She gazed up at Clay's face, he smiled down at her, and the stars rotated behind his dark head. She pulled him down and kissed him. His mouth was cold and tangy with booze. The field spun. They were the earth's axis. He kissed her back, and she wondered if this had been the idea all along.

Suddenly she didn't feel so hot.

"Shit," Justine said, pulling back from the kiss. Getting up unsteadily she staggered toward the trees. Branches scratched her face as she tripped over roots. Doubling over, she vomited.

Clay was there, hand on her back as she heaved.

She stood up, panting, bracing herself against a trunk.

He stroked her hair.

She leaned over and, for the second time in a week, threw up again.

Clay rubbed her back.

Justine stared down at the pool of puke in the weeds. She really hadn't had that much to drink, had she?

Her head pounded. She leaned against Clay, her cheek hot on his cold parka.

"Hate gin," she muttered.

Clay chucked the bottle into the darkness. It broke with a crash.

"Something's wrong with that stuff," he said. "A bad shipment or something."

He put an arm around her. "Let's head back," he said.

They wove through the woods. Justine prayed that she wouldn't get busted. If she could just make it into Claverly, past the common room, up the carpeted steps, up the ladder of the bunk bed, and under the covers, she'd be safe.

They arrived, and Clay held open the dorm's front door.

She only remembered snippets: the hallway lights glaring, a Celtics game on, a fuzz of raucous hollers, and flowered wallpaper.

Clay supporting her up the hallway steps, her room quiet and dark. Crumpling on Tierney's bed, she looked up at him. "Stay."

"Sleep," he said, stroking her hair gently off her forehead.

"Stay."

"Okay, a few minutes."

She lay on his lap, and he ran his fingers softly through her hair. As she relaxed, the gin seeped into her body; she was spinning, falling, grabbing for branches. The branches were arms, Justine reached for them, desperately grabbing for handholds, speeding past. One caught her and yanked her with a jolt. Her eyes flew open. She was in Tierney's bed. Clay was gone.

． ． ． ． ． ． ． ．

Mr. Winkler walked Eve home from The Mill. In another world, where they were just a man and a girl, he would put his arm around her. Past his threshold, the door shut behind them, he would abandon his self-control and tear her clothes off, fucking her on the sofa before they even made it to the bedroom. Then he'd do it again, more slowly the second time.

"I ate way, way too much," she said, clutching her stomach. "I can hardly breathe."

"It's you who leaves me breathless."

Eve was certain he had used that line before, but she didn't mind. "You know, in Kenya, lions don't eat for weeks and then when they kill a gazelle or an eland, they gorge themselves until they literally can't move. They lie on their sides with these huge bellies, panting with their tongues hanging out."

"I'd like to see an imitation."

She stopped and stuck out her tongue.

His voice deepened. "Looks like pleasure."

"Oh shush."

They kept walking. Eve paused at the edge of his porch, in the penumbra of the overhead light. Anyone could see them where they stood.

"Thanks for supper. I won't eat for days."

She waited. His breath was visible in the cold air. He took her hand in his.

In a moment he would pull her toward him into a kiss. She was about to close her eyes when he released her.

"Good night, Eve." He smiled.

She swallowed. "Good night, Mr. Winkler."

FIFTEEN

MONDAY MORNING THE WANKER STRODE IN AND SET HIS briefcase on the desk. Justine did a double take. He had shaved his beard, revealing the firm curve of his jaw. Justine shot Eve a look of surprise, but Eve stared ahead in silence.

Damon raised his hand.

"Yes, Mr. White?"

"Sorry, Mr. Winkler, just wondering if you got my paper. I slid it under your door over the weekend."

"I received it on Saturday afternoon. It was due Friday."

"I was in the infirmary Friday," Damon said.

"I've marked it late. But if you get a note from the nurse, maybe I'll reconsider."

Damon gave him a dirty look.

The Wanker paced. He cracked his knuckles.

He swiveled on his heels and faced them. "About your essays. Every year, I hope. Every year my hopes are dashed. To make matters worse, every year the writing quality decreases. The butchery, the lack of respect for the English language! It's a disease and it's spreading. But, you all know, it gives me great pleasure"—he ran his finger along the length of Eve's desk—"to whip you into shape."

With a dramatic turn on his heel, the Wanker unbuckled his briefcase and pulled out a sheaf of papers.

"Miss Huntington, a fairly respectable job." The paper landed on Irene's desk with a slap. "Mr. Comerford, truly dreadful. Make an appointment to come see me. Miss Harris, surprisingly well done. Mr. Adams, a train wreck. And, Miss Rubin, don't think I don't know when students rely on CliffsNotes."

The paper landed on her desk. B minus. As if she could afford CliffsNotes! She was paying the price for that weekend in more ways than one.

"Mr. Bradley, mediocre. Miss Straus, you can do better. Much better."

Justine glanced over, but Eve had leaned forward, arms covering her paper, lips tight. She always got As so maybe it was an A minus for once. The Wanker picked up a piece of chalk and tossed it from one hand to the other.

"Miss Straus," he said, and Justine detected a hint of menace, "please read the paragraph I highlighted in your essay." He beckoned with his finger. Eve glared and did not budge.

"Page three. Tell the class what your topic was."

"I wrote on Vonnegut's symbolism," Eve said, her voice barely audible.

Justine wondered what was wrong. Eve usually loved to be called on.

"Stand. Read on, Macduff."

Eve got to her feet and cleared her throat.

"In *Cat's Cradle*, appearances are deceiving. Through the use of irony and parody, Vonnegut endows even the most normal events with a sinister air. An innocent child's game for most, cat's cradle terrifies the children of the atom bomb scientist Hoenniker. Their father always neglected them, never played games, and barely speaks. But on the day when the atom bomb was dropped, he played cat's cradle over and over, obsessively."

"Continue," Mr. Winkler said.

Eve swallowed. "The children recognize the destructive power that their father holds over humanity because of his ice-nine invention. Ice-nine is a symbol for nuclear power. Scientists hold the power to wipe everyone out, even if it means they go down as well. Hoenniker's children know that he is not just playing a game with string, but that his irresponsible games will lead to everyone's death."

Eve put down the paper, staring at the teacher with her mouth compressed.

The Wanker surveyed the room, scanning the students' faces. "Thank you, Miss Straus, please be seated."

Justine gave her a thumbs-up, but Eve slumped in her chair, staring at the paper on her desk.

"Comments? Rebuttals?" he asked.

Silence.

"Come now! Do you agree with Miss Straus's assessment of Hoenniker? Is he merely a man acting like a child? Or is he a brilliant scientist?"

Jenny raised her hand.

"Miss Lake? Do enlighten us."

"He's kind of both," Jenny said, "like, he invents these amazing things, but he acts like a kid. Didn't he have all these weird games and toys in his lab?"

"He did. What do you think that means?" The Wanker's blue eyes flashed.

"That all adults want to stay kids?"

The class giggled.

Damon spoke. "Humans are like stupid kids playing games that kill."

"Mr. White, raise your hand. However, your point is well taken." The Wanker paced the room, rolling the chalk between his fingers. "What is Vonnegut saying about power?"

Justine raised her hand.

"Miss Rubin?"

"I think he means humans are weak. When they have power, they don't know how to channel it, so they end up destroying the things they care about."

"Excellent. Is Vonnegut taking a moral stance?"

Justine had to think about that for a moment. "Uh, he must be, but it's hard to tell what he really thinks."

Mr. Winkler nodded and looked around for another answer.

Eve's hand went up and the Wanker walked toward her desk.

"Miss Straus?" The chalk slipped from his hand and fell on the carpet next to Eve's combat boot.

"Vonnegut doesn't really talk about morality directly," Eve said. "I agree with Justine. I think he is saying that humans, adults, are weaklings, and so they destroy themselves and others. People in power always abuse it. I remember somewhere in the book he says, 'Think about what a paradise this world would be if men were kind and wise.'"

"Yes." The Wanker's grin spread in that Cheshire cat expression. "What a paradise indeed."

Eve and Justine walked across the footbridge. Justine tightened her jacket around her neck against the chill. Below the bridge, the ferns had dried into bare stalks, the trees had lost their leaves long ago.

"Where were you yesterday?" Justine asked. "I schlepped all the way up here and you weren't in your room."

"Library."

"I'd hoped you were with David."

Eve was silent.

"It's late October but it feels like it's going to snow," Justine observed.

"What difference does it make anyway?" Eve said. Justine glanced at her, suddenly noticing that her eyes were full of tears.

"What's wrong?"

"Fucking Wanker." Eve stopped midstep. "The asshole just gave me a B minus."

"Then why'd he ask you to read it in front of the class?"

"Because it's frigging good. Know why he gave me a crappy grade?"

Justine looked at her blankly.

"Because he wants me to beg. He's toying with me. He let me rewrite it, and I did, and then he said how much fun we were going to have. You know exactly what kind of fun he meant."

"When did he say that?"

"Saturday, at dinner. And then he didn't even kiss me good night!"

For a moment Justine thought Eve was joking, but she saw that tears were running down Eve's cheeks.

"I think he looks really good without the beard," Justine said softly.

"I don't know what's going on," Eve said, sobbing. "Maybe all this shit's in my head."

"If you weren't a virgin you wouldn't put all this pressure on yourself," Justine said, touching Eve's arm. "Why not take a breath and slow down? It's not a race." Justine knew she wouldn't have taken this kind advice, that it was easier said than done.

"I should just lose it to David and get it out of the way. I don't think I can lose it to a teacher. For the rest of my life I'd have to say . . ."

Justine pushed a wet strand of hair off Eve's forehead. "I lost mine to a much older guy. He was a partner of my dad's."

"*Really?*"

Justine nodded. "And he was amazing. He knew exactly what to do." Justine couldn't help but remember the thickness of Gerald's tongue in her mouth. The sharp pain and the bleeding. It had gotten better, but at first . . .

Eve looked anxious, pulling open the door to the arts center.

"Bet Wanker's a hot fuck!" Justine called after her.

Justine stood in the courtyard of the arts center and thought about Eve and Mr. Winkler. Considering the rumors, she wasn't surprised. The territorial way he would hover by her desk, how he always steered the class discussion in Eve's direction.

She felt wistful for the time when she had been as fresh and untainted as her friend. It had been a relief to mention Gerald, but Justine was still too ashamed to tell Eve about Bruce. She had gone over the details a hundred times in her mind like clues in a forensics lab, trying to think what she could have done differently. With Gerald, she should have been less available, less childishly adoring. With Bruce, she should have stayed on top, tied him up, had her way with him.

Justine turned around the athletic building to the smoker. Sitting on a bench, throwing stones at the goalposts, was Clay.

"Hey," she said lightly, sitting a few feet away and pulling out her cigarettes.

"Thought I'd find you here eventually," he said. A pebble hit the post. "How're you feeling?"

"Better. I can't believe how sensitive my stomach is." She exhaled a perfect smoke ring.

"I heard Alison Smith and Damon were both sick too."

"Who knew Alison drank?"

"Everyone drinks. There's nothing else to do in this prison." He chucked another stone at the goalposts. It missed.

Did he remember their kiss? He had been pretty drunk.

The remaining rocks in Clay's hand slid into the dust. "Ever feel like none of this is real?" He gestured across the playing field.

"Like everything is a movie and your Walkman is the sound-track?" she said.

He nodded.

They were silent. Justine blew a few more smoke rings. The bench chilled her through her jeans.

Clay was staring off at the field. "I just sometimes feel like I'm looking at everyone in a fishbowl. All they're doing is swimming around, eating, and shitting."

He slid down the bench. To her surprise, he put his arm around her.

"What if someone sees us?" She could kiss him. He was right there.

"They'd think I liked you."

"They'd never believe it." She pulled his arm off and stood up.

"Why not?" he frowned.

"You know exactly why. Clay, look, I'm not, I'm . . ." Justine struggled. What could she say, *I'm not at your level*? That thought was too horrible to verbalize. She saw pity flit across his face. "Don't feel sorry for me! I hate that!"

"I don't. I feel sorry for myself."

"What do you have to worry about?"

Clay stood up, placing both hands on her shoulders. His grip was firm.

"You've been to my mother's house, you've met her. And you don't understand?"

Justine was bewildered. What was there to understand? Barbara was the coolest mom she could imagine—a famous artist. And the family was rich.

Clay leaned closer. She reached out and brushed her fingers over his head. He was a wounded animal, she pulled him into an embrace. He held on to her tightly, soft hair on her cheek. His heart was beating so fast she could feel it through her rib cage.

SIXTEEN

December

EVE STRUGGLED DOWN THE STEPS OF THE SCIENCE BUILD-
ing with a crate of records digging into her fingers. Curfew was
eleven but she, Justine, and David had permission to be out an hour
later—for this, their first radio show.

The radio station was in a low-ceilinged basement with stained
red linoleum floors and garish fluorescent lighting. There were a
few metal tables and chairs, and beyond a wall of glass, the DJ
booth.

"Where the hell have you been?" Justine exploded. "This was all
Stanley's dumb idea."

Eve dumped the milk crate on the floor. She massaged her fingers, frowning at Justine's thunderous face.

"I thought David was going to help!" Justine said, pointing past
the glass wall where two guys worked the turntables. Eve gaped in
horror; it was like a cockpit, with hundreds of buttons they did not
know how to operate.

"Bonsoir!" David said, hurrying in the door. "So sorry I'm late,
my parents called."

He checked his watch then looked from Eve to Justine. He

pursed his lips. "Hey, don't worry! If those dopes can do it so can you. I'll cue up the song. Who's talking first?"

Eve pointed at Justine, who stuck out her tongue.

David held open the door to the booth. She was glad that he was here to help, and wondered if tonight might be their moment.

He was telling them to look at the ON AIR sign that lit up when you flipped a switch. Hold the edge of the album. Let the needle slide. Do that when the other person talks. Then he said to Justine, "When I give you the signal, start talking. NOW!"

He pointed to the microphone.

"Good evening, Grizzlies!" she said in a sultry voice Eve had never heard before. The voice she used with boys in bed, Eve thought.

"Justine and Eve here, spinning with you till the witching hour. We're transmitting over the underground radio waves of WGIZ with a brand-new show. Get ready, get wild."

David flipped the switch and the song began to play. Peeling off his leather jacket, he looked at Eve. "You look beautiful in head-phones." He turned and chose the next track.

At midnight, they closed the station and walked home. The show had been a brilliant success, with perfect segues between songs, several call-in requests, and not a moment of feedback or dead air. Eve was in such a good mood she barely felt the bitter cold. She and David dropped Justine at Claverly and took their time going to Londry. Even with permission to be out, Eve felt like she was breaking the rules, walking with a boy after midnight. The moonlight shone through the branches of the trees, casting shadows like tangled wire. David walked close beside her.

If he was going to kiss her, he'd need to do it soon, because she could see the dorm lights through the trees.

"Penny for your thoughts?" David asked.

"My dad says that."

"Hey," he said. David pulled out a small package in brown paper tied with twine and handed it to her.

Eve began to tear it open.

"Wait! Later, when you're alone." She couldn't meet his eye, and leaned on the railing of the bridge. The wind rustled the desiccated ferns.

"Eve," David said, leaning on the railing next to her. "I think I might be in love with you."

Eve swallowed.

"I'm obtuse, and I talk too much, I know, but . . ."

She turned and pulled him toward her, kissing him. When she released him, he looked dazed. Then she kissed him again.

A bird shrieked, and they broke apart.

"Nightjar," David said. "We should get back."

At the door of Londry, David whispered, "Wave to me." Then he kissed her again.

Eve climbed two flights in a dream state. Tabitha was asleep, the moonlight on her silvery hair. She looked like an angel. Through the window Eve waved to David. He placed his hands over his heart, bowed, and turned to walk back across the bridge.

Sunday afternoon Eve watched the raindrops streak the glass, like cells pulsing through a vein. *Diamond Dogs* played on the turntable and Eve wallowed in the wailing anguish of the saxophone. She could never decide which Bowie album she preferred. Stanley loved

Young Americans, but the apocalyptic narrative of this one might make it first for her. Perfect for a rainy Sunday.

Sunday. The dreaded day of homework. Maybe David would try to see her? It was funny that he had the same first name as her rock idol, and she had never made the connection until now.

Eve realized she had forgotten about the package that David had given her on Friday. She took it off her desk and removed the wrapper. James Dickey, *Poems 1957–1967*. The same book the Wanker had tried to read to her—it must be some kind of conspiracy. She wondered what Mr. Winkler would say when she told him she had a boyfriend. She chuckled to herself as she noticed a bookmark protruding from the pages and turned to the spot. David's elaborate scroll read, "This one reminds me of you."

"The Shark's Parlor." A swollen sea under cottage stilts after a storm. Boys baiting a shark, lashing a rope to the porch. From the water a massive, thrashing hammerhead. The shark fights, the porch splinters, groans. They run for more men and, slugging back beers, wage a tug of war, brutally pulling the slippery beast into the house, where it smashes the place to bits before finally giving up the ghost, white belly to the ceiling on the Persian carpet.

It was such a sad poem. A fierce and beautiful creature from another realm and the men killed it. Why? *Because they could.* Why on earth did David mean it reminded him of her? Was she the shark? Or was she the human baiting the beast?

Eve pulled on her wool coat and left the dorm. Damp tendrils of hair clung to her forehead as she walked across the footbridge and down the footpath, skirting the puddles in the courtyard of the arts center.

Across the playing fields, behind the athletic building, a lone hooded figure was huddled at the smoker. She imagined he'd rise, cloak billowing, and cut her down with his scythe. But it was just Stanley, bent over his boom box to protect it from the rain, his clothes dripping.

"You're soaked," she said.

"'Cleanse me and I shall be whiter than snow.'"

"Do you have a cigarette?"

He handed her a pack of Lucky Strikes.

"What was that from?" she asked.

"The Bible. Actually, I have no desire to be pure."

"Me neither."

They sat in the cold, damp air.

Stanley was humming a tune, patting his pocket, and chuckling. Eve waited for him to divulge. He did not.

Eve lit another cigarette. Stanley giggled.

"Okay, out with it," she said.

Stanley reached into the pocket of his coat and pulled out a small object. There, in his palm, lay a tuft of wiry blond hair, a miniature tumbleweed. "Admit defeat," he said.

Eve could not believe her eyes.

"You fucked Bruce?" she breathed.

"Get ready to dance. Naked, skin to the sky," he intoned.

Eve jumped up and twirled around. "Holy shit! How?"

"I had Damon take him a note," Stanley said, as serious as ever.

"*Damon*? That cokehead? What did the note say?"

"I believe the exact words were 'I think you're hot and I want to get it on.'"

Eve stared at him, dumbfounded, as Stanley described the sequence of events. After giving Damon the note, Stanley had waited in his room. Eve wondered why Stanley had entrusted a fuckup like Damon with such a delicate mission. What if he told someone?

But Stanley seemed to have known exactly what to do. After curfew he had climbed the stairs to Bruce's room on the fourth floor, a fifth of Jack Daniels under his sweatshirt. Eve had heard that floor of Crawford was less patrolled by the dorm master.

Bruce was already stoned when Stanley arrived, and after a few shots of whiskey he was wasted. It was easy. Bruce didn't mind at all as Stanley unzipped his jeans.

After it was over Stanley insisted on a snippet of pubic hair, saying it was a fetish of his, and, with the treasure in his pocket, had crept back downstairs.

Eve sucked in her breath. If it weren't for the proof sitting in Stanley's palm, she'd never have believed it.

Stanley seemed utterly unfazed. He could be in the CIA.

"I always had a vibe," he said. "It was just a matter of time."

Despite her supposed "worldliness," there was still so much that she had to learn. Was Bruce gay? But didn't he like Justine? It was all way too confusing.

Even worse, Eve couldn't keep her imagination under control. Bruce on his back, Stanley bent over, moving his head up and down. She shook her head, but the images persisted.

Then it occurred to Eve; she and Justine had lost the bet. They actually had to dance naked in the Skeets.

"Who's that?" Stanley pointed to a figure, mostly obscured beneath a large golf umbrella. Eve recognized the confident stride and the tweed blazer.

"Shit!" She threw the cigarette in a puddle where it fizzled.

But the Wanker lowered his umbrella and kept walking.

They remained silent as the teacher moved across the field, raindrops from the gutter of the athletic building making dull plips on the asphalt.

Eve understood the message Mr. Winkler had sent. He had seen her smoking and had turned a blind eye. She was off the hook with the school, but on the hook with him.

Eve headed straight for Claverly, stomped up the steps, and burst into Justine's room. Justine was sitting at her desk reading a textbook.

"We lost the bet!"

Justine jumped up and stared at Eve in shock.

"Stanley did it! He blew Bruce."

Justine stood there for a few moments, as the news sank in. "Do you have the proof?"

"Ugh! No way would I touch it!" Eve laughed.

Justine should have known. Bruce would do *anything* with *anyone*.

God, how she burned with hatred for him.

Justine looked up to see Eve eyeing her thoughtfully. Could Eve read her mind? But all Eve said was, "How are we going to be naked in this weather?"

"Indians used to be almost nude all winter," Justine replied. "I think you get used to it."

"We'd better smoke the peace pipe first."

Justine smiled a cheerless smile. "Apparently at night, the teachers sneak around the Skeets with flashlights. I heard they even use dogs."

Eve imagined the Wanker skipping from tree to tree on goat's legs. There was a game she and India used to play in Amagansett called German Spotlight; it was hide and seek in the dark, with a flashlight. Only now did Eve realize it had to do with the Nazis.

"What happens in a lie-detector test?"

"They shoot you full of stuff like in *A Clockwork Orange*," Justine said, throwing her chem notebook in the desk drawer.

"I'll tell them to ask me what my fucking English teacher is doing to me!"

"You can totally handle him," Justine said, slumping on Tierney's bed. She looked up at Eve. "And don't take it the wrong way. But this might be just the opportunity you're looking for."

Eve went silent.

Justine patted the bed beside her. "Come here, I want to tell you all about *my* older man." And she told Eve about Gerald, all about him, even the parts that didn't cast her in the best light, how he'd romanced her, their teas at the hotel, the music box, the first edition, the candy. How he had taken her virginity on the stage. She described how it had hurt at first, then felt better, even good. How Gerald had dumped her so soon afterward. For a fleeting moment, as she confided in her friend for the first time, Justine almost forgot about Bruce, about Clay, and about taking off her clothes in a frozen field.

SEVENTEEN

ON THE APPOINTED SATURDAY, THE RAIN TURNED TO SLEET
and then a fine snow. It drifted down steadily, and by suppertime it
was more than six inches deep. Tree branches were laden with soft
white piles, an occasional wind rustling the pine boughs and sending a shower of flakes down like pixie dust. The school looked like
a fairy tale.

Stanley had agreed to meet them at the Skeets at nine and provide the soundtrack for their striptease. Justine had fantasized on
more than one occasion that he'd tell them it had all been a joke.
Justine could not imagine what the encounter had been like, but
she had a feeling it hadn't taken long.

Her anger still felt more like pain.

Justine made Cup O Noodles for supper in the dorm kitchen.
Afterward she dug into the wardrobe for her snow boots, shiny blue
and secondhand. She would call them vintage and toss her hair if
anyone said anything.

"It's freezing out there!" Eve pounded on the door, stamping
her feet.

"This whole situation really sucks."

"It was your idea!"

"It was a sucky one," Justine admitted. "This'll help," she said, pulling a bottle of vodka from under her bed.

She still hadn't told Eve about the night in the Skeets with Clay.

They walked through the common room past Jackie and Tierney, envying their cozy evening nestled under a blanket watching *I Dream of Jeannie.*

Jackie held her nose as they walked past.

"I wish I could blink those bitches into oblivion," Eve whispered.

They trudged across the icy footbridge.

The fresh snow on the field was crisscrossed with footprints. To her shock, Justine could see several kids, including Christina, Damon, and Stanley, waiting for the show.

"I forgot about that part of the deal," Eve groaned.

So had Justine. What if Bruce had been invited? Justine scanned the field. Nobody else, at least not yet.

To make matters worse, the moon was almost full, its silvery light reflecting off the snow, transforming the field's velvety darkness into a luminous stage. Maybe, Justine thought, if she imagined this performance as theater, it would rise above pure humiliation. Unscrewing the cap from the vodka, she took a big gulp. It tasted like rotten potatoes. She took another, then handed it to Eve, who refused, making a face.

"Your choice," said Stanley, approaching them with his boom box, a zealous gleam in his eye. "Mozart or Chopin?" Again, coat billowing around his knees, Stanley reminded Eve of the Grim Reaper.

Justine protested, "You said a song, not a fucking symphony!"

"Who dances to classical music anyway?" Eve scoffed.

"I thought it might elevate the event," Stanley said, waving his arm. "Stars, moon, downy nymphets . . ."

David emerged from the trees a few yards away. "Shit!" Eve hissed. "I'm not dancing to Mozart naked in front of David!"

"How's 'Lady Grinning Soul'?" Stanley asked, pulling a cassette from his pocket.

"A waste of a fucking great song," Eve said, yanking off her jacket. Without another glance at the onlookers, she turned her back and said, "Let's just get this over with."

Stanley balanced the boom box on a hip and inserted the cassette, pressing the play button with exaggerated solemnity.

Justine took another deep swig of vodka.

Dark pines swayed, sparkling swirls of snow were airborne over the field.

The Bowie song began.

Justine took a bigger swig, forced it down, then threw the vodka in the snow. She whipped off her jacket, letting it fly. If they wanted a show, she would give them one they wouldn't forget.

Someone let out a howl of delight. She heard Damon catcall and yell, "Strip!" as she started peeling off the layers.

The frigid air made her pores shrink. She listened to the wind running through the trees that surrounded the open field. Anyone could be watching from that black circle. Justine took a step forward, toward the calls and hoots, snow crunching under her boots. Her nipples were as hard as pebbles, the moonlight gleaming on her skin. She glanced at Eve, who was covering her breasts and pubic hair with her hands.

Justine caught sight of Damon's pockmarked face, his jaw hanging open. Theater, just theater, she reminded herself, closing her eyes tightly, raising her arms to the sky, and starting to sway like the pines. Thinking of the stars above, Justine tried to imagine that she was part of some primitive ritual. She was Clay's sister in a cult, she was the high priestess of the moon, she was Hathor. The snow was getting in her boots. Her skin had turned numb, *and when the clothes are strewn, don't be afraid . . .*

Suddenly someone grabbed her by the hand and tugged her into the trees, dragging her across the snow. She opened her eyes, but the forest was dark.

"Quiet!" Clay's voice.

She tried not to stumble; her legs were numb.

"Sssh!"

Justine was aware that she was shivering violently, her teeth clacking against one another like joke plastic ones clattering across a table. She wrapped her arms around her ribs, hands like ice. She could hear angry voices. Was that the Wanker? Mrs. Tibbets?

"Hang on." It was Clay, gripping her arm, breathing heavy clouds of steam. They were in the forest. She looked back. The students had vanished and several teachers were arguing, their voices carrying through the clear dark air. Before them stood Eve. Alone. She was desperately tugging on her clothes in front of the Wanker, Tibbets, and a few others. Justine couldn't see her face and could only imagine her expression.

Behind a tree Clay held out her underwear and her sweater. "Should I turn around?" he whispered. She detected a hint of irony. The cold burned her like fire.

He put his hands over his eyes.

"Rules are rules!" A teacher, maybe the crew coach, stood with his legs apart and his arms crossed, like a referee. Eve was hugging her coat around her now, and Justine could see her trembling.

Where was everyone else? This was unbearable, it was like an execution.

"P-poor Eve," Justine chattered, fumbling with the string on her sweatpants, her fingers stiff with cold. "C-can you help me?"

Clay tied the string, his fingers brushing her stomach.

"We have to help her!" Justine started for the clearing.

"No!" Clay whispered, pulling her back. "It's too late. She's busted already."

Justine sagged against him.

"Let's get back."

They moved silently through the forest until they were well out of earshot.

Her teeth were still chattering.

"If it's her first offense, maybe they'll go easy on her."

Even the inside of her ski jacket was freezing.

"Cl-Clay."

"Yeah?"

"H-how-how'd you know about the bet?"

He paused for a moment.

"As if I'm too square to know?"

"No, no." She moved closer. She put her arms under his parka. "I'm so c-cold," she said.

Clay pulled off his ski hat and tucked it on her head, then un-wound his boy-scented scarf and wrapped it around her neck.

"You're so lovely," he said, admiring her.

"Hat head," she said, reaching up to fix his matted hair. He pulled her closer and kissed her cold lips. Her teeth chattered against his, then she lost her balance and they lurched into a birch tree.

"I've been th-thinking about doing that again," she admitted.

"Falling over?"

"Something like that."

. . . .

Struggling to keep up, Eve followed the teachers back to the dorm. If it had just been Mr. Winkler who'd seen her, there would be an easy fix; she would be on her knees begging right now. He would enjoy looking down at her, so willing, so compliant, but it would be a small price to pay. Mr. Winkler would be on her side, would fight for her.

The common room was deserted. The television was on. Soda cans and popcorn littered the table. The salty smell of instant noodles filled the air.

"Have a seat," Mrs. Tibbets said.

The Wanker was pumping up and down on the balls of his feet. Tibbets glanced at him. "Eve, would you excuse us for just a moment?" she asked. They walked across the room and began a whispered conversation.

Eve watched them, wondering if Mrs. Tibbets knew. About her and Mr. Winkler. About Mr. Winkler and other girls.

Eve stared glumly at the teachers. How on earth had Justine gotten away?

They would call her parents in a moment. She could see Patsy taking a message on the magnetic refrigerator pad. Eve pushed their angry faces from her mind and looked away, staring at the television screen.

"So, Miss Straus," Mr. Winkler said, startling her.

"Bob," Mrs. Tibbets said, twisting her gray hair around her fingers, "thank you, but I'll handle it from here."

The Wanker frowned, but started to walk away. He turned back once, looking as if he had been denied dessert, then disappeared through the door.

Tibbets sat down across from Eve, smoothing her corduroy skirt.

"Why don't you tell me what happened," she said in a gentle voice.

Eve looked at the center stone of a large Navajo necklace around Tibbets's neck. "A mistake," Eve said.

"I asked *what happened*. In your own words, please."

There were tiny ivory veins in the large lapis, encircled in silver fretwork.

"It was a bet."

"What about the vodka?"

How did Tibbets know that? Had Justine dropped the vodka when she fled? How had Justine escaped so fast?

"It wasn't mine and I didn't touch it."

The teacher shook her head in disbelief. "Who else was there?"

Eve did not respond.

The nostrils of Tibbets's nose were flared, her lips compressed and white. When she spoke, however, it was in a tone of measured calm. "Lying is a suspendible offense."

What? Eve had thought she was getting expelled. Suspension sounded almost desirable.

"But you have information," Tibbets said.

"What do you want to know?"

"If you help us out, tell us who was drinking, we might be able to settle on a lesser punishment. Perhaps just detention."

How had Justine just vanished?

"Nobody else was there," Eve said stiffly.

Tibbets searched Eve's face. "If you cooperate I might be willing to argue on your behalf." Despite her motherly tone, her mouth remained in a tight line.

"I was alone."

Tibbets regarded her suspiciously. "There will be a disciplinary hearing."

"Do my parents know?" Eve felt the beginning of a nasty headache.

"Bob's calling them. We'll get this resolved early so we have a clear verdict."

"You can't tell them I was drinking. Because I wasn't," Eve said. Only Justine could tell them Eve hadn't taken a drop.

"At Griswold it's innocent until proven guilty," Tibbets said. "Eve, think again. Think hard. You're a smart girl."

EIGHTEEN

JUSTINE LAY AWAKE ALL NIGHT, STARING AT THE CEILING while Tierney breathed softly below her. What would happen to Eve? She would be suspended at the very least, but what if she got expelled? It was so unfair. First thing tomorrow, Justine would find Mrs. Tibbets and tell her that Eve hadn't been drinking.

How on earth had the teachers found out? And of all people to have witnessed it, the Wanker!

At 7:15 in the morning, Tierney still asleep, Justine left the dorm and headed up the hill toward Londry. She knocked on Mrs. Tibbets's door.

"Come in!"

She opened the door into a living room with a Tiffany chandelier on a chain and a green parrot in a cage. A man she hadn't seen before stood up from the sofa.

"Looking for Alice?"

"Go ask Alice! Go ask Alice!" the bird squawked.

"I'm sorry," he said, "she's in New Haven at a seminar. Can I take a message?"

"When's she coming back?"

"Tonight. Maybe after supper."

"Alice doesn't live here anymore!" the bird cried.

"Hang on." Justine yanked a sheet of lined paper from her book bag and scribbled:

Dear Mrs. Tibbets,

Eve didn't drink last night. I swear.

Justine Rubin (Claverly 301)

She handed it to him.

"Now, don't worry," he said, folding the note and tucking it in his sweater pocket, "I'll make sure she gets this first thing."

The door to Eve's room was open.

"Oh, hi," Eve said.

"What happened? Are they sending you home?"

Eve jumped off her bed and walked to the closet.

"Eve"—Justine stared at Eve's back—"I just went to Tibbets. She's out but I left a note with a man."

"Her husband." Eve started rummaging for clothes.

"I'll tell Tibbets you're innocent," Justine continued.

Eve yanked a striped T-shirt over her head. "Thank you. But it's too late. How could I have been so fucking stupid? I suggested if we lost, we would do something simple, like eat sausages," Eve continued. "But no, that wasn't enough!" Eve threw her arms in the air. "I'm screwed. Tibbets had the nerve to say it was innocent until proven guilty. What a load of bullshit. They smell blood in the water and they won't give up."

Eve looked like she was about to cry, but she stormed out of the room. Justine followed, but as usual, Eve's long legs carried her ahead. As Justine hurried after, across the frozen spars of the bridge, she wanted to run, tug on Eve's coat, but at the end of the bridge Eve ducked sideways and disappeared into the trees.

· · · · · · · · ·

E ve forced down her rubbery eggs and bacon. Justine was going to stand up for her, but it wouldn't change anything. Her parents must know, and their silence was worse than their remonstrations.

Her hearing was scheduled for 10:00. In the Graves Room, the paneled library reserved for board meetings, important alums, and visiting scholars. James Dickey must have slugged down several bourbons there among back-slapping faculty. Go ahead, Eve thought, haul me in like the shark, watch me thrash on the carpet.

Eve checked her watch. 8:45 a.m. Dumping her tray she pulled her ski hat down and made her way down the hill to David's dorm.

Climbing the stairs of Strathmore, Eve felt her heart thumping in her chest. Down the hall to the left.

"Cookie?" David answered his door with a look of surprise.

She kissed him.

"What the . . ."

She kissed him again.

"Wait!" But she shut him up. His roommate wasn't there, they'd have time. She had nothing to lose. She would probably be expelled and would never see David again.

Eve slid her hand under his shirt, over his chest, hairless and smooth.

He held her at arm's length. "What happened at the Skeets? I saw . . ."

"Hush." She wrapped her hands around his hips. She looked over his shoulder at the room. The sole ornament was a gas mask on the wall, looming over the bed, its shadow like a snout.

She let David go and sat on his bed.

He dropped to his knees before her, cupping her chin and examining her face with concern. "Eve"—he rested his hand on her arm—"you okay?"

Justine would be ripping his pants off right now.

"Dandy. How much did you see?"

"Not a lot. As soon as I got there, someone tapped me on the shoulder and said there were teachers coming."

"Who?"

"I don't know. It was dark," David said, pursing his lips.

"It was as bright as frigging daylight!"

He shook his head. "It happened so fast. Everyone got out of there in seconds."

Eve glanced at her watch. 9:12. His roommate might be back any minute.

"Come here . . ." She pulled him toward her.

She reclined on the bed.

"Let's rewind the tape," he said. He leaned down and kissed her. She put her hands on his back.

9:24. At least a ten-minute walk to Meade.

Her shirt was off, then his. The glassy eyes of the gas mask gazed down.

9:27. 9:32.

David sat up. "Why do you keep looking at your watch?"

She covered her breasts. "I have to be somewhere at ten."

"Where?"

"The Shark's Parlor."

He smiled and took her hands off her breasts. He touched them, then kissed her, his hand moving toward her pants.

She glanced at her watch. 9:40.

"Hurry," she murmured, "let's get this over with."

He frowned. "This isn't something we can hurry." He turned her wrist over. "We have time." He moved on top, his hips between her legs.

9:48. "I have to go," Eve said.

David sat up and handed Eve her shirt. He did have that Michelangelo body. Justine had been right.

"Hey," he said. "Just come back later."

If there was a later, Eve thought as she picked up her coat and hurried toward Meade.

Eve skipped supper and stayed in her room, knowing word would have spread by now. Suspended. Going home until after Christmas. She didn't want to see a soul.

How had it come to this? She'd been caught and Justine had gotten off. Tibbets had tried to use the bottle of vodka to scare her into telling on her classmates. No matter what, Eve thought, she would not have ratted Justine out. Or anyone else, for that matter. But getting caught naked was enough for them to suspend her, and in the end they didn't bother to bring up the vodka.

The sky turned an intense cobalt, then bled into black.

Suddenly, Eve saw her parents' Mercedes wagon pulling into the parking lot. How different this trip was than when they dropped her off in September. They had all been full of hope and anticipation. Her mother slammed the car door. Eve watched her stride toward the dorm, and the sick shame she had felt all day turned to dread.

A minute later, Eve's door opened and Deirdre's skinny hip rested against the frame. Her face was a death mask.

"Ready?" she said in a cold voice.

"Oh, Mom!" Eve cried and leapt off the bed, flinging her arms around Deirdre's bony body.

Her mother pushed her away.

"I've seen your father cry only once before today, Eve."

Eve imagined tears running down her father's cheeks. His daughter had ruined everything, all of their lives, with one stupid move, and nothing would ever be right.

"Get your bag, the car's running."

Eve slumped into the back seat. Her father stared ahead, refusing to acknowledge his daughter. The car slid into the night with all the silence of German engineering. Eve pressed her cheek against the cool window as they drove down Elm. The lights were on at Mr. Winkler's. Tea with him seemed suddenly safer than going home.

Count Basie on the car radio, and the rush of wind past the glass. The headlights swept over the power lines, projecting them onto the asphalt like swinging halyards on a ghost ship.

From time to time Eve caught the flash of her father's angry eyes in the rearview mirror. He looked hurt, too. A strange kind of hurt that Eve hadn't seen on his face before. They were passing Greenwich when her father turned off the radio and cleared his throat.

"I want an explanation."

For a moment Eve remained in her sad fog. Her father raised his voice. "Eve?"

She sat up reluctantly and spoke in a monotone. "I bet a friend something. I lost the bet. The penalty was dancing naked."

Her parents fell into the kind of silence that is worse than shouting.

"I'm having trouble believing that you would do something so immature and vulgar," her mother said, her voice unsteady, as if still trying to convince herself it had really happened.

It was hard to think of a reply.

"And dangerous. What was it, twenty degrees on Friday night?"

Eve did not respond.

Frederick banged his hand on the steering wheel. "*Do you have any idea?* Any idea at all what I've had to do to get you into that school?"

"I'm so sorry, Dad, please! You don't understand how sorry I am!"

"You've barely been there four months! Did anyone else get in trouble?" Deirdre asked.

Eve shook her head.

"It's all because of that Justine," her mother said, and even with her back to her daughter, Eve could see her grim expression. "Don't tell me she wasn't involved. You would never have done that on your own." Deirdre turned and cocked an eyebrow. "And pray tell, why isn't your darling best buddy getting suspended?" Her mother's voice felt colder than the Skeets. "Are her parents driving *her* home right now?"

Eve did not respond. She felt as if she were pierced with arrows, like the painting of St. Sebastian at Barbara's.

Deirdre stared at her daughter.

"*Are they?* I'm calling those theater people tomorrow. No, actually"—she glanced at her gold watch—"tonight."

"No, please don't!"

Deirdre pushed a strand of black hair behind her ear.

"Her parents don't know anything about it," Eve pleaded.

We shall see.

Eve slumped back into the seat and watched the snowdrifts speed past. She tried to imagine Justine knocking on Tibbets's door. It must have been right after Eve ignored her at breakfast. But Eve couldn't muster gratitude yet, could feel nothing but pain and envy. Eve was envious of everything: Justine's confidence, her looks, and, above all, her freedom. Justine was free, totally free. Eve was a rat in a cage.

"And don't think you're leaving the house after dark," Deirdre was saying.

Eve let out an involuntary whimper.

"What, you think this is a vacation?" her father asked.

"Oh, right," Deirdre said, "just get home and call up India and flit off to Dancetastic or wherever you gallivant off to."

Danceteria, Eve thought, but did not correct them.

NINETEEN

THE TREES OUTSIDE JUSTINE'S ROOM WERE BLACK AGAINST the steely sky. The absence of Eve was as if a vital organ had been removed. But her pain was nothing, she told herself, compared to what her friend must be suffering.

Justine was about to put on her jacket when Clay walked through the door.

"Hey, how're you doing?" he asked.

"I should have told them I did it too," she said.

"That wouldn't have helped anything," Clay said, pulling her into his arms. After a moment, she pushed him away. She didn't deserve his affection. His or anyone else's. The dance had been her stupid idea, and she needed to pay the price.

"Everyone hates me," Justine said bitterly.

"Wrong. They totally admire you."

Justine shook her head.

"Seriously. You're the brave girl."

"You mean the slut." She struggled into her jacket and grabbed a scarf. Clay's scarf. She was going to be late to the radio show. Hers and Eve's.

"Can I at least walk with you?"

Justine nodded and they headed into the cold.

Students were hurrying back for curfew, and they passed Damon talking to a bunch of junior girls. They all went quiet as she passed.

"Yo, Gypsy," Damon called. The girls giggled.

"Why do they keep calling me that?"

"Barbara says Gypsy was some famous stripper."

"You told your *mother* what happened?"

"I was telling her about my girlfriend."

"Shit!" she said as she slipped and Clay reached out and caught her arm. Justine regained her balance. The snow had melted, only to be refrozen in a treacherous glaze.

Girlfriend? Nobody had ever called her that before.

Clay's breath billowed in the cold air.

"Can you come to the city?" he asked, still holding her arm. "My New Year's party."

Yes, Justine wanted to say, yes. But the train fare, the cabs; she couldn't afford any of it. And she had spent all of the money Cressida had sent her. "Remember the last time I was at your house?" She saw Clay nod. "You try to erase that."

"I know, I know. But he's going to be in the Caribbean."

She stopped walking. Clay sure knew a lot about Bruce's comings and goings.

Clay put his hands on her shoulders. "Look, it's just that you have to try to see the whole picture. I know he's awful, but his parents . . . He's had a really bad time."

"Lots of people's parents get divorced! They don't all end up leaving girls tied to bedposts."

Clay's arms dropped to his sides.

"I can't understand it," Justine said. "He's an evil person, and you're so, so . . ." She wanted to say pure, but he'd probably take it the wrong way.

Clay looked down at the icy ground. "I'm just trying to help him," he said quietly.

Was he trying to save *everyone*?

"You have so many options, you can't understand," he continued.

Options? What was he talking about? "You're the one who has money," she muttered.

"Money?" Clay spat the word out like a bad piece of fruit. For the first time since he had found her in Barbara's loft she saw real anger on his face. Anger she had caused. "What does that have to do with anything?"

Justine felt the itch of tears behind her eyes.

They were in front of the science center. She would be late for the radio show, but she needed to make Clay understand. "You take it for granted, Clay. Like, tonight, imagine you want to go to the city, drink booze at some cool club, and come back in the morning? That's an entire month of rent from my parents' tenants. And yeah, they don't live in the whole house, because they can't afford to."

He frowned, then gripped her shoulders again, and looked hard at her. "As if drinking at some club would improve anything?" His face was contorted with disgust. "Look at my family. Having money doesn't change that."

Clay pulled her closer to him, his grip almost painful. "You'd drink at the club, and then the morning would come," he said, his flushed face inches away. "*Like it always does.*"

He kissed her then, with a fierceness she hadn't felt before. He pulled back and whispered, "And you'd be in the same fucked-up world you were in the night before." He released her, roughly this time, turned, and walked down the hill.

Yes, he had to save everyone, Justine thought. Everyone but himself.

The basement of the science center was empty and David was nowhere to be seen. Justine grabbed the headphones and put the needle down on "The Man with the Child in His Eyes" by Kate Bush. What was so bad in Clay's life? She had seen his family but it didn't seem fucked up to her. She was missing something major.

"Sorry!" David burst in. He looked around, worried. "Where's Eve?"

"Very funny," she said, pulling the crate of records toward her.

David stared at her blankly.

Did he live under a rock? "She got suspended." Justine was too sad about it to be exasperated.

David rested his fingers on his temples and closed his eyes.

"She didn't say goodbye to me either."

He shook his head slowly. "But you're not in love with her," he said.

No. She was just my best friend, Justine thought, putting on the next song, setting down the needle, and flipping the switch. *Was.*

"You've never been in love, have you?" David asked, his eyes shining with tears.

She didn't respond. Girlfriend, she thought. *Girlfriend.*

"I saw Clay leaving."

"You mean my boyfriend."

"You're going out with him?"

"Why are you so surprised?"

"He doesn't seem very sophisticated. Especially for a rich kid. No offense."

Justine wasn't offended because David was so clueless. She kept searching through the albums in the crate. Eve's albums.

"Sorry. I'm happy if you are. Clay just seems so insubstantial."

TWENTY

INDIA CLARKSON WALKED UP PARK AVENUE, TUCKING THE collar of Kiki's fur coat around her face in case anyone recognized her. Kiki Kristoff had spent most of her short life here, even after becoming Mrs. Clarkson, but India didn't often come to her old neighborhood. The December air was crisp and cold and made India feel alive. She couldn't understand why her father preferred Florida.

Poor Eve, getting suspended. Nothing bad had ever happened to her until now. Not that India wished bad things on her friend; on the contrary.

She nodded to Eve's doorman and rode the elevator to the Straus apartment.

The foyer was dark, the apartment quiet.

"Hello?"

India heard a noise from the bedroom wing. Eve rushed from the hallway and flung her arms around her. India endured the hug.

"Wow, I'm glad to see you," Eve said. "The wardens are out, but we only have about a half an hour. I'm supposed to be at the Met." Eve's hair was unwashed, and she was still in her flannel nightgown.

"You look amazing," she said, admiring India, who would never have entertained a guest in sleepwear. Mademoiselle had raised her that way.

"Want anything to eat?" Eve asked. "I'm famished."

"No, thank you, I just ate," India lied.

"Well, I need sustenance." Eve took her hand and pulled her toward the kitchen. India slid off her fur and folded it neatly over a kitchen chair as Eve began flinging the cabinet doors open.

"Fucker," Eve said. "Sandy finished the Froot Loops. God, you're lucky you're an only child." She poured herself a bowl of Corn Pops, and India wrinkled her nose at the thick, sugary smell.

They sat at the kitchen table, Eve shoving spoonfuls of cereal into her mouth. A drop of milk spattered on the table. India regarded it, but reminded herself that it wasn't her house.

"So? How's life?" Eve said.

If that was what you could call it. "I have a new apartment," India said, moving her mother's handbag away from the spilled milk. "On the West Side."

"Whoa!" Eve said, through a mouthful. She swallowed. "That's pretty radical. I thought you needed a permission slip to even visit. Where?"

"Fifty-fifth between Tenth and Eleventh."

Eve gaped.

"I'm subletting from a friend," India explained. "I actually like the place. Come see it."

Eve gestured around with her spoon. "I'm incarcerated, in case you hadn't figured it out. Nurse Ratched will be thrilled to see you." She shoved another mouthful of Corn Pops in her mouth. "I can't imagine your dad living in Hell's Kitchen!"

India sighed. "I'm alone. We were robbed."

"On Fifth Avenue!"

India nodded. They had been overly confident about the security at 984 Fifth. Who would imagine burglars getting past the several doormen on a Saturday afternoon? The housekeeper had been the only one home, thank goodness.

"Did they take everything?"

India shook her head. She couldn't bring herself to tell Eve that after Kiki's death her father ran through what Kiki had left him, then had sold most of her mother's jewelry to buy drugs. India had hidden the pearls, but the rest was already gone. "They took my mother's wallet."

Eve looked confused.

"I know," India said. "She's dead. She doesn't need it anymore."

"But," Eve said, "you have all of her stuff besides that still, right?"

"Her wallet was the object that she touched every single day. Of all her things, even her pillbox hat, it was the one that I really cared about."

Eve put her hand on her friend's arm. India had to admit her touch was warm, comforting, even. What did she have left now except her friends and her horse?

"I'm so sorry, India."

India shrugged. "I try to tell myself it was just a piece of leather."

"How's school?" Eve changed the subject.

"I'm not in school," India said.

"What? What are you doing?"

"Figuring things out," India said. She didn't want to talk about it, and wondered for a moment if she should have come prepared with a story, but Eve was her closest friend. India couldn't bear to lie to her. "After the burglary my father and his girlfriend sold the apartment without telling me. They moved to Palm Beach and I wasn't invited. They just left, and the next day the broker opened the door and told me someone else was moving in. Daddy doesn't know where I'm living, and I moved my inheritance to a new account. Otherwise he'll try to take it. Please, Eve, don't tell anyone. Keep my secret."

Eve nodded. "I will, I promise."

India left the Straus apartment and walked to the Metropolitan Museum. Clipping the button to the lapel of the mink, she wandered through the Greek and Roman galleries toward her grandmother's amphora. "Attributed to the Berlin Painter. Generous Gift of Charles and Genevieve Kristoff." India remembered her grandparents' apartment on Seventy-second and Park, the spotlit front hall, the scents of mothballs and her grandmother's Shalimar perfume. Now India gazed at the painted musician holding his lyre, his head thrown back to the sky. The angle of his neck had always seemed both gay and macabre.

She headed for the Saint Laurent exhibit. The burglars at her father's had had no idea of the worth of her mother's couture, or else the gowns had been too bulky to steal.

A sixties Mondrian print dress, a theatrical ostrich cape, a fabulous red and black lace evening gown with chiffon and marabou jacket. 1980. Her mother would have been thirty-five if she had lived. India moved farther along, toward a silk ruffled taffeta gown she recalled seeing at Yves's studio on the Avenue Marceau. She recalled the bolts of colorful fabric stacked on white shelves, the designer's sketches strewn across his lacquer desk. Her mother had told the designer that the dress made her look like a cupcake. 1977. The winter before Kiki died.

Her mother had spent long afternoons in the hotel suite with its velvety gold carpet, the damask curtains drawn to block out the light of the Place Vendôme. They had seen the real column the next summer in Rome.

"India?" a throaty voice broke her reverie.

"Hi, Mrs. Bradley."

"That was my mother-in-law. Call me Barbara," the woman chuckled, pulling India into a patchouli-scented embrace. India tried not to stiffen.

"What brings you to this neck of the woods?"

India gestured to the mannequins.

Barbara sighed. "Ah, yes, our materialistic zeitgeist."

India knew exactly what she meant.

"Come," Barbara said, taking India's arm and leading her out of the exhibit and into another gallery. They stopped before a painting of fields. "Look at those clouds, those miraculous clouds." India read the label. Jacob van Ruisdael. "He was from a family of painters. The craft was in his blood," Barbara said. "We can learn so much from Ruisdael's clouds." As they strolled toward a Rembrandt self-portrait Barbara explained how after RISD she and a few other painters had been looking at artists who had fallen out of favor: Reni, Murillo, and Cabanel. The academic aesthetic had enthralled them, and, though out of fashion, their work had laid the foundations for Barbara's technique. "New Masters" was just a marketing term coined by Margot Moore, the savvy gallerist adept at detecting undercurrents. Barbara's paintings were now in high demand. Even so, Barbara added, "New Masters" was a bullshit label.

That evening, Eve sat down at her parents' dining room table and stared at the pink slabs of lamb. Usually it was one of her favorite meals, but these days she had no appetite.

Her father rang a little silver bell.

"Patsy, could you open the Margaux that's on the bar?" Frederick called to the maid's retreating back.

"Which one is that?" Patsy asked, turning around. She winked at Eve who gave her a weak smile.

"How was the Met?" her mother asked, slicing her meat savagely into tiny shreds.

Eve shook her head. "I was too tired to go." She reached for the mint jelly.

"I see," her mother said, pushing her massacred meat under a raft of potatoes. Eve thought about the fancy meat market on Lexington, where you got a ticket and waited for them to call your number. The butcher was beefy and red-faced but he was sweet on Deirdre, always saving her the best cuts.

They ate in silence. For a moment Eve wished that Sandy was here, but he was at a sleepover. How could she ever be part of this adult world? Despite how horrible India's father was, she envied her friend living on her own, not needing to answer to any of them. Teachers, parents, all in league with one another, watching Eve thrash around like that shark on the carpet. It was a cult. She would not join it, she vowed, forcing the soft meat down her throat.

"What are your friends doing for the holidays?" Frederick asked, shaking the bell again.

"Too bad we had to cancel our plans," Deirdre said.

"Sorry"—Patsy poked her head in from the kitchen—"I'm having trouble with the cork."

"It's an old one, I'll give it a try," Frederick replied. He rose and headed through the swinging door.

The moment he was gone Deirdre leaned over and grabbed Eve's wrist.

"Stay away from Justine."

"Ouch!"

Deirdre dug her claws in farther. "You want to end up like this?"

"Like what?"

"I didn't start out at Tufts."

"What?" Eve squeaked. She had no idea her mother's skinny fingers were this strong.

"I went to Pine Manor first."

"Pine Mattress?"

"I was much smarter than those girls. So are you, and you know it. Get out there. Be an important part of the world. *Be something.* Don't end up like your mother, dependent on a man for every bite you eat."

Jesus, Pine Manor wasn't even a real college. It was a finishing school for girls being groomed to be wives of rich men. How could her mother, seemingly erudite and discerning, have gone there? And how had she only admitted this now, years later?

Frederick walked back into the dining room carrying the bottle. Deirdre dropped Eve's arm.

"What's going on?" asked Frederick.

Neither of them said a word.

The silence continued. What if Eve simply asked to go back to Beaverton in January? Eve remembered who her parents were.

Even if they thought it was a good idea, they would deny her, just to teach her a lesson.

"I had a very pleasant chat with Justine's mother," Deirdre said.

Eve almost choked. "You called her?"

"I said I would, didn't I?" Deirdre wiped a smear of lipstick off her wineglass.

Eve squinted at her mother. Was she making this up?

Deirdre set down her glass. "Eve," she sighed, in that you-never-learn way that drove Eve up the wall. "Think what you will, but as your mother I have responsibilities. They may not always be welcome, but I have to fulfill them to the best of my ability."

Eve stared.

Deirdre waved a hand in the air. "We both know none of this would have happened if Justine weren't in the picture. I can't choose your friends, but I can prevent you from fraternizing with the bad ones. I'm not going to stand on the sidelines and watch as you go down the tubes!"

· · · · · · · · ·

Justine woke before dawn, emerging gradually from a dream. Stanley had been dancing in the Skeets, which, in the landscape of her mind, had become a glassy, frozen pond. He was holding his boom box aloft and gliding across the glossy surface. When Justine joined him, they skated in synchrony, before they found themselves passing over Clay, who was floating just beneath the surface, staring at them with milky eyes.

Sitting up abruptly, Justine felt sick. She tried to get the vision of Clay under ice out of her mind. What had that meant?

In the dim light, she noticed that Tierney's desk drawer was ajar, could just see the makeup bag through the crack. Peeking down, she saw Tierney on her side, mouth open, eyes closed.

Justine crept down from the upper bunk. A creaking rail made her freeze for a moment but Tierney slept on. It took her several moments to pry open the desk drawer without making any noise. Heart pounding, she unzipped the bag, examined several orange vials of pills. Ranitidine. Diazepam. Acyclovir.

Tierney's bed creaked and Justine whipped around. But Tierney had merely shifted to her back. Justine rezipped the makeup bag and returned the drawer to its former half-closed state.

Tierney's eyes flew open. "Can't you be quiet?" she hissed, looking like an expensive doll under the patchwork quilt. "And by the way, I knew it wasn't true."

"What wasn't?"

"That you're dating Clay. I didn't believe Jackie for a second."

Justine leaned down. "Jackie was telling the truth," she whispered back.

"Then it's only because he knows you're an easy lay. Now go away, your breath stinks." Tierney turned to face the wall.

Justine ate her Lucky Charms while Stanley and David argued about which Brian Eno song was the best distillation of his work. Had David talked to Eve? She was anxious for a report. If Justine did, by some miracle, get money from her parents and make it into the city, would she see Eve at the party?

Maybe Eve's parents wouldn't even let her go to Clay's. Then Justine would just have to contrive a way to see her.

The fields looked like yellow tundra under an ice-blue sky. Clay,

Stanley, and Bruce all lived in Crawford, a large brick building where you got your own room. Psycho singles, kids called them.

Billy Comerford slouched in the common room watching a basketball game.

"Hey, Gypsy," he said.

"Which room is Clay's?"

"Gonna strip?"

She gave him the finger.

Billy let out a snort. She waited.

"205."

She knocked. No response. She knocked again, louder.

She was just about to leave when Clay answered the door, shirt unbuttoned.

He glanced up and down the hall, then pulled her through the door. She kissed him. He hadn't brushed his teeth. She didn't care.

"What are you doing here?" he whispered.

"Have you spoken to Eve?" she asked.

"Nope."

She kissed him again.

"Let's get breakfast," he murmured.

"Hmm?" she said, moving closer. "Can't we . . ."

They kissed more.

She looked up at him. "What are we going to do about each other?"

Clay pushed her hair off her face. "We have all the time in the world."

All the time in the world, she thought, looking around. Clothes and books were everywhere, the bed unmade, an untucked bottom sheet revealing a striped mattress. The walls were bare, except for a poster of the Nike of Samothrace.

"I love that sculpture."

"Got it in Paris."

Amazing that the sculpture looked about to take flight, even without arms.

"Who'd you go to Paris with?" she asked.

"Barbara."

"Just the two of you?"

"And this Italian guy. A painter friend of hers. They watercolored all over the place while I went to the cemetery where Jim Morrison's buried."

Justine imagined Clay contemplating a tombstone in the dusty silence. The chill of that image reminded her of the frozen Clay of her dream. What she wouldn't give to have been in Paris with him.

TWENTY-ONE

NEW YEAR'S APPROACHED AND EVE'S PRISON SENTENCE STILL hadn't been lifted. She remained on house arrest except to visit "approved cultural institutions," which still only included the Met, the Frick, and the Modern. To think, the Strauses lived in the cultural capital of the universe and, in their eyes, only three museums passed muster? Her parents were art collectors—what about all those galleries from which they purchased art? Eager to break out of jail, Eve concocted a plan. She would tell her parents she wanted a summer job in a gallery—SoHo was practically at the other end of the city.

At first, they were surprised. Then, to Eve's satisfaction, they became encouraging. Deirdre even offered to take her to SoHo herself the following day to meet and network with some of the dealers. Perhaps their shamed daughter's life would go on after all. Improve, even. Finally they might stop acting like Eve was dying of an incurable illness.

The plan was brilliant and might even provide an opportunity to see one of her friends. Eve was desperate for company, and as it was school break, she might contrive to bump into Clay or India. Her mother would have no choice but to let her talk to them, at least. She called India immediately after supper.

India, ever loyal, agreed to "bump into" Eve in Margot Moore's gallery the following day, and to bring Clay with her. It was a safe bet that Eve and her mother might linger in the gallery. Deirdre was dying for a Massimo Sforza painting and would seize the opportunity to chat up Margot, his dealer.

Eve kissed the receiver as she hung up.

....

Rain pounded on the windows of the Rubin house, threatening to freeze and turn to sleet. Miles stood up from the table and ambled over to stir the fire. Leftover pizza from Sally's sat on the dining room table, with an open bottle of white wine and a terracotta pot of paperwhites. In Justine's opinion, the scent of those flowers always fluctuated between sweet and putrid. She lounged on the tattered chaise, smoking cigarettes and reading mystery novels.

"Can I go to the city for a New Year's party?" she asked.

"Whose fete?" Cressida asked from behind a copy of *Madame Bovary*.

"Clay Bradley's."

Cressida put down the book.

"As in the *Bradley Arts Center*?"

Justine did not flinch. She was a private-school kid now, going out with a wealthy, good-looking boy. Her mother's excitement was a reminder that this was not normal, but fuck it, she would pretend it was.

"Is his mother that artist Barbara Bradley?" Cressida persisted.

Justine rolled her eyes.

"Which Barbara, dear?" Miles asked his wife, leaning the poker on the massive stone fireplace.

"Remember, the one who paints those violent Bible scenes?"

"So, can I?" Only a week into Christmas break and Justine was already going bonkers. Three Agatha Christie novels in, and she was about to start a fourth.

"Where were you thinking of staying?" Cressida asked.

Justine extended her woolly socks toward the flames. I guess not with Eve, she thought. Eve was incarcerated.

"What about chez Gretchen?" Cressida suggested.

"I'm allergic to cats, remember?" Justine felt itchy just thinking about the fur in Gretchen's messy brownstone. "I can stay with Clay."

Cressida and Miles exchanged a smile.

"Is Clay blond like his mother?" her mother asked.

"Dark hair, pale, green eyes."

"Sounds divine."

The most beautiful boy alive.

Justine wondered what Clay would think of this house. Her parents had bought the brownstone for three thousand dollars, part of one of the many failed "urban renewal" projects in the blighted city. Cressida had excavated the basement and the first floor to create a double-height space with exposed brick and hanging plants in macramé, adding a river-stone fireplace and a salvaged stained-glass window in reds, greens, and blues. A mixed-up, eclectic mess, but home.

"Miles?" Cressida asked hopefully.

"Yes, dear?"

"Your only daughter wants to go to the city for New Year's to be with her boyfriend. Care to weigh in?"

Miles peered at Justine over tortoise demi-lunes. "Are you paying your way by posing for his mother?"

Cressida laughed.

"Don't act as if this is all within the budget!" Miles added, closing his paper with a snap.

Cressida ran her fingers over her forehead.

"We can't really give you much more than train fare, but we don't want you to be in an uncomfortable position," he continued.

Justine watched the wheels of her mother's brain grind forward as she stared into the fire. "We'll find a way," Cressida murmured. "We'll find a way."

Justine waited for her parents to creep off to bed, but by 10:30 they'd made no sign of shifting from beside the fire. Still drinking, reading, fussing with the logs. She tried to stare them down, willing them to fall sleep. It was no use, they were intractable, and she couldn't wait any longer to call Clay and deliver the news.

In the kitchen Justine picked up the phone and dialed. The whir of an answering machine tape responded. "Salutations! You've reached Barbara. Actually, you've reached her newfangled answering machine. Leave a message. It *likes* messages." Justine hung up and slumped down behind the counter, her arms hugging her knees. Maybe Barbara could tell who called. Maybe she was sitting there with Clay right now, staring at the machine, listening.

Don't be a fool, Justine admonished herself. He invited you.

An image of Gerald floated before her, getting out of bed, pulling up his pants, straightening his bow tie. The day he'd told her they had to call the whole thing off. Of course, while she had been between his thighs she hadn't known it was the last time. He told her he had met someone else, someone his age. It had been inevitable from the get-go. Surely she'd realized that?

Had Gerald known all along how things would end? Now Justine imagined Clay out at parties with Eve, and that exotic India whatever her name was . . . Her mother's voice interrupted her thoughts.

"To think you'll be in some fancy Fifth Avenue apartment while your parents sit around at Walter's. *Again*. To you shall we raise our meager goblet, my darling," Cressida continued, sloshing her wine.

"They live in SoHo."

Cressida waved her hand into the air. "The details may change, but the reality stays the same. Our child is a child no longer." Cressida downed the rest of her wine in a gulp.

TWENTY-TWO

DAYS PASSED AND CLAY DID NOT CALL JUSTINE BACK. CHRIST-mas came and went. The Rubins had stayed in New Haven because the heat was better. Miles hated to pay the bills for the cavernous barn in Woodstock.

It was December 30 when the phone finally rang.

"I'm really sorry," Clay said. "I *just* got your message."

Justine paused, processing this information. She had spent the last few days trying desperately to quell the ache in her chest by burying herself in Baudelaire, listening to as much Kate Bush as she could, and wishing she had invited Stanley to come to New Haven with her instead of staying at Griswold.

"My parents gave me the green light for New Year's," she said weakly, even though it was tomorrow.

"Party's canceled. We have no heat."

She had no clue how that was possible.

Clay explained that Barbara had had some big moral argument with her landlord and he had turned it off.

Who has a moral argument with a landlord? Justine wondered, while the relief of hearing his voice, of realizing that his feelings hadn't changed, slowly seeped into her consciousness.

"We had to go to the Hamptons."

"Oh, that sounds beautiful." Justine imagined crashing waves, gray beaches, and scrabbly hedges. Clay in a fisherman's sweater, smelling of damp wool and shampoo.

"Nah, it's cold and boring. Nobody's around this time of year."

Justine would have given her firstborn to be at the beach with him. She could see them walking hand in hand across the sand, dipping their toes into the freezing surf, boiling lobsters and cracking their claws by the fire.

"What're your plans?" she asked.

"Char's home. I haven't seen her in two years." Did she escape from the cult or was she allowed to visit? "Barbara's going to Keith's," Clay continued.

"Who's Keith?"

"Family friend. Huge party." He fell silent. She waited.

After a long pause he said in a voice that was barely audible, "I miss you."

"Me too," she admitted.

He did not seem to hear her. His voice was a whisper. "I wish you were here."

At the sound of this, Justine closed her eyes, feeling herself dissolve into the phone.

"I can hear the waves," she said.

"They never stop," Clay said flatly.

"You make it sound like that's a bad thing."

For a moment he did not respond, and she listened to the consistent crash in the background.

"When I'm out here it starts to drive me nuts."

What was causing this unhappiness? Clay was in his beach house with his cool mom. It was incomprehensible.

Justine imagined, by contrast, how Stanley must be feeling, trapped at Griswold, having his holiday ham or whatever with Tibbets and her family. What did he do all day at school with nobody around? Even the library was closed. Sit at the smoker? Wander into Wormley and talk to the toothless guy in the deli?

"I need to see you," Clay continued, sounding bleaker than she had ever heard him sound.

"It's only a week." Walking on the beach in winter, strolling the streets of Paris, all of that would come true one day when they were older. Right now she didn't have the money. "I wish I could visit."

"Yeah, me too. See you in a week?"

"Yeah."

"Bye."

TWENTY-THREE

January

EVE WATCHED MR. WINKLER TURN TO THE CLASS.

"Lovely to see you so refreshed after such a *long* break." His gaze flicked across Eve's face. "Has anyone ever been to Salem, Mass.?"

Tierney raised her hand, her hair in Bo Derek cornrows.

"Enlighten us, Miss Worthington."

"What's that mean?"

Mr. Winkler's eyes flashed. "Any connection between Salem and Nathaniel Hawthorne that might be lurking in the recesses of your gray matter?"

"Uh, no," said Tierney, adjusting the rope bracelet on her arm. "I went to Salem for a crew race with my dad when we were looking at boarding schools."

"And?"

"So what, I've been there," Tierney said casually.

The teacher paced. "Salem is the birthplace of Nathaniel Hawthorne." He stopped and turned, rising onto the balls of his feet. "It is also one of the most important New England towns from the Puritan period. And Hawthorne is, arguably, the most influential American writer to describe that time in history."

Damon's arm went up in the air.

"A raised hand, Mr. White, congratulations!"

Damon scratched his buzz cut. "Isn't Salem haunted? Where all those witches were burned at the stake?"

"Indeed." Mr. Winkler's heels sank back to the floor. "Salem is the site of those famous witch trials, and legends about hauntings continue to this day."

Justine passed Eve a mimeographed sheet.

ENGLISH 10-01   MR. R. WINKLER   OFFICE HOURS: M 4–6

THE SCARLET LETTER, NATHANIEL HAWTHORNE
ASSIGNMENT 1: ORAL REPORT

1. Damon White/Justine Rubin
   "Evil in The Scarlet Letter"
2. Irene Huntington/William Comerford
   "The Role of Nature"
3. Eve Straus/Tierney Worthington
   "Sin and Knowledge"
4. Jenny Lake/Alison Smith
   "Night and Day"
5. Clayton Bradley/Christina Porter
   "Identity and Society"
6. Mona Harris/Kevin Adams
   "Pearl"

Each team will have 10 minutes to present, and the presentations will span two classes, allowing time for discussion in between. A portion of your grade will be based on your ability to work with another student.

Everyone was talking at once. Sin and knowledge? Eve thought. Across the classroom Tierney was looking ill.

"Silence!" Mr. Winkler cleared his throat. "Once you crack the book, these themes will become clear. We have more than a month to go over them. I'm available during office hours, and I'll be prepared to discuss any issues you may have. Issues relating to the project, that is."

Tierney had her hand up.

"Yes, Miss Worthington?"

"Your office hours are at the same time as my volleyball practice," she said.

"Volleyball?"

"I'm captain. First sophomore in twenty years," she added proudly.

"That's quite an accomplishment. I coach soccer; you should go out for it in the spring. Speak to me after class and we'll arrange another time."

There was a hard rime on the footbridge, coating the planks in a treacherous layer. Eve paused for a moment and zipped her jacket all the way up. She gazed into the forest beside the footbridge. The branches had a glaze of ice on them, as if melted sugar had been poured from a giant ladle. Birdsong rang through the wintry tangle, and she saw a flit of wings.

"Wait up!" Tierney called.

Eve turned, watching Tierney's new cornrows bobbing as she jogged toward her. "What are we going to do?" Tierney panted in a cloud of steam.

Eve frowned at Tierney's fresh-off-the-beach tan. "Let's see, read the book?"

"I mean, when should we get together and start?" Tierney's blue parka had a polo player stitched over the breast.

"Why not start by reading as much as we can. It will probably take me at least two weeks. That gives us a bunch of time after."

Eve knew Tierney could take months to read it. This was going to be a nightmare. Had Mr. Winkler assigned her a thick-skulled partner on purpose?

"I'll have a head start anyway, since I just got invited to tea at his house," Tierney smirked.

Ah ha, thought Eve, he'd moved on. The Wanker's new love interest was standing before her.

"Make sure to find out how to get an A."

Tierney nodded, looking conspiratorial, then tossed her hair with a clack of plastic beads. Tender scalp shone between the rows.

"You've heard the rumors," Tierney said.

Eve couldn't think what to say.

"He'd never dare. Come on! My parents have given this place a ton of money!"

Eve was silent.

Tierney's eyes widened. "Did he try anything with you?"

For a moment Eve thought of confessing, but Tierney wasn't worth it. And after all, nothing had happened.

"Of course not!" Eve scoffed, feeling warmth rise to her cheeks.

Tierney leaned in. Eve could smell her perfume, Anaïs Anaïs. "Between us," Tierney whispered, "I've heard he does actually do things with students. But only the ones the administration would never believe. You know . . ."

All Eve could do was nod.

"I'll fill you in on what I learn tonight. Glad we're on the same team. Ta-ta!" Tierney turned and walked down the footbridge.

Eve watched her go. Tierney's affability wasn't fooling her, the girl was just hoping Eve would do all the work.

TWENTY-FOUR

EVE KNOCKED ON MR. WINKLER'S DOOR JUST BEFORE SUPPER.

He opened it and grinned. "I hoped you might stop by."

"Is it a bad time?" It occurred to her that another girl might be there. She peered past him but could see no one.

"Not at all! I'm glad to see you. Come in," he said, standing aside in mock chivalry.

She entered and he took her coat.

"Can I offer you something?" he asked.

"What's available?" She looked up at him.

"Anything your heart desires," he said, and his eyes swept over her, taking her in. Eve relaxed a bit; Tierney or not, he was still interested.

"Bourbon?"

"Coming right up."

He walked into the kitchen. The portrait of the old headmaster stared down at her from above the mantel. A log shifted and sparks flew up the chimney.

Mr. Winkler handed her the drink and she sat on the sofa. He was only a few inches away.

"What an ordeal you've been through," he said. "How are you holding up?"

"Okay, I guess." She took a slug of bourbon. It burned her throat.

They looked at each other.

As if in slow motion, her teacher reached out and gently took the glass from her hand. He set it on the table, where one of the ice cubes fell onto the other with a clink. Eve was frozen in a film still, but Mr. Winkler was moving, leaning toward her.

And then he was kissing her. She couldn't believe it, it was actually happening. In a moment she started to kiss him back, hoping she was doing it right. Eve was aware of her teacher's hand on her back, the smell of wood smoke, his corduroy knee. He was excellent, she thought, smooth, this must be the way a man kissed. How had she waited so long?

Her teacher's hand moved under her shirt, across her bra, his fingers cool from the glass as he caressed the nylon. Eve kept her eyes tightly shut. Mr. Winkler eased her onto her back, leaning his weight against her side.

His fingers slipped beneath her waistband. She tensed.

"Hush," he whispered, like a lullaby at bedtime. His hand on her hip bone, across her stomach, then into her underpants. Eve willed herself not to move, not to act like this was unusual. Should she be doing something to him? His fingers were inside her. She tried to focus on the kissing, keep things up there, but as he kept at it she stopped caring, she couldn't worry anymore. Eve's head fell back, lips apart, but at the last moment she covered her mouth and masked her cry as a cough.

Mr. Winkler pulled his hand out of her pants, looking gratified. "I've been wanting to do that for a long time."

Eve could not trust her voice.

"This isn't safe," Mr. Winkler said. "We need to meet at night."

She tried to speak normally. "I have a radio slot on Friday night from ten to midnight."

The night she had permission to be out past curfew. They'd have plenty of time. Justine could host solo next week and would understand, probably even applaud. She'd have to lie to David, tell him Eve wasn't feeling well.

"Brilliant," Mr. Winkler agreed. "But it will have to be in two weeks. This Friday I have a dinner and a concert."

He could go out at night and do whatever he wanted. She imagined him in a theater with red velvet seats and a classical string quartet on stage.

"Do you have a girlfriend?"

"You're so sweet to ask. No, I don't, not at the moment." He stroked her cheek softly with the back of his finger.

"Great, then the following Friday."

"It's a date."

He took her face in his hands and kissed her tenderly. Surely, this was okay. Surely, she didn't need to be afraid of a man who would kiss her like that.

Eve walked to Londry in a daze. She had hidden two more of her mom's pills in a vial in her bag. Maybe she would take one now, just to prolong her bliss.

....

That evening, Justine headed to Clay's dorm. It had started to snow, the second big storm of the season. "I need to see you," he had said on the phone. Words she had replayed over and over in her head. She floated up the steps and down the hall in a haze of happy anticipation.

Clay's door was ajar, the desk lamp the only illumination.

There he was, leaning back in his chair, cradling a football. He was smiling broadly. She almost didn't want him to see her; he was so lovely when no one was looking. Then he threw the ball and Justine pushed open the door farther to see Bruce catch it. He was reclining on Clay's bed as if he were at some Roman banquet.

Clay's chair legs landed on the floor with a bang.

Bruce aimed the football. *He's not going to throw it at me.* But it left his hand, whizzed past her ear, and flew down the hall.

"Nice catch, Gypsy," Bruce said.

"Shut up," Clay warned.

"Sorry, I just . . ." Justine mumbled.

"Come in!" Clay said.

But she waffled in the doorway.

Bruce patted the bed next to him. "Let's snuggle." His shirt was riding up, golden hairs encircled his belly button.

"Give it a rest, Underwood." Clay's smile faded. "And go and get the stupid football before someone takes it."

Bruce hoisted himself up and ducked past her into the hall.

"Please, please, come here," Clay said, more softly. He stood up and kissed her. She tried to think what he tasted like. Sweet, with a slight tang. Like plums. Ripe, purple plums. He pressed her against the wall and she could see melted snow from her coat making spots on his shirt.

Bruce guffawed, seeing them, and landed back on Clay's bed with a thump.

Justine looked up, wishing she could blink and make him disappear.

"Mind getting lost?" Clay said, not unkindly.

Bruce ignored him, toying with the football.

"I said get lost."

Bruce tossed the football at the ceiling and caught it. "Threesome?"

She was starting to sweat in her parka. She shouldn't have come.

Bruce stretched toward the shelf above the bed and flipped on the radio. Justine saw a bit more of his muscled torso.

"Don't be an asshole." Clay pointed to the door. "I mean it, Bruce. GET OUT!"

Bruce sat up and stretched lazily.

"If you change your mind, just whistle," he said, and threw Justine the football. She missed, and it bounced across the desk.

"God, I'm sorry," Clay said when he'd gone. "The guy was almost crying when he got here. I had to cheer him up. Sorry he acted like such a dick."

Justine collapsed onto the bed. Bruce always acted like a dick.

Clay sat beside her.

"How'd New Year's end up?" he asked, stroking her damp hair.

She shrugged. "How was your sister?"

"It was weird. She came with this lady called a minder who never left her alone with us. Char even went to the bathroom with her."

"Why?"

"In case we tried to deprogram her. Ha, that would never work anyway. Char is the most stubborn person I know."

Did Char look like him?

"I told her about you."

"What'd you say?" Justine managed.

"How beautiful you are. And that"—he gazed in the direction of the window—"I'm a sucky boyfriend."

Not true, she wanted to say, sinking into his bed.

"Like, I didn't call you and tell you the party was off." His eyes were full of sorrow.

Justine pulled Clay closer and kissed him. They could do it now, she didn't care if she got busted in here. She unbuttoned his jeans. His pants were almost off when there was a knock at the door.

"Fuck," Clay said, hopping up and fumbling with his fly. "Get under the covers!"

Justine pulled the blue duvet over her head. She was breathing fast, and it was hot and airless underneath.

"It's Coach Jellinek. You asleep?"

"I was, hang on."

Justine heard the door open and the *thwap* of a hand on skin. A conversation about crew ensued. Justine caught only snippets. She heard the coach say something about someone and a torn ACL.

The quilt was heavy, there was no oxygen.

A racket from the hall drowned the conversation as students rushed in from the snowball fight. The overhead light shone through a bare patch in the navy comforter. Rumpled clothes were stuffed at the bottom of the bed and the pillow smelled unwashed. Justine felt like she might slip into unconsciousness if she didn't breathe fresh air.

She heard the door close.

Clay whipped off the duvet.

She smiled at him.

"Could you breathe?"

Justine nodded.

He ran his eyes over her but shook his head. "That was too close a call. We'll get busted," he said, helping her up. She wobbled to her feet and leaned on him to steady herself. Why was it always like this? she wondered. Justine hadn't figured on boarding school being this shitty for her sex life.

"Sorry again about Bruce," he said, "but he brought amazing news."

What, she thought, Bruce was getting recruited a year early?

"Bowie's playing a surprise concert at Toad's. In New Haven."

Toad's Place? The venue was tiny, like only a hundred people. Bowie? Eve was going to go wild.

"Oh my God! How did he find out?"

"His dad—and he said he can get us on the list."

Her elation faded, her face fell.

"I'm not taking gifts from that asshole," she said, feeling like she would start crying just thinking about it. "When is it?"

"Friday. And you're being insane," Clay continued, pulling her into a hug. He whispered in her ear, "Bruce owes you."

"No!"

"It's late," Clay said, "we have to go."

The storm was getting worse, wind kicking snow in gusts across the campus. On the way back to her dorm she huddled against Clay, her fingers and nose numb, her hair encrusted with snow. They arrived only minutes before curfew. Clay would barely make it back to his dorm in time.

"Don't torture yourself," he said. "For Bruce, it's just a snap of the fingers." He kissed her on the nose, then on the lips, and without a word hurried into the night.

The common room was deserted. Justine tiptoed upstairs to her room, hung her sodden parka on the back of the door, and took off her wet boots. Tierney was asleep, Rapunzel braids on the pillowcase. What Justine would have given for a pair of scissors so she could lop them off.

For Bruce it's just a snap, she thought.

Justine pulled on her pajamas. First thing in the morning she would find Eve and tell her about the concert. Eve was going to lose her mind. Toad's Place. Why would someone as famous as Bowie play there instead of the Hartford Civic Center? But her parents were friends with Todd Rundgren and he did those surprise concerts from time to time. So did Bob Dylan. Then it dawned on her. Her parents! Couldn't Miles be useful for once? The man ran a theater! New Haven was the size of a nickel. Surely, he must know someone connected to Toad's Place.

Happy, Justine lay in bed. Snow pounded at the window. She hoped Clay had made it back safely. David fucking Bowie. At Toad's. It would be a dagger in her gut if she and Eve couldn't go.

Justine had barely fallen asleep when her alarm went off. She jumped up and grabbed clothes from her drawer.

The snow was at least a foot deep from last night's blizzard and it felt like wet concrete as she trudged up the hill. She saw a figure approaching and her heart lifted when she realized it was Eve, on her way to breakfast. Justine tried to run toward her but the snow was too deep and she made slow progress.

"Bowie's playing at Toad's!" she called out.

"What the hell are you talking about? What's Toad's?"

Panting, Justine filled her in on what she'd learned from Clay. Eve stared at her for a moment, then let out a howl of joy that reverberated up into the sky.

"Oh my God, oh my God." Eve was hyperventilating. Tears of joy shone in her eyes.

Students tramped by, giving them odd looks.

"I'm going to DIE! Oh my God! *This* Friday?"

Justine put her arm around Eve and waited for her to compose herself.

When she was breathing normally they walked toward the

dining hall and devised a plan of action for the escape. They agreed to record a radio show in advance on a tape and play it in the station while they were at Toad's. There were risks. What if there was a malfunction and a teacher was listening?

"Too bad you and David are a bust," Justine said. "He could do the whole show for us!"

Eve was too jazzed up to bother discussing David. "We're definitely using Bruce's dad. That asshole owes you!"

Justine shook her head no. She intended to call Miles right after breakfast.

Eve stopped walking, crossed her arms, and pursed her lips. "For Bowie I'm willing to be a total whore." Justine knew that Eve didn't begin to know what being a whore meant.

. . . .

E ve lay on the floor of her dorm room gazing at the ugly popcorn ceiling. It was hard to believe that her teacher had really done that to her. And with such ease. Would it be like that with other guys? Finally everything was coming together. The date with Mr. Winkler, the Bowie concert even sooner. Eve was going to see her idol and lose her virginity at last, all in a matter of weeks. And only days ago she had been imprisoned in her parents' apartment, feeling like a royal fuckup, and now this huge step forward. It was as if some karmic wheel were turning after months of stagnation.

This was one of those moments in her life that would always matter, Eve thought, reflecting on other times of monumental change. The summer of 1976, the Straus family had rented a house in Connecticut with a pool. Besides watching the Montreal Olympics, Eve had gone to day camp, picked up each day by a pimply counselor named Alan who drove a blue station wagon. Eve sat in the front listening to music on the radio and looking at her reflection in the side mirror. It was the first time she'd heard music in a car, and this new world of pop aroused something in her that had lain dormant until then. Alan told her about a crush he had on a female counselor, and suddenly it made sense why the boy in her swim group was staring at her all the time. It wouldn't sound like much, she thought, if she told her friends, but the whole summer had been an awakening. Eve suddenly belonged to a larger world, to a world of music and romance.

These shifts weren't just big, they were seismic. And this Friday was going to be another one.

Bill's Taxi dropped them off in front of Toad's. Justine pulled the tickets from her pocket and showed them to the bouncer.

"ID?"

She flashed her fake one and Eve did the same. He stamped the back of their hands and they were in.

The place was packed, a throng pressing forward toward the stage. Some secret, Justine thought. Eve grabbed her arm and pointed to Bruce and Clay at the bar.

"Want a drink?" Justine asked.

"No fucking way. We need to be up there," Eve said, pointing to the stage. Justine gave Clay a wave and they headed into the crowd. She felt sorry for poor Stanley missing out on this.

When they finally made it to the front, roadies were scurrying around the stage, plugging in amps and leaning electric guitars on stands. Eve, her eyes shining, looked at Justine and held her hand.

They stood there for at least forty minutes, defending their tiny spot. Finally the lights went down, and the audience began to scream. The musicians took the stage. Eve spotted Carlos Alomar slinging his guitar over his shoulder.

Eve saw the glow of the cigarette first. Then Bowie himself, in black trousers and a T-shirt, his hair canary yellow.

He was more beautiful than she could have imagined, all hip bones and animal grace. "I love you!" Eve screamed.

Bowie smiled over their heads, gazing around the ecstatic crowd.

He pulled the mike to his lips. The musicians waited. "Lavender blue, dilly dilly," Bowie sang in his deepest voice, the one Eve loved so much. "Lavender green. When I am king, dilly dilly." He looked down, and pointed his cigarette at Justine, "you will be queen."

Then he began to sing "Heroes," and Eve thought she might die.

She was unable to move, watching Bowie, watching him throw back his head, his lips drawn, his eyes half closed. *We can beat them, just for one day.* Being with him was the most amazing thing that had ever happened to her. A religious experience. Wouldn't he see her there, gazing at him with adoration and love? Eve was shooting hot flames toward the man. Surely it had to make an impression? Then Bowie sat astride a chair and a roadie handed him a human skull, the crowd roared, and he began to sing "Cracked Actor." *Suck, baby, suck, give me your head.* He started to make out with the skull. Eve was so close she could see Bowie's tongue, the lights on its gleaming surface, as it darted in and out of the bony mouth. It was intolerably sexy. This is it, she thought, the way desire is supposed to feel. Would sex with her teacher be this incredible? She shivered as Bowie stood up and strode toward her. Eve looked up at him, frozen. Then he knelt, showed her the skull, and snapped its jaws in her face.

———

After the final encore, after they had screamed themselves hoarse for more, they gave up, and shuffled away. Every inch of Eve's body was pulsating with happiness. It had been the best night of her life, and it would remain so forever. Clay spotted them and gestured for them to come to the bar. His hair was damp and his T-shirt clung to his sweaty skin. He was breathing fast, smiling. He kissed Justine and ordered more beers from the bartender. Bruce was nowhere in sight.

"That was fucking amazing," Clay said, turning back to them.

Eve could not speak, and just nodded her head. Words did not do Bowie justice.

Justine and Clay chatted about which song they liked best, while Eve saw the skull jaws snapping over and over. Bowie had felt her energy, her love. He had done that just for her.

Clay handed them each a cold bottle and they clinked them in salute. Eve took a swig of the beer and closed her eyes. She wanted to see Bowie over and over again in her mind. Imagine herself as the skull.

Just then Justine grabbed her arm. *"Get down,"* she hissed. Eve whipped around to see what Justine was looking at. Her stomach twisted as all joy drained away. Standing by the exit sign were Mr. Winkler and several other teachers. She ducked, but not in time. The teachers had seen her. Eve's head was spinning, she couldn't hear through the buzzing. All was lost, irrevocably lost.

She was going to pass out, her ears full of a loud rushing noise. What the fuck was the Wanker doing here? The look of surprise on his face. Why had she been such an idiot, imagining him at a *classical music concert*? Eve recalled him offering to play Steely Dan. *Shit.*

Justine pulled her up by her sleeve. The teachers had vanished so fast it was almost possible to believe they hadn't seen her. But they had. Eve knew it was over. She would be kicked out without a doubt. Out of school, her world, her life.

Justine was saying, "He won't bust you, what about your date next Friday night?" But Eve couldn't bear to hear the empty words.

If it had been just him, without other teachers, Eve thought ruefully, tears falling freely, but no.

No tryst with her teacher, no Clay, no Justine.

Game over.

PART
....
two

ONE

New York City, June 1984

INDIA CLARKSON EYED THE DIRTY DISHES IN THE SINK, the full ashtray beside her on the kitchen table. Justine was arriving in an hour and the apartment was a sty. Well, India thought, she couldn't ask her father's housekeeper to come and clean because then her father would find out where she lived. And if she asked her parents' friends it might get back to him.

India wondered what her new housemate would think about this shabby railroad flat. Her current housemate, Dino, didn't care about the mess, or the peeling paint, or the stench of urine on the sidewalk.

India pulled a handmade broom from the kitchen closet, purchased at a gift shop on Martha's Vineyard. It reminded her of a Russian fairy tale her nurse Mademoiselle had read to her when she was little, about a witch living in a hut who roamed the forest on chicken feet, the whole house squatting down to scoop up naughty children. One little girl who had gotten lost hunting turnips had swept the witch's hut, then cooked the witch supper, but still ended up in a pot on the stove.

Had the girl been eaten or had she escaped in the end?

The living room was more pleasant. It had three windows facing the street, and plenty of sun. India's only furnishings were the up-right piano from her grandmother's house and several silk throw pillows that had been in her mother's library. Dino had found a coffee table on the street—a hideous concoction of tubular brass and cheap glass, but India hadn't felt she could object. He paid his rent, and she detested conflict.

Foster had moved out, the poor junkie, last year. It was for the best; India had spent too much time fearing break-ins and being held up at gunpoint with a heroin addict in the house. Maybe at last she could unlock the real china and wear her mother's pearls.

It was going to be nice to have another girl here, but India worried about Justine, a blond beauty, being hassled in this neighborhood.

． ． ． ． ． ． ． ．

The buzzer on West Fifty-fifth Street read "Clarkson/ Cherubino/Reynolds." Justine was pretty sure that Reynolds was that guy Foster, the heroin addict now in rehab. She hadn't realized there was a third roommate.

The door had been painted British racing green years ago, but was covered in dents, stickers, and graffiti. It was kind of beautiful.

A voice crackled over the speaker. Then India Clarkson leaned from the fire escape, her soft-spoken instructions rendered inaudi-ble by the noise of a garbage truck. A bunch of keys landed on the sidewalk like a dead bird.

In the dim hallway, piles of newspapers, flyers from Chinese restaurants, and discarded mail covered the floor. It smelled stale, Justine thought, as she lugged her bag up the stairs. After several clicks, the door opened a few inches, a metal rod blocking it from opening farther.

"Hang on," India said, fiddling with the lock, which looked like an instrument of medieval torture. "The true sign of a shitty neighborhood," she apologized as the door swung free.

India stood in the doorway, looking smaller than Justine remembered. Her dark hair was in a smooth ponytail, her shirt neatly pressed. Justine felt flustered and sweaty in comparison.

India refastened the door behind them.

"Who's there?" a voice trilled. A man walked in, wrapped in flame-colored silk. He had carefully exposed one shoulder and his black chest hair curled above the vibrant material; a red dot had been painted between his eyes, and he wore a pink Jackie-style pillbox hat. "Namaste," he said to Justine, placing his hands together in prayer.

"Dino, what are you wearing?" India demanded.

"It's called a sari, darling. In the country you're named after, women wear these to stay cool," he replied, fanning himself.

"You know what I mean," India insisted.

Dino touched the hat. "This little thing?"

India stamped her foot. "That was my mother's! You're getting Brylcreem all over it!"

"Don't be so old-fashioned, darling," Dino said. "Nobody has used Brylcreem in years." He handed her the hat, removing bobby pins from his lustrous locks. "A girl could work up a sweat trying to introduce you to modern inventions like pantyhose and condoms. Refreshment?" he asked Justine, touching the handle of an ancient refrigerator.

"That thing works?" Justine gaped.

"Perfectly. They don't make them like that anymore," said India, grimly wiping the rim of the hat with a paper towel.

Dino offered Justine a beer.

"It's barely lunchtime," India frowned.

He placed his hand on his hip, like a mannequin in a dress shop. "It's always five o'clock somewhere. Wait! We have champagne." He shoved the beer back into the fridge and began rummaging around, his bright orange rear held aloft. Finally emerging with a bottle, Dino popped the cork and filled three glasses. "To your arrival," he said, winking at Justine.

The summer had begun.

. . . .

Eve lay on her bed listening to the soft hum of the air conditioner and the vague sounds of traffic outside on Park Avenue. Her mother was out, her father at work, her brother at camp.

It was when she was alone that the full shame of her fall from grace descended on her, pressing her down like a heavy weight. Eve felt it spread through her now like icy liquid. Expelled from boarding school. Her chances at college ruined, her record tainted forever and ever. She would have to tell her boyfriends, her husband, her children.

These were dark times in the Straus household. And Eve had had to beg to be readmitted to Beaverton.

Forced to sit before a council of teachers, interviewed. *Why should we let you back here, why should we be convinced that you have mended your ways? How do we know that there will be no further infractions*, and on and on. And to think, Eve had been first in her class before she left to go to Griswold. Maybe they hadn't forgiven her for leaving, for trading up.

Eve wondered what Mr. Winkler was doing right now. She reread the letter she had received yesterday.

WORMLEY, 14 JUNE 1984

Dear Eve,

I hope this letter finds you well. It's blazing hot in Connecticut, I can only imagine how infernal it must be in New York.

English class was successful despite your absence. I always enjoy teaching Romeo and Juliet—*it is often the first Shakespeare play my students read. I regret missing the opportunity to teach it to you.*

What are you reading these days? I just finished Eco's The Name of the Rose. *Truly brilliant—you'd like it.*

What are your summer plans? I teach a survey course in the summer program—it's not too onerous and leaves me plenty of free time. Perhaps you would enjoy a break from the city one weekend? You could take the train up to New Haven and we could have lunch and see the Yale Art Museum. I am a big fan of the building, I'd love to show it to you.

Let me know, and I look forward to hearing from you.

My best,
Bob Winkler

Visit? It would be hard to make an excuse to travel, unless she and Justine said they were going to visit Justine's parents.

If they were just walking around New Haven, she and the Wanker wouldn't have a chance to do much. Eve wasn't sure she wanted to see him if they couldn't finally wrap up loose ends.

A car honked below and Eve rolled on her side to face the wall. She often imagined what having sex with him would be like, especially after that evening last January when he did that to her on the sofa. Eve still couldn't believe it had actually happened.

The phone rang.

Patsy would answer it.

But it kept ringing. Eve jumped off of her bed and hurried down the hallway, past the sailor-boy photo of Sandy, through the limestone foyer, and into the library. The ringing stopped.

Eve stared at the phone. It did not ring again. She picked it up and dialed India.

········

India answered the phone.

"Hello? Oh, hi, Eve. Yes, she just got here. Yes, it's absolutely boiling."

Justine sipped her champagne. It would be an even better summer if she had more than thirty-five dollars in her pocket.

"We're celebrating," India continued. "No, just André. They can't tell the difference. She's right here." India handed Justine the receiver.

"How's the pad?" Eve asked.

"Haven't made it past the kitchen." Justine looked around. The narrow room had one window that opened onto an alley of blackened brick. Dirty dishes sat in the sink under a rusted tin ceiling. A colander over the bare bulb served as a shade.

"Don't you love Dino? When do you start work?"

"Not till Tuesday," Justine replied.

"Meet us for lunch Monday?"

Justine wondered who "us" was, sipping her André.

"My treat," Eve added.

Her friend was clairvoyant. "Okay, bat time?"

"Nobody eats lunch earlier than one. Get directions from Dino, India's never been below Forty-second Street. Ciao!"

Justine's room was high-ceilinged, yet barely large enough to contain the futon that sagged under the window. A poster of a lurching Janis Joplin was pinned to the wall. No wonder what's his name Reynolds was in rehab.

She eyed the stains on the futon, pulled a bedspread out of her suitcase, and threw it over them. Placing Henry on the pillow, Justine lay down under the cracked ceiling and clasped her hands behind her head.

It was incredible that she was actually here, in the city, for the whole summer. Justine thought about the conversation with her parents in May. Cressida suggested she work at her friend Flavia's gallery in Woodstock. Flavia had discovered a lot of prominent artists, a few of whom had hightailed it to Margot Moore's in the city—coincidentally, the very gallery where Eve was interning this summer. Now Flavia mostly sold paintings of Hendrix on black velvet.

"I can't stay here, I'm totally claustro," Justine had said.

Her mother had turned to Miles with a knowing look. "I was waiting for this to happen."

Miles had lowered the play he was reading and moved his gaze from Cressida to Justine.

"It's that Clayton Bradley," Cressida added.

Justine groaned.

"What, aren't you still going with him?"

Nobody had said "going with" since the fifties. *We're in love*, Justine might have told them, but her feelings were none of their business.

Yes, and Clay was working at a bank in the city.

Cressida had replied, "I guess I shouldn't be surprised. Smile, Fortune, and turn thy wheel."

"'Fortune, good night. Smile once more,'" Miles corrected.

And fortune had smiled on Justine. Cressida had made a call to her friend Gretchen Lermontov, and, miracle of miracles, the loony Russian woman needed help in her prop warehouse in Chelsea. Justine envisioned potted palms, marble busts, and suits of armor.

She examined the funny cracks in her new bedroom's ceiling, the curl of peeling paint. Maybe, finally, she and Clay would have sex on this futon, and while he was on top of her she'd look over his pale shoulder and have this same view.

Justine hopped up and went back to the living room.

India was sitting on the floor in front of the coffee table, rolling a joint. Opposite her, a battered upright piano stood along a wall, and several garment racks lined the other.

"What's all that?" Justine asked as she grabbed a pillow and sat down.

"Most of it was my mother's. Some of it's Dino's new line."

India lit the joint.

"Eve said he worked at a hotel."

"He makes clothes at night." She offered Justine the joint, but Justine shook her head.

Justine stood up and wandered over to the garment rack. There were ruffled blouses and swingy skirts and a pink suit she recognized as Chanel. There were a few floor-length gowns that looked itchy. Farther along was a jumpsuit of fake leopard fur with a gold lamé sash, a pair of suede overalls with silver buckles.

India tapped the joint on the ashtray and inclined her head toward Dino's closed door. "Thank God for cocaine," she said. "He'd never be able to do it otherwise."

"Where does he get the money?"

India drew herself up primly. "Dino pays his rent, and he doesn't bring strange people home, so I don't have a reason to pry." She took a long drag as her eyes closed.

A breeze swept in.

"Fuck, it's going to pour," Justine said, glancing at the sky.

India exhaled a pungent cloud. "We need it. To cool things off."

Justine's stomach growled. Breakfast had been a long time ago. "Is there anything to eat?"

But India was meditating. Justine went into the kitchen and opened the cabinet: spaghetti, Kraft Parmesan, and a few half bottles of Mouton Cadet. Justine filled a pot with water and glanced at the clock. 8:45 p.m. She set the pot on the dirty stove and was about to call her parents when the phone rang.

"Hello?"

"It's Clay. How are you?"

Happiness filled her. "Great. You?"

"Working."

"Did you know the Reynolds guy?" she asked.

"Foster? Sure. We all grew up together."

Justine was getting sick of everyone knowing everyone from childhood. She twirled the phone cord around her wrist. "Come over, I'm cooking."

"I'm going to be at the office really late. Can I call you tomorrow?"

"It's Saturday!" she said, untwirling it. And he had said all he was doing was Xeroxing.

"I know, but I have stuff to get done." He was silent for a moment. "Jus?"

"What?"

"Miss you," Clay said, and hung up.

Justine replaced the receiver and pressed her forehead into the wall next to the phone. How could she wait another day to see him? It had been weeks—one more day shouldn't make a difference. But working on a weekend?

She started to clean the pile of dishes in the sink. They were mismatched, some were fragile and encrusted with gold, others swiped from Howard Johnson's. Justine set them in a drying rack, uncorked the wine, and poured herself a glass.

When the pasta was drained, Justine dished out three plates and carried them to the living room. Dino was lounging on a cushion, wearing tiny shorts. His legs were dark with hair. India was smoking another joint and the humid air was thick with smoke. *Dressed to Kill* had just started on the TV. They ate in silence.

"Can I finish that?" Dino asked India, who hadn't touched her pasta.

She handed him the plate.

"Honey, you need to eat," he said, poking India's scrawny arm.

"Shh, this is the elevator scene," she replied.

"Angie's so fabulous," Dino said through a mouthful.

Justine didn't get it; the actress was tacky and gave her the creeps.

When the movie ended, India switched the channel, sat back, and lit another joint. She smoked them like cigarettes.

"I'm going to bed," Justine said, getting up.

"But this is *Midnight Blue*," Dino protested.

She'd never seen the show but was exhausted by the journey and the newness and excitement of it all.

As Justine shut her door, lightning crackled and illuminated the room like a strobe. One Mississippi. Two. The floor shook with the baritone of thunder. She heard a shriek from the television. She lay down with Henry and closed her eyes, inhaling the familiar smell of his tufted belly. It was still hard to believe that she was in an apartment, in New York, by herself.

Rain erupted from the sky and spattered the window like beads from a broken necklace. Lightning again. Justine sat up. Her window was open, and raindrops were splashing over the sill. On her knees, she pulled it shut, watching the columns of rain against the streetlights. Water sloshed through the gutters, carrying trash, which bobbed like toy boats, into the sewers, and off to sea.

TWO

MONDAY MORNING EVE TOOK THE SUBWAY TO HER FIRST day at Margot's gallery.

She felt slightly sick. To celebrate her first day as a "working woman," Patsy had force-fed her eggs and bacon, like one of those ducks in France they stuff until they explode into foie gras. By the time she climbed up the steps at Spring Street, Eve felt like vomiting it all onto the sidewalk. An artistic statement of her own.

The gallery air-conditioning was set to an arctic temperature, and Eve stopped at the front desk to introduce herself. The guy behind the desk with sculpted hair studiously ignored her.

"Eve Straus," she said, "for Margot."

He put his book down, then picked up the phone and spoke in a library voice. He hung up and pointed toward the back.

Eve walked through the gallery, passing small abstract paintings by Carolyn Heller. She wasn't a fan of her work, but the summer was reserved for painters low on a gallery's list. September was reserved for the A-listers like Massimo Sforza. Eve couldn't wait to work on his show.

In a separate room at the rear of the building, a young man sat at a long table concentrating on papers. He wore khaki pants and a blue Oxford. Margot Moore sat next to him, one elbow on the table, in a tight red sleeveless dress and high suede heels. Thick dark hair curled in her armpits.

"Good morning," Eve said, staring.

"Greetings," Margot said briskly, standing up.

Eve would have to train herself not to look.

The man nodded in her direction. Margot didn't bother to introduce him.

"Let's get started. What do we do here?" Margot demanded.

"Represent artists?" Eve quavered.

"We *sell*." Margot tapped her heel on the floor. "Other galleries are run by brats with trust funds, donations, and dishonesty." There was lipstick on one of her front teeth. "This is a *business*."

Eve nodded. Everyone here knew that Eve's parents had gotten her this job. What was Margot trying to say?

"Where's your Rolodex?"

"Uh, I don't have one."

"What?" Margot barked. "Nobody works here without personal contacts. Take your mother's off her desk, for heaven's sake. Raymond!" She clapped her hands. "Show her a few of yours." Margot stalked into the back, high heels jabbing the floor.

So, Eve thought, I'm a conduit to my parents' rich friends. No wonder Margot didn't care that Eve had been expelled.

"Isn't she amazing?" Raymond breathed. He was biracial, stylish, and handsome.

"What's the story with the underarm hair?" Eve asked.

"She makes us braid it." Raymond laughed. "Here"—he slid his contacts toward her—"all yours."

"Thanks," Eve said, shivering in the chair. "So, what are we supposed to do?"

"We pick up the phone, we call people, we sell them art," Raymond explained. Eve glanced around, feeling instantly intimidated. They would hear every word she said in the open room. Maybe working here was a big mistake. She should have tried to sell clothes at Charivari instead.

"Don't let Margot fool you," Raymond warned. "She acts like she's all business, but that woman lives and breathes art. How old are you anyway?"

"Almost sixteen," Eve replied.

"Bullshit."

"No, really! I'm going into eleventh grade."

"You're just a kid! Margot's going to eat you like a baby bunny."

Eve pointed to the phone. "Show me how."

Raymond smiled and sat down at the desk. He flipped through the cards, picked up the phone, and dialed.

"Hello, may I please speak to Mrs. Theodoracopulos? Raymond Rathbone from the Margot Moore gallery." Eve thought she heard a slight accent. The Midwest? "Mrs. Theo? Hi, darling, it's Raymond! Fabulous, fabulous. Yes, of course, it's reserved for you. Has been for months."

She could never be that smooth, Eve thought, watching in awe. "Oh, of course, he called me about it but you know I'd never sell it to that crook. You'd better come today. There really is not a moment to spare." Raymond waved an elegant hand in the air. "I could meet you at the gallery; you know his studio address is top secret. Perfect! See you then. Ciao ciao, darling."

Raymond hung up. "See? Easy."

She did not see. "What's she buying?"

"A brand-new Massimo Sforza."

"Isn't the show after Labor Day? That's what I thought I was working on."

Raymond nodded. "Margot sells everything before the show is even up. She picks which paintings go to which collectors. It's how she creates the advance frenzy. Mrs. Theo wants to see hers before the show goes up. I've seen some, but nobody has seen the Susanna. It's rumored to be his greatest yet."

Which one had her mother and father been assigned?

"So," Eve asked, "what if you're some rich guy from Chicago, and you walk in here and want to buy something?"

"No dice." Raymond crossed his legs, exposing a sockless ankle. His collar was artfully frayed.

"Wow." Eve thought about having all the money in the world and still being denied your prize.

"Look through here and see if you know anyone, then let's talk." He pushed the Rolodex her way and headed into the back.

Nothing looked familiar under *A* or *B*, but under *C*, she found Dino. Dino Cherubino. Odd, she thought.

Eve glanced toward the wall at the back. She walked over and peeked around it.

There was a conference room containing an oval marble table and bookshelves stacked with books on Diebenkorn, Agnes Martin, Cy Twombly. Ahead was a closed door. To the left was a kitchenette with a gleaming espresso maker. Eve still hadn't had coffee this morning—Patsy always gave her milky tea, as if she were a small child. Her head was starting to ache. She turned to go when the door opened and Raymond emerged.

"Need something?" he asked.

"How do you know Dino?"

"I could ask you the same thing."

"He's my friend's roommate."

"Small world."

She waited for him to elaborate, but he just looked at her, a wry smile on his lips.

"I wouldn't make that your first call, Eve. Dino doesn't buy art."

· · · · · · · ·

Justine woke up slowly. It was barely eight, but sun was already pouring through her unshaded window. She went to the kitchen and was boiling water for tea when the phone rang. Justine jumped. One day, no matter what, she swore she wouldn't do that every time. Who was calling so early?

"Hello?"

"Hello, dear," Cressida's voice wafted through the receiver.

"Oh, hi." She should have known; her mother only called when the rates were lower.

"How's the apartment?"

"Awesome. No food though. India doesn't eat," Justine said.

"That goes with the type," Cressida said. "If you've never had to worry about your next meal, well . . ."

"Mom, the world isn't just rich people and people like us."

Cressida emitted one of her world-weary sighs. "Don't think I don't see the nuances in the human race. It was a manner of speaking. How's Clayton?"

"Fine," Justine lied. Would he call her today?

Silence ensued.

"I'll check back in a few days. Maybe your foul humor will have passed." Cressida hung up.

Justine stood there and stared at the phone. Her mother could always tell when she was in a bad mood, she thought, and usually made it worse. The receiver started beeping.

"Oh, fuck off," she said, and slammed it down on the cradle.

"Who was that?" India asked, walking into the kitchen.

"My mother."

An odd expression passed over India's face.

What would it be like to lose your mother, get kicked out of boarding school, and be left to live on your own? Had India really tried to ride a horse into the city?

"You look great, India," Justine offered meekly.

India wore a striped shirt and jeans and held an alligator clutch in one hand. Her hair was pulled into a tight ponytail, her cheekbones sleek and sharp.

Justine entered the Margot Moore gallery on West Broadway. Beyond the entrance, freshly painted gray letters read CAROLYN HELLER—NEW WORKS. India drummed her fingers on the counter of the reception desk. Reluctantly, the young man behind it asked whom she and Justine were there to see. Slowly he stood up and led them to a room with red-tiled floors like in a Florentine palazzo.

Eve sat at the far end of a long table, with a Rolodex, a pad, and an ashtray in front of her. She was dressed in a pencil skirt and flats. A cute guy sat next to her on the phone.

"What took you so long?" Eve asked, stuffing things in her purse as soon as she saw them.

"We're fashionably late," said India.

"I'm starvacious."

"Where are you going?" the man asked, hanging up.

"Dunno, that cool place called FOOD maybe. This is Raymond. He knows Dino."

"What a small world," said India politely. "How?"

"From around," said Raymond. "Excuse me," he said, moving to answer the phone again. Justine watched him fingering the spiral cord. He was suave, but she had a sense he had invented himself from scratch, and recently.

Raymond hung up. "Massimo's on his way."

"Oh my God! Can you please introduce me?" Eve implored.

India crossed her arms in protest. "Aren't you working here all summer?"

"My stomach can wait!"

"He's just a person," India said.

"Just a person? He's the most important painter Margot represents!"

"That's not why he was on the cover of *New York* magazine," India said, smoothing her hair back. "He's a womanizer and his paintings are vulgar."

"Who thinks my paintings are vulgar?"

A bear of a man stood hulking in the doorway.

He stepped forward and took India's hand in his paw, bending down and kissing it with a grandiose flourish. He had a tangled bush of caveman hair. He murmured something in Italian, his voice soft enough to soothe a frightened animal. "Hello, Mimi."

"That's not my name," she said stiffly.

Massimo spread his palms heavenward. "Of course it isn't. But you know my name for you is Mimi."

India did not respond.

Massimo looked crestfallen.

"Please excuse us," India said, stepping toward the door, "we're late for lunch." Eve made a weak gesture of farewell and they followed India out onto the street.

. . . .

G od, India thought, wiping her hand on her jeans, nothing had changed. Everything about Massimo lacked subtlety. He, like his crucifixions and martyrdoms, was exaggerated and melodramatic.

"Mimi? Explain!" Eve demanded.

India shrugged. "I've met him before."

"And you never told me?"

India did not respond. She wasn't about to list all the famous people she had met with Kiki. She wasn't a name-dropper.

"Where do you guys want to eat?" Justine asked.

"India never wants to eat," Eve said.

Justine opened her bag and reapplied her fuchsia lipstick. She was such a luminous beauty, India thought. She really didn't need to cheapen her looks.

"Did you see the way Massimo looked at you? He *loved* you," Eve said.

"He's nothing but a playboy," India replied with disdain.

"Can you loosen up for one millisecond? That was Massimo fucking Sforza. And you need to eat something!"

"Isn't he married?" Justine joined in, remembering a magazine article she'd read at the dentist's office. His wife was a beautiful Italian aristocrat, and she could have sworn he had a few picturesque offspring too.

"Yeah, but he sleeps around," Eve said. "All those Euro guys have mistresses. India, I say go for it. Don't look a gift horse in the mouth."

India had always hated that expression. It reminded her of Christmas last year at the family house in Bedford. Her father and his girlfriend Courtney had had one of their spectacular fights on the stairs. After the screaming there was a *thunk*, a couple of sickening whumps, and silence. India sat tensely in the kitchen. A thin cry arose. She went running.

There Courtney was, standing on the stairs, a Ming vase in her hand. India's father was lying on the landing, blood streaming from his forehead onto his silk ascot and Jermyn Street shirt.

"Is he . . ." India had gasped.

"Breathing."

"Oh, thank God."

"Don't look a gift horse in the mouth," Courtney snarled. "Call an ambulance."

· · · · · · · ·

E ve glanced at India. That faraway, haunted look broke her heart, but it also enraged her. It was true, India's mother had died tragically, and her father was debauched and louche, but the girl needed to live her life. Not this half-life, a ghost in the shadows. India had friends. She had money of her own, for God's sake. And she was stunningly beautiful. Here was her chance!

Gerald, Massimo, Bob Winkler. Eve giggled to herself. An older man for each girl.

When they reached Da Silvano, all the outdoor tables were empty.

"Let's sit outside!" Justine chirped.

"Nobody sits outside," Eve replied, walking ahead. Lulu would give them a good table.

But Eve had never seen the woman behind the podium, with her pale face and thick waxy makeup.

"Hi," Eve said, "three of us."

"Reservation?"

Eve said, "My parents, Deirdre and Frederick Straus, eat here all the time. They never need one."

The waxwork consulted her list.

"I'm sorry"—she shook her head, and not a follicle budged—"totally booked."

Eve spotted Sylvia Miles in the back and blew her a kiss, praying she'd remember who Eve was. Sylvia winked and gave a slight wave.

Wax woman clocked this exchange.

"Right this way," she said, giving Eve an unpleasant look.

I saw that, Eve thought as she followed the skinny derriere past a large, empty table. She thought of asking to sit there, but didn't want to give Waxy the satisfaction of saying no.

"Enjoy!" the hostess said, unceremoniously dumping three menus on the table and striding off.

"What a bitch," Eve said, sitting down and pulling out her Marlboros. "She'll never last." She lit a cigarette and noticed there was no ashtray.

"Au contraire," India mused, "she'll probably go far in this city."

"It's like they get paid to be rude," said Justine, who was looking around the restaurant in awe.

"So downtown," India said.

Eve ashed on the floor.

"Isn't Hell's Kitchen downtown?" Justine asked.

"No," India replied, opening her menu.

Eve took another drag and looked around for a waiter.

And then she saw them. Massimo and Margot, kissing Silvano, both cheeks. She had definitely picked the right restaurant.

Massimo was looking in their direction. Margot was still chatting with Silvano.

"Oh, for God's sake," India said, looking back at her menu.

"Should we leave?" Justine asked anxiously.

"No, I have as much right to eat here as he does," India said, running an elegant finger down the list of entrées.

Eve consulted her menu. God, she had never really noticed the prices when she'd been here with her parents.

"Compliments of Mr. Sforza," the waitress said, bringing a tray with three flutes.

Eve beamed at her friends. This was going to be the best lunch ever.

"Which one of you is Mimi?" the waitress asked.

Eve pointed to India, who was turning pink despite her poise.

The waitress handed her an envelope, which she stuffed in her clutch.

Eve wanted to ask why she didn't tear it open and read it but India looked furious.

"Cheers!" Eve said, holding up her glass.

The waitress pulled out a pad.

"Veal Milanese, please," India said.

Justine sipped her champagne. It was a lot better than that plonk at India's.

"Pappardelle, please," she ordered.

"What's the special?" Eve asked.

"It was baby lamb chops, but Mr. Sforza just ordered the last ones."

"Fine. I'll have the puttanesca," she said, and then glanced over at their table and saw Margot reapply her lipstick. Massimo was waving a hand in the air as he tried to explain something.

"Going to the beach this weekend?" India asked.

"Huh?" Eve asked, staring at the artist.

"Hamptons?"

"Oh, yeah, no choice. You?"

"Staying here."

"India's apartment is awesome!" Justine said.

Yeah, maybe for you, Eve thought, having never understood why India lived in that shithole. Whenever she went over, she always asked the taxi driver to wait until she was safely inside.

"Seriously, Indi, why do you live in that neighborhood?" Eve asked.

"Nobody can find me there."

"What does that mean?" Justine asked.

Eve glanced back at Massimo, who was leaning forward, his arms spread wide like Christ in that Caravaggio painting.

"At first it was to be near Mr. Ed's stable," India explained, "but then I realized my father can't find me there."

"Is he dangerous or something?" Justine asked, untangling her feather earring from a blond curl.

"All fathers are," Eve said, waving a new cigarette. "It's like that whole generation didn't have mothers and we have to suffer, raised by wolves or something."

"Like me?" India asked.

"You know what I mean. Oh my God!" Eve was staring across the room.

Massimo was heading toward them from the back of the restaurant, wiping his hands on his enormous, expensive-looking shirt.

"*Ciao ragazze.* Enjoying the champagne?"

"Oh, thank you so much, Mr. Sforza," Eve gushed. "It's absolutely delicious. Is it Moët?" She could see other patrons pretending not to stare.

"A pleasure. Mimi, what do you think?" Massimo said, turning his soft eyes on India.

"I don't care for champagne."

"And my note?"

India nodded.

"Allora?"

"I need a day or so," she replied, sitting up very straight.

"Cara Mimi, *non c'è problema."* His hand was on her chair. India looked down at the table. Eve glanced over and, with a rush of happiness, saw Margot watching them. I bet she was impressed, Eve thought. First week at work and already the intern was rubbing shoulders with her most valued artist.

"Arrivederci," Massimo said, walking back toward his table.

"You didn't even read it!" Eve hissed.

"I know what it says."

THREE

WHEN EVE RETURNED FROM DA SILVANO, RAYMOND WAS ON the phone again. India and Justine had gone home directly from the restaurant and Eve was still reeling.

"Oh my God!" she exploded when Raymond hung up. "Massimo was at the restaurant and he sent champagne and then he sent India a note! I feel like I'm . . ."

Raymond held up a hand. "Breathe."

"I just practically had lunch with Massimo Sforza!"

"Margot will be back any second," Raymond said. He pointed at the phone. "Calm down and do your job."

Sitting, Eve tried to regain her composure, and flipped through his Rolodex until she found Keith Wilson. This was a stroke of luck; Keith was her mother's friend who had married well and started collecting. Eve picked up the phone.

It rang and rang. Didn't they have that butler? She dialed again. A Brit answered, "Wilson residence."

"Alisdair! Its Eve Straus, is Keith there?"

"Miss Straus! What a pleasure!"

"You too. Is he around?" She stabbed her Bic repeatedly into her pad.

"Hold the line." Eve could hear footsteps. The Wilsons had those inlaid stone floors, brought over from some château in France.

"Hello?" Keith picked up.

"Hi, Keith, it's Eve."

"Eve, darling! How are you?"

She imagined him wearing a soft velvet smoking jacket, sitting at his mahogany desk. "I'm calling you from work, at Margot Moore's."

"Ooh! Does that mean you can sell me something great?"

Eve dropped her voice to a whisper. "Maybe I can snag you something from Massimo's show before it goes up."

"God, you're good. I have a message somewhere from Margot, let's see." Eve heard Keith rummaging through papers. "Here it is. It says 'Urgent; call about M.S.' But we know how Margot works. She's probably chosen it for me. Can you snoop and find out which painting it is?"

"Done." Eve dropped her voice further. "There's also a beautiful Fischl watercolor that just came in. Raymond was going to try to sell it to that countess in Lugano, but I'm giving you first crack."

"Send me a transparency and I'll tell your mother and Margot what a good job you're doing. It may be a while before I get down there. I haven't been feeling well."

"What's wrong?"

"Oh, summer cold. Nothing to worry about. Ciao, darling." Keith hung up.

Eve's thoughts were on Massimo in the restaurant, and how pleased her boss would be about Eve's successful first day. She smiled to herself, thinking, I can do this art-selling thing, no problem.

"Where's that Straus girl?" Eve heard Margot's shrill tones before she saw her stride across the room, looking murderous.

Eve's smile disappeared.

Margot glared, nostrils flaring, then motioned for Raymond to follow her into her office.

Eve knew she was in trouble but had no idea what for.

Margot strode back in, wiping her nose. "Who were you talking to just now, on the phone?"

"Keith Wilson."

Margot leaned down and bared her teeth like a foo dog.

"Let's get a few things straight. I call Keith Wilson, not you. And I eat lunch at Da Silvano, not you. You and that little slut made me look like a fool. I had serious business to conduct with Massimo and all he thought about was the little lost heiress and his hard-on."

A tiny blob of saliva landed on Eve's cheek.

"I'm sorry, I thought I was doing my job—"

"You don't know what that means!" Margot interrupted. "I started without a pot to piss in. I built all of this." She waved her arm in the air, and Eve kept her eyes averted from her pits. "With no help from Mommy or Daddy. Your first day of work and you're eating at an expensive restaurant? How spoiled can you be? You think you just sit around drinking champagne with your friends, flirt with artists, then pick up the phone, and voilà!" Margot slammed her fist on the table, making the pads jump.

"Keith wants the Fischl," Eve squeaked.

"Oh, he wants the Fischl, does he?" Margot replied. "Well, he can't have it!"

Eve blanched.

"As I've been saying, I sell him art, not you!" Margot's face was as red as her dress. *"Now he'll never get it."*

What was she going to tell Keith?

"He *is* getting one of Massimo's, isn't he?" Eve asked hopefully. Margot turned and walked away.

· · · · · · · ·

India closed her eyes, feeling the marijuana seep into the furthest reaches of her consciousness. Finally she could think clearly. That note. India recognized his thick creamy stationery. It was from the Pineider store near the Trevi Fountain. Her mother had had some as well, with smaller cards and envelopes in jade green.

Perhaps Massimo would still smell like Prosecco and linseed oil. Every man, woman, and beast had their particular odor. Eve was smoke and apricots, Justine more floral. Dino grapefruit and olive.

Her father had smelled like an addict's nervous sweat and the Drakkar Noir he used to cover it up.

India drifted into thoughts of her father, remembering a visit to her grandparents' in Rhode Island, in their old mansion overlooking the sea. She knew it had been in September, because she was two weeks late to start third grade. Kiki stayed behind with her parents and her father had driven her back to the city. On the way he had pulled off the highway at a Burger King. She was thrilled. At eight years old, India had never been to a fast-food restaurant. Her father had let her order whatever she wanted—she had a Whopper and a Coke. Then he said he had to run a quick errand and told her to stay put for a bit.

After a few hours, the manager had come over to inquire why she had been alone in a booth for so long. India made something up about a game with her father. It was dark when he returned. She did not ask where he had been, because she knew he'd been doing drugs again.

. . . .

Oh my frigging God, it's like Calcutta in here!" Eve said, clomping into India's apartment.

It was true. Couldn't India afford an air conditioner?

Eve unbuttoned her mechanic's shirt and sat down in her black bra and cutoffs. She reached out as Justine passed her the bottle of white. "Margot ripped me a new one after lunch."

Eve described Margot's livid face, how molecules of spit had landed on her cheek. Raymond had explained that Massimo was hideously behind schedule on the paintings for the show. How hysterical it was making their boss. Eve stopped to swallow a big gulp of wine.

"Why was she angry at you?" India inquired.

"Massimo's boner at the restaurant pushed her over the edge."

They were all silent for a moment.

Justine hoped working at a prop warehouse wouldn't be so complicated.

India stood up and played a bar of something familiar on the piano. Then she wandered over to the garment rack and rearranged a few ball gowns.

Eve lit up, exhaled, and leaned back on an elbow. "Adults say they want us to grow up"—she gestured with her cigarette—"but they just want to keep us down."

"How old do you think Margot is?" Justine asked.

"Old," Eve replied. "At least thirty. Speaking of old, where's the note from you-know-who?"

India ignored her and took a joint from a carved sandalwood box. She lit it; exhaling, she traced the carvings. A gift from Morocco, to her mother, years ago. India stretched her legs on the pillow in front of her. She lay her fragile figure on the pillows and closed her eyes.

The phone rang, startling Justine.

Eve got up to get it, then leaned in from the kitchen holding the receiver toward Justine.

"Hey," Clay said, "can I come over?"

"Please!" Justine said, the receiver under her chin. Clay was so polite all the time, never wanting to impose. Even if they hadn't seen each other in days.

He asked if she needed anything from the bodega.

"Smokes?"

"Camels, right?" he asked.

"Benson & Hedges."

Justine hung up.

She walked back into the living room.

"Clay's coming," she said, trying not to sound too excited.

Eve handed her a glass of wine. "Do you mind if he sees my tits?"

They downed another bottle, but the pot was wearing off. It had been at least an hour and the sky had darkened. Justine was wondering if she should call Clay back, when the buzzer finally rang. He was breathless at the top of the stairs. Justine kissed him, then he hugged her.

"I've missed you so much," he said into her shoulder.

She held on to him.

"Clayton, baby doll!!" Eve shrieked from the living room.

"Everyone's pretty fucked up," Justine murmured.

"Yeah, welcome to India's," he said, looking past her into the living room.

"Do you have any beer?" he said, throwing a pack of Camels on the table. Hadn't she said Benson & Hedges? No matter, Clay was finally here, and she could live with another brand.

Eve was hovering over the turntable in the living room. The needle hit hard, and "Blue Monday" began to play. Eve stood up and frowned at Clay.

"You look terrible, you need a weekend at the beach," she said.

"I've been working really hard," Clay said. Justine realized he was proud of it.

"That's ridiculous. You're in high school, for fuck's sake!" Eve rolled her eyes and started dancing in her Sophia Loren bra.

Justine handed Clay his beer. He did look pale, Eve was right. Why on earth? If Justine were in his position she'd never work. She'd hang out here all day, smoking and reading poetry, maybe even write some.

India gave a sluggish wave from the floor, curled on her side, her hair streaming over the silk pillow.

"It's so great to be here," Clay said, cracking open the can.

Justine wanted to ask why it had taken him so long but didn't want to sound like a nag.

Dino came in through the door, loosening his tie with one hand, a beer in the other. "Ciao ciao, kitten boy," he purred. "Oooh, now the party's starting."

"Good evening, Dino," Clay replied, not smiling.

"Don't 'good evening' me. How's work, honey, with all those sexy little boys in their suits?"

Clay gave him a sour look.

Dino ignored it and tossed his pin-striped jacket aside. "I'll get you, my pretty! Where'd you put my snow, ice princess?" he asked India.

India shrugged.

"Oh pwetty, pwetty pwease, tell poor Dino?"

India took a deep, steadying breath and pointed.

Dino clapped in delight. Opening the piano lid, he took out a shard of mirror and a velvet bag.

Seven years' bad luck, thought Justine.

Eve sat cross-legged at the table as Dino cut five lines of coke on the glass. He handed Eve the straw, and she snorted a little up each nostril.

Clay bent over the table and did a line, his face reflected in the mirror like Narcissus at the pool.

Justine watched his technique carefully. He handed her the straw and she bent low over the mirror, inhaling the powder. It pushed into her brain and there was a rushing sound in her ears, like the inside of a shell.

Her pulse was throbbing through her veins. What time was it? Fuck, already nine. She'd be up all night.

Dino stood up, kicked off his loafers.

"Dance with me," Clay said to Justine, jumping up. The bass of "Blue Monday" pounded; it was the best dance song ever.

She joined him.

Eve started dancing again too.

"Here, kitty kitty," Dino said, blowing Clay a kiss, rubbing his fingers together and slinking toward him. Dino cocked his hips to one side like an Italian film star about to wade into a fountain. Clay moved toward Justine, who wrapped her arms around him and danced closer. The coke was trembling through her.

Eve cranked up the music. *How does it feel? To treat me like you do?*

Justine would have her way with Clay tonight on the futon. Was the coke making him horny? How long were they going to dance before she could pull him into her bedroom? Didn't Eve have a curfew?

Clay whispered in her ear, "Let's get out of here!"

She agreed and ducked into her room. In the mirror her face looked crazy, pupils enormous like a cartoon character's, her nose twitchy and rabbity. Where was he taking her? Her hands shook as she pulled off her dirty tee and put on a silk tank top—a favorite secondhand special. It still smelled of someone else's perfume. Everything was magnified, the pores on her face visible, she could feel her skin suck in air. She grabbed a comb to tease her hair, and microscopic cuticles stripped back, furry scales ripping from the cortex. Was she hallucinating? *It's not the side effects of the cocaine, I'm thinking that it must be love* . . . She teased her hair higher into a knotty yellow pile, gave the sculpture a shot of Aqua Net, shoved her feet into her flats, grabbed her fake ID.

Clay and Justine tore down the stairs and burst onto the street.

She grabbed him and they kissed. Stumbling and regaining her balance, she heard a coughing sound.

A prostitute stood a few feet away. Sequined bustier, torn fishnets.

"What's so funny, Romeo?" the hooker taunted. "How about a ménage à trois?"

Justine stared at the greasy pink lips, the massive blond Afro. Those lashes had to be glued on.

Clay tugged her away.

"Go ahead, pretty boy, turn your ass on me!"

Justine sucked in her breath; the hooker's hands were a dead giveaway, she was a man, not a woman.

"You think you're so hot!" the hooker spat toward them. "But you're not and you're the real thing!" She cackled as Clay pulled Justine down the street.

. . . .

Eve left India's a few minutes later. The coke was making her jittery, but her mind was clear as a bell. Clay and Justine were probably going to Danceteria or the Underground, or someplace wonderful that Eve couldn't go. Actually, that could describe all of New York City.

As Eve headed down the stairs of India's apartment building, she felt a familiar sinking feeling in her chest. Justine was living the life she wanted. These were Eve's friends, this was Eve's city. Justine had slipped in as if she had always been here. And she was having more fun than Eve ever had.

And Justine hadn't gotten expelled from boarding school. And why was that? Because Justine had had permission to be at the Bowie concert, and Eve had not. Justine had been allowed to smoke, and Eve had not. If only her parents had been more lenient, Eve wouldn't be forced to break the rules. Didn't they realize that?

Eve did a calculation as she headed toward Tenth Avenue. Two more years and she would be in college. That meant about eight hundred days until she was free of her family. Eve glanced around to make sure no muggers were lurking in the shadows. The neighborhood was foul, but she'd live here in a second if it meant freedom.

. . . .

Clay hailed a cab on the corner of Eleventh Avenue. "Seventh and A," he told the driver. "Please," he added.

Clay leaned closer and they started making out. The wind sped in one window and out the other as they hurtled downtown. Justine's pulse was pounding so hard she felt like an artery in her throat would erupt. She clutched Clay's shoulders as they kissed, she was convulsing. The cab driver's eyes were on them in his rear-view mirror, flicking away each time she looked up. She pushed Clay off, gasping for breath out the window.

"It's the coke," he said, stroking her back. "Dancing'll help."

They pulled up in front of the Pyramid Club and Justine flashed the bouncer her ID. A dirty door covered in stickers led to a narrow room packed with people. She held Clay's arm as he pushed his way toward the bar. Transvestites gyrated on its surface, as shirtless bartenders with superhero pecs handed people drinks between their dancing legs. There was Wonder Woman, a Darryl Hannah mermaid, and a sexy squaw with a tomahawk and Cabbage Patch doll papoose, all grinding to the beat.

Clay ordered but all she heard was Coke. Coke! Coke! Coke! The word reverberated in her head with the throbbing bass. The floor heaved as if she were at sea. A black stiletto stepped in front of them, a thick yellow python coiled around the guy's torso. He wore a blond wig and had a beauty mark. Clay handed Justine a drink—it tasted like cool twisted toffee. The snake's head hovered, its forked tongue flitting at Clay.

"She likes you," the dancer said in a husky voice.

Clay stuffed a bill in the dancer's G-string.

"Thanks, preppy."

"Anytime, Marilyn," Clay replied, and took a sip of his drink.

Justine's hand was shaking, rattling the ice cubes.

"Let's dance," he said, and they shoved their way through the crowd to a staircase leading to a basement dance floor. She stumbled into the primordial throng, the only girl for miles.

Her drink sloshed all over her tank top. She wasn't wearing a bra.

Clay took the glass and vanished.

The colored lights streamed over her face like rays of the sun. She closed her eyes and raised her arms over her head. The song was the best she'd ever heard. *There's seventy billion people of Earth, where are they hiding?* The cocaine coursed through her organs in time with the pounding bass. Her eyes stung, she was pouring sweat. A voice inside her head called her name. *Where are they hiding?* She clenched her teeth to stop them from chattering. Her hands were shaking like falling leaves.

Justine! Someone tapped her shoulder.

She opened her eyes. "Stanley?" Her voice sounded so far away, it could not have been her own. She flung her arms around his skinny, sweaty body. "What are you doing here?"

Something about a cheap room in the East Village, his father and a shotgun, escaping on the bus. It felt like a hallucination, Justine felt her wet shirt clinging to her, she was going to fall over.

"Are you high?"

She chewed into her lip, trying to remember where she had come from. "Spilled."

"I came with Ted but I can't find him either," Stanley shouted into her ear and danced in a wriggle around her. "Give me your number."

She patted her hips in vain.

Stanley's eyes darted around the crowd, burly shoulders jostling around him.

"Be right back."

Dancing with myself . . .

A strobe went off. Justine looked at her legs. Small bluish lice made of lint clung to them. They were crawling up her body. The strobe jolted everything into a stop-motion film and she was falling through slices of light.

Two men were making out next to her. One was old, bald, and

unshaven, in a poufy strapless. The other was a delicate boy in a tank top and shorts. She couldn't tear her eyes away, their tongues roiling in each other's mouths.

Stanley reappeared out of the crowd with a pen. Holding his skinny wrist, she etched her number in blue jags on his arm. But it looked wrong. Stanley stuck a piece of paper in her jeans pocket, and then he was gone.

Clay came back, slipping his arm around her, and the two of them moved in a sweaty sync. For a few moments they were the only people in the world.

The crowd jostled him and Clay glanced around, noticing the men kissing. He stared, and in a second he pushed past Justine, past the crowd, clawing people out of his way as he tore up the stairs. Heart like a hammer, Justine hurried after him, reaching the top stair to see a commotion by the front door as Clay stumbled out.

On the sidewalk he punched a metal gate on a bodega and it shook like thunder.

He lurched away.

Justine tried to ask what was wrong but her teeth chattered so hard she couldn't get the words out. She needed to come down off her high, right now.

"My dad!" Clay said. "That fucking tranny was my dad!"

She shook her head. No. Not that old guy with the skinny kid?

Clay slumped against a graffitied wall, his eyes glowing jade. Then he slid down, covering his face.

She touched his hair, soft as down and damp with sweat. The coke was still ricocheting through her body, her hand was unsteady.

Clay got to his feet. "I'm sorry," he said, wiping his face.

"D-don't," she chattered.

"You shouldn't have to see that. Nobody should."

"S'okay." It wasn't. That man was Clay's father. Mr. Bradley, in taffeta, with a boy.

"I need a long walk. I'll put you in a cab."

"I can take the b-bus."

"It's one in the morning! And you're half naked!"

She looked down to see her breasts, perfectly visible through her soda-soaked silk shirt. Justine quickly crossed her arms over her chest.

"I'll put you in a cab," Clay repeated, heading toward the curb.

"Wait!" she insisted, following him, shivering. She was freezing, even though it was at least ninety degrees. And tomorrow was her first day of work and she didn't have cab fare home.

Clay hailed one and it pulled over.

Fine, she'd get off in a few blocks and walk. Let the muggers attack her. She'd tear their throats out with her clattering teeth.

Clay held open the taxi door. "Promise you won't tell anyone."

She stared at him in confusion.

"I've learned to think the worst," he explained, "about everything. Now you know why. Fifty-fifth and Tenth," he said to the driver. She got in, and he handed her a ten. She pushed it back but he folded her fingers around it.

Clay closed the door. The cab started to move. She turned and watched him walk down Avenue A.

FOUR

A PIERCING CHIRP WOKE JUSTINE, AND SHE FUMBLED FOR the button of her alarm clock. Then she remembered last night and pushed her face into the pillow. Images appeared like flash cards. Mr. Bradley, his tongue jammed into that boy's mouth. Clay's tragic face. The hooker. Justine's mouth was dry, her eyes gluey, and she realized with a jolt that today was her first day of work. She hauled herself off the futon and limped toward the shower to wash off the stench of sweat and cigarettes.

Props for Today was on the ninth floor of a warehouse on Twenty-fourth Street and the Hudson River. Justine stepped off the freight elevator and stopped dead, gaping at the Piranesian scale of the room. Shafts of light streamed through factory windows, illuminating metal shelves stuffed with props: a green plumed headdress, a copper cauldron, a steamer trunk inlaid with mother-of-pearl.

In a corner was a small trailer with a droning air conditioner punched into its side. She threw her coffee cup in a garbage can as Gretchen Lermontov swept out of the trailer in a blast of arctic air.

"Justine, darling!" she trilled, pressing the girl to her soft, capacious bosom. "You look exhausted. Are you getting enough sleep?"

"It's just so hot in our apartment," Justine said.

"No air-conditioning?"

Justine shook her head.

"I, for one, never believed in AC. We Europeans find it unhealthy."

Justine's eyes strayed to the unit poking from the trailer.

"Oh, that! The employees take breaks in there. It just gives me the grippe, it really does," Gretchen said, rolling her *r*'s like a cat's purr. "Come, I shall give you the grand tour."

The warehouse was piled with miles of shelves that towered to the ceiling. Objects Justine could not imagine anyone would ever need. A coat of armor, a pink Victorian telephone, a machine gun. It was hot and dusty, but, as Justine soon realized, meticulously cataloged and organized.

"Each prop has my own system of numbers," Gretchen was saying proudly, "and as with the Dewey Decimal System, those numbers correspond to a number in the card catalog." Justine nodded. Her head ached. She wondered if Clay was at his desk, and how he was feeling this morning.

"If a client calls . . . let's say he's directing the stage adaptation of *The Seventh Seal*. We did that last summer. Well, then, he'd want a scythe and a chess set. In which case, what would you do?"

"Um, I'd look in the card catalog?"

"Right, and what would you look under?"

"Um, scythe?" Justine recalled seeing Stanley last night; what was he doing in the city?

"Well, that would be a start. But our system is even better than that. Scythe would be cross-referenced under 'Tools comma Harvest' and also under 'Symbols comma Political.' Without a system as effective as mine, finding anything here would be a nightmare."

Justine did her best to look at once impressed and enthralled.

"Let's get started. See those boxes? They're for Williamstown. The request is in the office, should be right on the desk. Find the props they want. By the time Seymour rolls in, he can show you how to pack them."

"Uh, Gretchen?"

"Yes, dear?"

"Could I use the phone? I just want to tell my roommate that I got here safely, I'm new to the city and she worries."

"How sweet! Of course, it's in the office."

It was at least thirty below in the trailer. Papers were everywhere, on the carpeted floor, on the metal desk, on an old brown filing cabinet. Justine picked up the phone and dialed.

"Hello?"

"Eve! Thank God you're not at work!"

"Galleries don't open till eleven. Maybe I can come over after work?"

Justine desperately wanted to tell her about last night. She wondered if she'd have the guts to do so. "Only if you can hang out with no air-conditioning and pot smoke," she said.

"Always. Ciao for now."

After an hour of hunting down props by combing the aisles, riffling through the card catalog, and staring at the instructions, Justine was covered with sweat and dirt. She consulted the next item on the list. "Oil lamp," and then "Whips, large." Wiping her face on her T-shirt made it look like the Shroud of Turin. Where would that be filed? "Textiles, biblical"?

Flipping through the card catalog, she found the listing for oil lamp, jotted down the number, and trudged over to grab an Aladdin-esque one off the shelf.

Gretchen's head popped around the corner.

"What's that, dear?"

"An oil lamp?"

"Heavens no, it's a Chekhov play. Look under kerosene."

Later, Justine was at the card catalog when she heard Gretchen's voice ring out over the shelves.

"Aisle *P*, as in Pierre!"

The sound seemed to be coming from a stuffed grizzly at the end of the row. She found Gretchen standing behind it with an ancient, stooped man.

"Goodness, I've been calling and calling! Justine Rubin, Seymour Oliphant."

Seymour must have been over ninety, with watery pale eyes and a gash of a mouth set in a tired face. She shook his veiny hand and watched a crooked smile suddenly illuminate his features.

Gretchen put her arm around his little shoulders. "Seymour is our majordomo, anything you need, he's your man. Rats! That blasted phone."

Seymour shuffled closer to her, taking her wrist in his fingers with surprising strength. "I have a theory that Gretchen hears the phone when she wants to escape. But, then, I'm a little deaf."

"I didn't hear it either."

He smiled and let her wrist drop. "It's just ten. What's she got you doing at this ungodly hour?"

"I've been here since eight!" she said.

"That will have to change. We all need our beauty sleep."

She wondered how Clay looked today. If only they could have woken up together. If only none of last night had happened. If only the whole horrible thing could bring them closer. If only she wasn't convinced it would push them apart. He'd been so eager to be alone, to ship her home.

"What did Madame Tsarina assign you?"

"Williamstown."

"What do those cretins need now?" Seymour grumbled.

"All these weapons—guns, rifles, shotguns. And they're all over the place."

Seymour shuffled closer to her. A whiff of mothballs hit her nostrils.

"Smart girl. The place could be completely reorganized. I've been thinking that for years. In fact"—he reached into his pocket—"I've been keeping this notebook with my observations."

"Justine, darling," Gretchen called, striding over, "Williamstown asked for a whip. You put a riding crop aside?"

Justine admitted that she had passed the crop on the shelf when she was looking for the decanter.

"We must always look things up. There are great subtleties in props. Oh no, the phone again!" and Gretchen was off.

Justine walked up Tenth Avenue toward home. She'd finished work at six, having finally found the proper Chekhovian lamp, escaping after Seymour had shown Gretchen his pocket watch and cleared his throat meaningfully. She was sweaty, dusty, and needed a shower. She hoped the bathroom didn't reek of Dino's Paco Rabanne cologne.

Eve was coming over this evening, and there was nothing to eat in the house. Justine dug in her pocket. After paying eight of Clay's ten dollars to the taxi driver, she had two dollars left. Passing a McDonald's as she continued north, she went inside. The woman behind the cash register had vicious glue-on fingernails. Justine ordered a Big Mac and fries, skipping the soda to save money. As she continued home, she devoured the fries from the bag.

India was not home, neither was Dino. Justine set the McDonald's bag on the counter and picked up the phone. She dialed the Bradley house. The answering machine. She headed into her room, tearing off her damp T-shirt. The buzzer rang. Justine grabbed another shirt and chucked the keys out the window.

Eve arrived and Justine admired her shoulder pads and narrow skirt. She seemed older all of a sudden. They were both growing up, but Eve, glamorous and groomed, looked like she was having a much better time of it.

Eve held out a cold bottle of white wine. It looked expensive.

"Where'd Clay take you last night?"

"Pyramid. And Stanley was there, I think I gave him India's number," Justine said.

"I wonder how Stanley ended up in the city. What's he living on? He's even more broke than . . ."

Eve did not finish her sentence. "Well, we have to find him," she said decisively as she pulled open a drawer looking for the corkscrew. "He's probably living on the street." Eve found it and peeled the lead off the top of the bottle. "Big Mac?"

Justine gave her a feeble smile. "Want some?"

"No, thanks. How was Clay?"

Justine almost choked. Did Eve know?

"I still think the guy leads something of a charmed life," Eve said. "He's been given everything, after all. How important are mom and dad anyway?"

Pretty important, Justine thought as she took a big gulp of wine.

"I watched the whole family fall apart," Eve continued. "It was like a Greek tragedy." Eve paused, looking pained as she reflected on the demise of the Bradley family. "You know what's weird about parents, though," she continued, setting her glass down, "once I got expelled, even though I was barely allowed to leave the house, it felt strangely comfy. They still drive me up the wall and my mother is like the evil queen, but I dunno . . . I felt *safe*, like if I fell and scraped my knee, Mom and Dad would be there."

They sipped wine in silence, Justine wondering whether Eve knew about Clay's father, whether she'd known all along. Justine couldn't bear to ask.

"God, I'd love to go to the Pyramid," Eve said, psychic as ever.

"Yeah, but I'm totally fried today." *And Philip Bradley was kissing a boy as young as your brother.*

"Any good drag queens last night?" Eve asked.

"There was one with a snake that almost licked Clay's face," Justine said.

"That must have freaked him out!"

Justine took another bite of the burger.

"Mind if I smoke while you eat?" Eve asked.

Justine nodded as Eve took out her Gauloise tobacco and started to roll a cigarette. She licked the paper, spitting a tendril of tobacco out of her mouth with a *pfff.*

"Don't you think it's weird that Dino and Raymond know each other?" Eve lit her cigarette.

Justine wasn't sure. It seemed everyone knew one another and had for ages, like Tierney and Jackie and Christina and Bruce and so on. Justine was the only one who didn't know them all from way back when.

She got up, feeling unsteady. Maybe a burger and wine on an empty stomach had been a crappy idea. Staggering to the window, Justine took in huge breaths through her mouth. Heat and the stench of garbage wafted up from below.

Eve was beside her in a moment. "You okay?"

Justine's eyes filled with tears. No, she was not okay. She just wanted to go home.

"You need to get out of this insane heat," Eve said, stroking her arm. "We'll find a way to get you out to the beach."

FIVE

Dear Mr. Winkler:

Happy Summer Solstice!

Thank you for your letter. Sorry it was so hot there, and not to talk about the weather or anything, but it has cooled off here.

I'm working at the Margot Moore gallery. It is on West Broadway and I'm extremely busy helping prepare for the upcoming Massimo Sforza show. It's exciting work, and I feel lucky. It's also fun being in SoHo every day.

What are you teaching this summer? Is it mostly high school students from around the United States? I'd love to know what's on your syllabus.

I bought a copy of the Eco book you recommended. It looks perfect for me, so thanks.

I just finished The Sheltering Sky *by Paul Bowles. I loved it—it completely transported me to that part of the world. I did go to Morocco with my parents four years ago, and the book really captured the exotic atmosphere. A strange thing happened there, I was only twelve and my mother and father had to literally hold my arms on either side so that men in the souks did not try to grab me. Mom and Dad were terrified but I thought it was funny.*

Then, in the Atlas Mountains a shepherd tried to trade a goat for my younger brother. We are still laughing about that. I still remember the tangerines we ate there, and the incredible sweet mint tea.

I'd love to visit you, but I'm not sure I'd be allowed. When did you have in mind?

Thank you again for writing, it was great to hear from you.

Love and other indoor sports,
Eve

On Friday afternoon Eve was admiring Raymond's slender figure at the espresso machine.

"Want one?" he asked.

She glanced around and nodded. He handed her a black demitasse just as Margot stormed in.

"Right!" her boss snapped, looking at Raymond. "Take a look at Eve, would you? Sipping espresso on the biggest day of the summer. Does she have any idea where that coffee comes from?" Margot wheeled around to face Eve.

Eve shook her head.

"Tazza d'Oro," her boss said.

"The one in Rome?" Eve asked.

"*'The one in Rome?'*" Margot mimicked. "Let me guess, you were there on some teen tour?"

Eve nodded. It was her favorite espresso place, near the Pantheon, she thought, as she set the cup down on the table.

"Drink. It cost a fortune."

Eve picked it back up. "Mom and Dad are coming at three."

Margot glanced at her watch. "They're getting the Salome. It will look great in their foyer next to the Horace Anders. Slasher sculpture, slasher picture."

"I saw a really great Salome at Barbara's loft," Eve said.

Margot's eyebrows shot up. "Barbara Bradley?"

Eve nodded.

"You know Barbara Bradley?" her boss asked in a voice of controlled calm.

"I grew up with her son," Eve said, finishing her espresso.

"Interesting. Raymond, my coffee?"

"I'm just making it."

"Bring it to my office. Eve, stop hogging the oxygen and come with me."

Eve followed her into a room painted lipstick red, with a red Venetian-glass chandelier and a sofa shaped like lips. It was like being inside of Margot's mouth.

Margot pointed to the sofa. "Please have a seat." Eve wondered if she was about to get fired.

There was a tap on the door.

"Come in!"

Raymond placed another cup on the table and scurried out.

Margot folded her hands on the desk and looked at Eve. Her lipstick had run into small fissures and she reminded Eve of Sekhmet, the Egyptian goddess with the head of a lion who had drunk rivers of blood. "I'm sure you've noticed I'm not exactly thrilled with you."

Eve nodded, feeling a lump in her throat.

Her boss waited.

"Please, Margot, I'm trying—"

"If there's one thing I must insist on," Margot interrupted, "it's disclosure."

Eve looked at her in confusion. Didn't she mean closure?

Her boss stirred the espresso with a tiny spoon. "You must share all information pertinent to the success of this business. You have to be an open book here, or else you are of no use and might as well sell handbags at Bonwit's."

"I understand," Eve lied.

"Why have you been hiding this?" The spoon landed in the saucer with a clatter.

Eve started to stand up.

"Sit down! Everyone knows I've been trying to lure Barbara away from Holly's for years, and I can't understand how . . ." Margot's voice shook with emotion. "How could you not tell me you know her?"

Eve stared at Margot's livid face, recalibrating. Her boss had been trying to get Barbara to her gallery for years? As understanding dawned on Eve, she began to panic. Did Margot think Eve would be able to convince Clay's mother, a famous artist, to move galleries? *Oh, hi, Barbara, I was just at the Earth Room, thought I'd drop by, oh, and did you know I'm working at Margot Moore's? Margot's such a visionary.* Barbara's bullshit detector would go off instantly. It was one thing to call up her parents' friends and try to sell them art, but getting Barbara Bradley to switch galleries? She'd almost rather get fired.

"I can definitely help."

"Good," Margot said, narrowing her eyes at Eve, "and maybe, just maybe, I'll get that Fischl back for Keith."

"Thanks." Eve sagged back onto the sofa with relief.

"Don't get comfortable," Margot said, pointing at the door.

Movers hauled in Massimo's paintings as Margot stalked, her heels like firecrackers thrown across the terra-cotta tile. Eve hurried after, trying to learn how it was done.

"Why the black walls?" Eve panted. "I mean it looks great!"

"I will not succumb to the tyranny of white!" Margot said. "Curly," she addressed an art mover who was so covered in tattoos that he resembled a Persian carpet, "the Magdalene goes there." She turned to Eve. "I'm having them hung higher than usual, minimum sixty inches; it's more intimidating. The black walls, the biblical figures erupting from the canvas, it will be a phenomenon! We are manipulating the psychology of desire." Her boss traced a majestic arc in the air like a conductor. "No other living artist besides Sforza can make a collector feel he is buying a piece of history."

The art mover sliced open the plastic, revealing a huge canvas of reds and oranges, with an angel soaring over what looked like a hillside with shepherds. Instead of sheep, they were tending large tufts of hair tangled with paint.

Eve was stunned by the painting's beauty. What a master, she thought. Raymond had been right. It was like being an apprentice in the studio of one of the greats—a Rubens or a Titian.

"Human hair's a new medium for him," Margot said, chewing on her pencil. "It's top secret! Keep your mouth shut because the critics are going to eat this up. If any of this leaks out I'll know it came from you."

"Isn't it very Joseph Beuys to use hair?" Eve asked hopefully.

Margot rolled her eyes. "That was completely different." Margot shook her head, gazing at the canvas. "We are all just his sheep. But," she said, frowning, "I wish he would hurry up and finish the

Susanna. The crown jewel of the show! You'll be happy to know your best buddy Keith is getting it." And then there Massimo was, lumbering toward them like an elegant giant. The art movers hushed as the artist passed.

"Ciao, *cara*." He kissed Margot. "Sorry to miss you last night," he said. "Ah! How's our intern?"

"Turning over a new leaf. Massimo, darling," Margot continued, her voice softening, "this is our best show ever. I feel like a young girl visiting the Sistine Chapel for the first time."

"You flatter me." Massimo bent to kiss Margot's hand.

Margot held on to his for a moment longer and gave the artist a look of worship. "I never exaggerate. But we are still waiting for your star piece . . ."

Massimo scratched his forehead. "I need a small favor," he said, turning to Eve. "I need to speak to your intern. Alone."

Margot started to giggle hysterically, then stopped abruptly and stalked off.

"Miss . . ." Massimo turned.

"Eve," she reminded him.

"I need to speak to Mimi." Massimo's famous face was inches away from Eve's. He did have beautiful brown eyes, she noticed, with golden flecks and long lashes. He took her arm. "Give me her number. Please."

Eve was torn. She couldn't just hand out India's number without her permission.

"Hey, Eve, hon!" Frederick Straus was striding across the gallery, Deirdre close behind. Massimo dropped Eve's arm. Her father stuck out his hand. "Frederick Straus, huge fan."

"Enchanted," the artist said.

"We can hardly wait to see our precious Salome." Deirdre clapped. *"Possiamo vederla?"*

"Where is the painting?" Massimo asked Eve.

"Not sure, I'll find out." She fled to the back room, where Raymond was sitting at the table flipping through paperwork.

"Can you believe what a genius Margot is?" he said, shaking his head. "The black paint, the height of the pictures, making it look all museumy. Incredible!"

"Oh, shut up. My mom's out there babbling in Italian to Massimo and I need the Salome, or I'm going to get killed!" Eve glanced back toward her parents in the gallery.

Raymond put down his papers as slowly as possible and stood up.

Even from this far away Eve could hear Deirdre. *"Anni fa, ho passato un'estate a Firenze. É stato meraviglioso!"* Eve wanted to dive into one of the paintings and disappear.

Raymond asked a mover, "Can you find the Salome for those customers?"

The mover turned and pointed to the back of the gallery.

Raymond lowered his voice. "Not a good sign. I hope she isn't foisting the worst of the show on your poor parents. Come on, introduce me."

Raymond was already shaking Frederick's hand.

"Mr. and Mrs. Straus, Eve has told me so much about you. I'm Raymond Rathbone. I've asked one of the movers to locate your painting. Can I offer you anything to drink while you're waiting?"

"We have espresso from Tazza d'Oro," Eve said.

"The place with the great granitas?" Frederick piped in. Eve cringed again.

"Ah, you know the Eternal City?" Massimo observed.

"*Certo,*" Deirdre said, moving her hand higher on Massimo's arm.

What if Massimo's Salome turned out to be a piece of shit? Would they know?

"*Un espresso per me,*" her mother said.

"Pardon?" Raymond said.

"She'll have an espresso," Eve said.

"I'll tell Margot you're here," Raymond said.

Deirdre wasn't listening, gazing up at Massimo.

"*Signora*, Massimo will give you a preview," Massimo said, and tucked Deirdre's arm under his.

Eve stared at his powerful figure as they walked away. It was pointless to try to protect India. Massimo would find a way to her, with or without Eve's help. That was a man who got what he wanted.

· · · · · · · · ·

I ndia was in the bath when the phone rang. Sinking farther beneath the bubbles, she let it ring. Underwater, it sounded like a church bell tolling in a dream. She closed her eyes and remembered.

She had been eleven years old, in Rome with her mother at the Hotel de Russie. One morning after breakfast India heard shouts in Italian from her mother's suite, a phone ringing, a room-service cart rolling across a carpet, glasses colliding and smashing. Mademoiselle ordered India to stay put in a cold voice India had not heard before.

India remembered the water seeping under her door, spreading across the pale carpet in a dark stain. Huddled on the bed she watched as it approached.

A violent wail rose from the hall, a keening, ungodly sound. India flung open the door and fled. Nobody noticed as she left the hotel and hurried down the Via del Babuino.

India slipped into the darkness of Santa Maria del Popolo. It took a moment for her eyes to adjust to the gloom of the church.

The air was pungent with burned incense. A black-robed priest was extinguishing the lights in the nave, and a praying old woman was the only other occupant.

India walked to a side chapel and fished in her wallet for a lira coin. It fell into the metal slot with a thunk, and the chapel was illuminated. She ducked under the velvet rope.

Sitting cross-legged on the worn stone floor, India gazed up at the painting. She had never understood why the man was splayed on the ground, but she wasn't here for him. It was the horse, massive and powerful, that dominated the canvas. The man spread his arms, holding them up to the gentle beast as the light flooded onto the scene. Once upon a time, many people had horses. To have a horse of her own was the dream of India's heart.

But what had happened at the hotel? When would they tell her?

The last few days had been hot, shimmering afternoons of ochre stone and dripping gelato. Her mother and Massimo the painter, holding hands and throwing coins into the Trevi Fountain. The rainstorm, taking the three of them by surprise, Massimo sweeping India's tiny mother into his arms as they dashed into the Pantheon. The bright column of rain tumbling into the oculus.

India already suspected the truth. She had watched her mother for the past few months, refusing to eat, speaking only occasionally, staring into the sea with eyes that reflected no light. Kiki had tried it before.

The lira coin dropped, and the light in the chapel was extinguished.

Opening her eyes, India swished her fingers through the water. It was getting cold.

Eventually she learned the truth. Her mother had run a bubble bath at the Hotel de Russie, and while the water was filling up the tub, she had swallowed a handful of phenobarbital.

Had India seen her that morning? She had ransacked her brain for the last five years, but the truth was always just out of reach. India could see her mother's long dark hair swirling in the water around her naked body, but perhaps years of wondering had created that vision. A child's memory was unreliable, shadowy, patched together from photographs, hearsay, and nightmares. The bathroom had been caramel marble with a relief of Neptune; of that she was sure. But Mademoiselle was now back in France, and her father had been in New York with his mistress that day. There was no reliable witness.

India looked just like Kiki, they said, only taller. She got out of the tub, dried herself, and looked in the mirror. Her breasts hung from her rib cage. She knew she was too thin. But it was the only way she could fit into her mother's clothes.

The phone rang again, and she wrapped the towel around herself and padded into the kitchen.

"Hello?"

"*Cara* Mimi, Massimo Sforza."

"How did you get this number? From Eve?"

"Darling, no, your friend was very loyal. Eve would never have done that. Raymond gave it to me."

Right, friends with Dino. And a traitor.

"What do you want?"

"To paint you."

India did not respond.

"There is only one painting left, a Susanna at her bath. I need you."

"Why should I care?"

Massimo exhaled. "Because the show won't be complete without it and your friend Eve will get blamed. Margot thinks Eve is convincing you to pose for Massimo, but I am a far better judge of character. I know Eve would never pressure you. So, I had to do it myself."

"I'm not interested."

"Please, if not for Massimo, if not for Eve, do it for Kiki."

India froze. "How dare you mention my mother's name?"

"I was with her that morning. In Rome. At the hotel."

Shock paralyzed her for a moment. Massimo had come aboard *Mata Hari* for a day, and then spent time with her mother in Rome. India had thought he was just a friend. She had been so naïve. He had been Kiki's lover.

"Your mother had a sadness that no man could touch. You know you've grown to look—"

"Why didn't you tell me?"

"How could I have? In the gallery? In the restaurant?" Massimo sighed. "I was deeply in love with her. Please, Mimi."

India hung up on him.

She stood there for a long time. Then she went back into the living room and pulled the beaded silk caftan of her mother's off the garment rack. She held it to her face and inhaled deeply. India imagined her mother wearing this on the *Mata Hari*, gazing at the Adriatic while Massimo's huge hand caressed her tiny one.

. . . .

On her way home from work, Eve stopped at the Strand bookstore. Down an aisle, she pulled a worn copy of *To the Lighthouse* off the shelf, read a few lines, then looked up and halted. Mr. Winkler was across the aisle, his back to her. Had he seen her? Eve ducked around the shelf and watched him.

Hadn't he received her letter? How come he hadn't tried to see her if he was in the city?

He was dressed in shorts and sneakers, and watching his hairy legs as he shifted from one foot to the other, she wondered if he didn't want to see her here, on her turf.

Mr. Winkler reached up to the shelf, revealing sweat stains in his armpits. He pulled a book down and was about to turn toward her when Eve ran from the store.

SIX

JUSTINE GAVE STANLEY HER ADDRESS AND HUNG UP THE phone in India's kitchen. She went back to studying the Hampton Jitney schedule. It looked like there was one every hour from Fortieth Street near the public library. Eve had promised to figure out their ride, but Justine was not convinced her friend would succeed.

When the buzzer rang, Justine threw the keys down to the darkened street. Stanley appeared, unshaven, his complexion like a dead fish but for an angry pimple on his nose. Speaking of needing a weekend in the Hamptons, Justine thought. He handed her a cassette tape and a perspiring bottle of Colt 45.

"Play the tape."

"Talk first."

He followed Justine into the darkened living room where candles were burning and India and Dino were draped on cushions in a haze of pot smoke. India's limbs poked out at an angle that reminded Justine of the keys on the sidewalk.

Dino pushed himself up on one arm, wearing a bustier. The light from the kitchen spilled onto his hairy, fishnetted legs.

India swayed. "Pleased to meet you," she said, offering a hand.

Justine kept her hold on Stanley's arm. "I'm stealing him for a sec," she said, "but he brought tunes," and handed Dino the cassette.

In her room, she closed the door and they sat down on the futon. She pulled out a pack of cigarettes and groped around for a light.

"Smoking in bed? That's how Edie died," Stanley said.

"No, she died from drugs." Justine had read the book three times.

"Here," he said, flipping a matchbook in her direction. It was black with a cross-shaped dagger. She lit the cigarette, trying to remember where she had seen that design before.

Stanley forced the cap off the Colt 45. He took a slug, and as he raised his arm a wave of rank body odor hit her. He offered her the bottle, but she shook her head. The guy looked contagious.

"How'd you end up in the city?" Justine asked.

He took a sip from the bottle. "My father found out about me."

Justine looked at him, but Stanley kept his eyes on the futon. "He intercepted a letter."

Justine wanted to ask from whom.

He offered her the bottle. She declined.

"He told me I was going to infect the whole family with 'the AIDS sickness' and threatened me with a shotgun, then he locked me in the garage."

Stanley described how he had finally escaped and hitchhiked to the bus station. He'd been working as a janitor in a public school on the Lower East Side.

"Where are you living?"

"East Village," Stanley said.

Muted sounds of conversation and music were on the other side of the door.

"Clay's dad's gay," she said.

Justine was used to Stanley's eyes bulging, but this time they almost popped out of his head.

"We saw him in drag, making out with a boy," she continued, "right after I saw you. Clay freaked."

Stanley shook his head. "Must have been shocking to you too."

It was a relief that he understood.

"It's ironic." Stanley let out a long breath. "Mr. Bradley, as in the arts center donor? A friend of Dorothy?"

Justine nodded.

"Was the guy younger?"

How did he know? That must be a thing.

Stanley took another gulp of beer. "How's Clay holding up?"

"I haven't heard a peep from him since." She stubbed out her cigarette, thinking about Clay sobbing.

"Have you called him?"

"Isn't he supposed to call me?"

Stanley wiped his mouth and shifted on the futon. "Think of how humiliated he must feel. His own father didn't tell him!"

Clay humiliated? Justine wondered how she would have felt if that man had been Miles. It was impossible to imagine. Despite all of Miles's and Cressida's faults, their flimsy finances, the lack of guidance or structure, their marriage was something she took for granted.

"And imagine being Clay's dad," Stanley said. "Pretending to be something you're not, lying to everyone, even to your own kid." Stanley pointed to the door. "Call Clay. I'll go play nice nice with the queen in the living room."

The phone at Clay's rang for a long time but the machine did not pick up.

"Ah, *la belle* Justine!"

"Hi, Mrs. Bradley."

"*Barbara.* Are you packed?"

"Sorry?"

"Caravan departs in an hour," Barbara replied.

Justine was confused.

Barbara heaved a sigh of disappointment. "Clayton didn't invite
you." She called into the depths of the apartment, "'Tis the lovely
Justine!"

A muffled conversation ensued. At last Clay came to the phone.

"Hey," he said. She strained to interpret his tone.

"Hey." Silence fell. Music pulsed behind her in India's living
room. Her heartbeat was out of sync.

"I didn't think you'd call," he said.

Someone in the living room turned up the volume. "I've tried. I
didn't leave a message. I'm sorry."

"It's okay." She listened to his soft breathing, and the sound of
talk radio near the phone. Maybe he was in Barbara's room, sitting
on those satin sheets. She thought she could hear Reagan's voice. "I
mean about your dad," she said.

"Philip?" Clay said flatly. "He's not my dad anymore."

"Because he was with a boy?"

"No. I've known for a long time. Just never had to see it up close.
It's because he left us."

"He must have been very unhappy." Justine thought about what
Stanley had said about living a lie. And then she thought about
having everything in the whole world and still being miserable.

Through the phone she could hear the president more clearly.
He was congratulating the Space Shuttle. India's buzzer was ringing again. Dino scurried by her in the kitchen, followed by a flurry

of squeals at the front door. Raymond was kissing Dino on both cheeks.

"Sounds busy over there," Clay said.

She glanced into the living room at Dino and Stanley dancing, Stanley's T-shirt rolled over his skinny shoulders and Dino pumping his lacy pelvis.

Raymond was leaning down, pushing India's hair aside, whispering into her ear. Her eyes were half closed as if learning the secret from the serpent.

"Stanley's here, and this guy Raymond just arrived."

"The dude from the gallery?"

"How do you know that?" Justine asked.

"He's a coke dealer, everyone knows Raymond."

She should have figured it out.

"Jus, I would have invited you but . . ." She heard Clay sigh. Resignation? Maybe it didn't matter anymore.

"But what?" she asked.

"I . . . after my Dad . . . I guess I wasn't sure you'd be able to deal with my mom too."

How could Barbara be worse than Philip? "You should see my parents!"

"Sorry, I'm sure it's all in my head. Would you please come?"

"Uh, sure, why not?"

"Pick you up in an hour." He hung up.

Justine pulled an army surplus bag from her closet and examined what she had. Parachute pants, a tattered jumpsuit, and a pair of jeans with safety pins jammed up one side. She threw them onto the futon. As she did, she noticed Stanley's matches, turned them over, and opened them. But the minimalist design divulged no clues.

In the living room, Stanley was lounged out poring over a book of Dino's Pasolini poems. It was hard to imagine him cleaning toilets in a janitor's uniform.

He looked up.

"Thanks for the advice," Justine said. "Clay's on his way over."

"Do unto others," Stanley said, and returned to the book.

Dino looked at her duffel. "Going somewhere?"

"I'm about to split for the Hamptons." God, it felt good to say that.

"Want some blow?" he asked, handing her a small plastic bag. "Raymond was generous. Take it for the road."

The buzzer rang again and Justine leaned out the window. Clay was leaning on a wood-sided station wagon, under a flickering streetlight. He had on white shorts with a sweater loosely tied around his waist. She motioned for him to wait.

"Indi, Clay's here!"

"Cannnn't," India slurred from the floor.

"You packed?"

"Wablingda."

"Barbara's waiting, come on!"

"Gowitoutme." India's eyes were half closed, the whites showing.

"What about Mr. Ed?"

"Miss 'im. Sssssooo much."

Justine grabbed India's hand but it slipped from her grasp, and the limp arm flopped to the floor with a thud.

Justine ran to the window and gestured for Clay to come up-stairs. She unlocked the metal rod and left the door ajar.

"India's too fried to get up," she said when he came in. He did not try to kiss her.

"Since when's she coming?"

"Sorry. She was going to take the Jitney, I think. Can't we just drop her at her house when we get there?" It suddenly occurred to Justine that she had no idea where India's summer house was. She didn't begin to understand the geography out there.

Clay knelt down and touched India's forehead.

He sighed. "Her house isn't too far, but Barbara's not much of a driver. Not when she's been smoking."

I can drive, she thought. Anything to help India. Clay scooped his hands under India's back, and picked her up in his arms. "Wow, she weighs nothing," he said.

Justine followed Clay down the stairs as he carried India like an awkward bundle of sticks. Barbara climbed out of the station wagon as Clay was folding India's legs into the back seat.

"Sleeping beauty?" Barbara trilled.

Justine said, "Hope it's no trouble."

"Nah," Clay said, straightening up, not meeting her eye.

"So glad you're joining, dear!" She embraced Justine in a cloud of perfume and stale pot smoke. "No, no, both of you ride up front with me, let the girl sleep. Clayton, be a doll and sit in the middle."

They drove through the Midtown Tunnel and onto the Long Island Expressway in silence. Clay's warm leg was touching hers. The foot well was a mess of magazines and 8-tracks. Miles seemed to think a clean car would result in its longevity, and kept the Volvo spotless, despite the faulty wiring.

Justine picked up a copy of *New York* and scanned the cover story: "AIDS." The article called it a "gay men's epidemic." She tried to imagine Stanley's father wielding a shotgun and locking him in the garage.

Barbara was humming along to an opera. "How's work?" she asked between arias.

"Good," Justine said, letting the magazine slide back to the floor.

"Theater, right?"

"Prop warehouse."

"And the apartment?"

"It's great."

"Such an interesting neighborhood."

"You mean sleazy," Clay muttered.

"Speak up, Maria Callas is drowning you out," his mother said.

India groaned from behind them. Barbara yawned.

"You okay to drive?" Clay asked.

"Just a little sleepy," Barbara replied, her eyelids drooping. The tape ended with a loud click. "Find me Act Two, dear."

Clay bent over and started scrounging in the foot well. Barbara reached across and patted Justine's shoulder. "He really likes you a lot, you know," she said, "but his father never taught him how to treat women. You'll have to be forgiving. Cigarette?"

Justine pulled her pack out and gave Barbara one. She pushed the car lighter in as Clay straightened up and inserted a cassette.

Barbara pulled the glowing lighter from its hole and lit the cigarette dangling from her coral-lipsticked mouth. She balanced it on the steering wheel as she cranked the window open and exhaled into the night.

"You shouldn't smoke," Clay said.

"Darling, this cigarette is a life-saving device, so I don't career off the road," Barbara replied, waving it in the air and swerving slightly. The oncoming headlights glinted off her bangles. Barbara flicked her ashes in the ashtray. "Oh, hush, this is right before she stabs him to death." She turned up the tape player.

Clay turned it down. "God, I hate opera," he said.

"You'll change. I think there's some rock down there somewhere," Barbara said, and chucked her half-smoked cigarette out of the window. They had left the highway and were on a narrow country road. Their headlights illuminated scrub pines and a sandy verge.

"How much farther?" Justine asked.

"Not much." Barbara yawned again. "Rats, we should have stopped at the last gas station. Want to drive, Clay?"

Justine thought Barbara was slurring her words slightly.

"That's only a felony," he said.

"Better in jail than dead," Barbara said.

Justine showed him the small packet of coke.

He shook his head.

"Whatcha got?" Barbara asked.

They did not respond.

"Divulge, children."

Justine glanced at Clay again. He shrugged in defeat.

"A little coke from a friend," Justine admitted.

Barbara sat up straighter. "Set me up. Use the back of one of the tapes. I'll replenish your supply when we get home."

India groaned again.

Justine picked up a tape from under her feet.

Justine cut the line on the 8-track case—*Rumors*, the powder dusting the balls hanging between Mick Fleetwood's legs. She didn't have a straw. "Clay, hold this a sec."

He took the tape and balanced it over the dashboard, his lip curled in disgust. Justine dug in her bag for a bill.

"Just hold it under my nose," Barbara said.

Justine could feel Clay's resistance just by the touch of his thigh. She wondered how she would feel if this were Cressida. The thought made her sick.

"There's no shoulder," Barbara said, "and I've done this a million times."

"You've snorted coke while driving? Before or after Philip?" Clay asked.

Barbara let out a sigh of exhaustion. "Just stick it under my nostril, darling."

"I'll do it," Justine said.

Clay handed her the tape and bent into a tuck, his head sideways on the dashboard. He glowered at Justine, who held the cassette and the bill for Barbara. What choice did she have, Justine wanted to ask. Still holding the steering wheel, Barbara quickly snorted the line and sat back up, wrinkling her nose.

"That's great stuff. Who's it from?"

"Raymond," Justine said. "Shit. I shouldn't have told you that."

"Why not?" breezed Barbara.

"He works for Margot."

"That makes sense."

"Why?"

"Margot's a coke addict. No doubt that's why Raymond works there."

At the end of a driveway between high hedges, the station wagon's headlights swept over India's large shingled house with white columns. Barbara killed the engine, leaving the lights blaring on the garage doors. It reminded Justine of a drive-in.

Clay nudged her. She climbed out, inhaling the smell of ocean and salty dune grass. Stars glittered in the moonless sky.

Justine wondered why India would live in a walk-up when her dad had a spread like this, then she remembered India saying, "Nobody can find me there."

India was sprawled in back, half off the seat.

Clay bent in the door and shook India gently. She stirred but did not open her eyes.

"We might have to carry her," he said.

"No, s'okay," India mumbled, sitting up unsteadily. She pulled a tendril of hair from her mouth and slid toward Clay.

He helped her to her feet, and Justine took her arm on the other side.

"Hi, Barbara," India said. Clay's mother was scissoring through yoga poses in the headlights, her silhouette projected onto the garage doors like a shadow play.

"Justine, dear, give her some of that candy cane. It gave me a fabulous second wind," Barbara said, lunging.

Justine and Clay helped India up the porch. Clay tried the door, but it was locked. India collapsed onto the bench.

"Keys." She pointed under the porch.

Clay hopped down and peeked under the side.

"Of course Barbs wouldn't have a flashlight," he muttered. His mother had folded her hands like a massive praying mantis.

Justine tossed matches to Clay.

He slid under the porch. She heard a sulfurous flare, and Clay emerged holding a metal key.

The moment he opened the door, the stench of rotting food hit them. A grand stair hall painted glossy apple green led to a kitchen with an enamel stove and marble counters. The place was a pigsty, glasses overflowing with cigarette butts and dishes encrusted with food. It was as if the police had shown up and the partiers had fled.

"She can't stay here," Justine said, wondering what kind of person would leave such a mess in this beautiful house.

Clay pulled the offending trash bag from under the sink. "Just open a few windows and let's get her into bed."

Justine couldn't leave India here alone, to wake up to this wreckage, however much she wanted to be with Clay. She followed him back to the porch.

Together they helped India up the stairs. At the top was a black-and-white photograph of a woman with a sixties hairdo and big dark eyes, naked except for a pair of go-go boots. She looked just like India.

Clay headed down the hall and opened the door to a bedroom. They helped India into a canopy bed with frilly covers. A Hardy Boys poster was taped to the wall. India's breathing was ragged, her eyes half open. Clay pulled up the covers and tucked them under her.

He took Justine's hand and led her from the room. "What if . . ." Justine suddenly remembered how Edie Sedgwick's boyfriend had described her breathing as if there were a hole in her lung. In the morning, Edie was dead.

"She's on her side," Clay said.

"You're psychic."

"Let's go home."

"Don't kill me but I think I have to stay with her."

He leaned down and kissed her. Geishas winked at them from the wallpaper.

"Can I have my matches back? I need a smoke if I have to clean up all that shit."

He handed them to her.

"Sorry," she said.

"For what?"

"Giving your mom coke."

"Don't ever apologize for saving my life." He kissed her again and headed down the stairs.

SEVEN

INDIA WOKE EARLY, HER MOUTH STICKY AND HER ARM stiff. She dragged herself to the pink-tiled bathroom with the gold taps shaped like leaping dolphins, the handles like mermaids' tails. Holding her hair back, she drank water from the dolphin's mouth.

India looked in the mirror, her hair like a tangle of thorns. Mademoiselle used to be the only one who could get rid of the knots. Mademoiselle used to tell her the story of the man who sold his watch for a comb, his wife selling her hair for a watch chain.

India went back to her room, where she put on her jodhpurs and riding jacket. Down the hall, past the Scavullo portrait of her mother. *Your mother had a sadness that no man could touch.*

Vague memories of last night filled her mind, the smooth vinyl of the back seat, the headlights, Mrs. Bradley, Justine tucking soft covers around her. Perhaps Justine was asleep in the guest room, or maybe she was at Clay's. India would be back well before anyone else got out of bed.

A low mist hovered over the fields, still deeply green. The sun was just above the horizon, the sun that would turn these fields to brown by August. As India strode down the road, she could hear whinnying from the barn and quickened her pace.

Nobody was at Toppings stable this early, and India hurried past stalls with shiny ribbons in blue and canary yellow tacked up to their drab doorways, the brass plaques that read SCARBOROUGH FAIR, MONTSERRAT, and RUDOLPH VALENTINO. Even though he didn't have a fancy name, Mr. Ed was Toppings's best horse, a thorough-bred descended from Harpagon of Chantilly.

Mr. Ed recognized her from afar and jerked his head in excitement. India hurried to him, kissed his brawny jowl. As she un-latched the stall door and attached his harness, she was pleased to see he had gained weight and his coat was almost shiny again. Standing on a stool, she mounted Mr. Ed's bare back and rode him across the Gibson Lane path. Although he snorted with impatience, she held him to a trot, his hooves clopping on the blacktop as they headed toward the beach.

The mist was starting to burn off as the sun moved higher, and Mr. Ed's hooves sank into the sand as India steered him to the water's edge. Sunlight glinted on the silver waves that muscled their way onto the beach. Far away, almost on the horizon, a white yacht was visible. Maybe it was the *Mata Hari*.

India gave the horse a nudge and Mr. Ed broke into a gallop. As they flew over the swirling water, she grasped his mane, her thighs hugging his flanks. India's spirits lifted, and she concentrated on the rhythm of human and horse. She would never need anything else. Jubilant, that's what her darling was. If only Kiki had experienced happiness like this, maybe things would have been different.

They galloped toward Sag Pond. At the edge Mr. Ed slowed, but India encouraged him and the horse waded in. Water rose past

India's boots, then her thighs. It lapped over the horse's shoulders, and just as the water reached India's waist, Mr. Ed's hooves lifted and he began to swim. She held on to his neck as they glided across the surface like some forgotten mythological creature.

India remembered coming here with Mademoiselle, tying raw chicken necks onto twine, lobbing them as far as they could into the water. They'd wait, motionless, until they felt the gentle tug. Slowly, gingerly, they'd reel in huge blue crabs, checking the tummy to make sure it wasn't a female with eggs. Later Mademoiselle would boil the males in Old Bay seasoning.

Had her mother been at those dinners? India could remember her mother's soft dark hair and perfume. Most of the people who had been close to Kiki were dead. Her father was useless—drugged or hungover. Massimo Sforza must have information, he could fill in so many of India's blanks. She knew she would go to him, and soon.

The ripples spread across the brackish water. Gulls argued above. She had always wondered if her mother had fallen asleep before sinking under. Or had she held herself beneath the bubbles as the warm bath filled her nose and lungs.

They were nearing the opposite shore and Mr. Ed touched bottom. As they emerged, dripping, a woman with two children was lugging a cooler onto the beach. The three of them stared at India with incomprehension. A lot of people looked at her that way. India was a strange creature, outside the rhythm of life. Farther down the beach, a man was casting a fishing rod into the surf. Justine and Clay at home, tangled in her mother's sheets. Her father would be snorting his first line in Palm Beach. Everyone starting their day, going through the motions, trying to distract themselves from the knowledge that someday all would come to an end.

"Wakey, wakey," Deirdre sang, ripping back the chintz curtains. The rings clattered over the rod and daylight streamed into Eve's Hamptons bedroom.

"Clay's on the phone."

"Muuh," Eve said, rolling over.

"Clayton, sweetie?" Deirdre breathed into the cordless phone. "She'll have to call you back." She hung up and tore the covers off her daughter. Eve squinted up at her, goose-pimpled and naked. "What have you done?" her mother hissed.

"I shaved off my pubic hair."

Deirdre looked disgusted. "Why on earth would you do such a thing?"

"Like everything I do. To piss you off."

Deirdre frowned. "You wanted to go out to supper this evening? You're on thin ice. Sleep tight."

As if she weren't already awake.

Deirdre slammed the door. Eve lay in bed, recognizing that this was the most dialogue she had exchanged with her mother since getting expelled.

Eve dialed Clay back, looking up at the ceiling, where striped fabric was draped in folds so that the room resembled a sultan's tent. Clay's phone rang and rang. She examined the intrusive tan line on her breasts. If only she were in the south of France, her boobs would be tan too.

"Hello?"

"Oh, hi, Barbara. It's Eve Straus. How are you?"

"Wonderful, how's the gallery?"

"Working for Margot's an incredible experience."

"That woman's a master of commerce." Coming from Clay's mother, this was not a compliment. "You might as well work at Brown Brothers with Clayton."

There was a miserable silence. Barbara must know that Margot had always wanted to represent her.

"Is Clayton there?"

"I'll check." There was a receding clatter of clogs.

Eve scratched her itchy pubic stubble, then stretched out on the sheets under the warm sun. There might have been something dreamy, Brigitte Bardot–esque about lazing in bed nude and talking to a boy on the phone. But it was only Clay.

"How's stuff?"

Clay filled her in on the disaster they had found at the Clarksons'. "Justine insisted on staying over." Eve envisioned Justine and India in that mansion, the pool, no curfew, no rules, no parents to speak of. India's house was gorgeous, done by some famous Italian decorator. Fucking hell. Justine's good fortune was a tape playing in an inexorable loop.

"Is Barbara driving you over there for a swim?"

"I'll use my thumb."

She imagined him hitchhiking by the side of the road, the preppy little man-child.

"Wait!" This might be a chance to see Barbara face-to-face. "My mom can take us. She loves Mr. Clarkson."

"He's in Palm Beach," Clay said dully.

Eve wouldn't tell Deirdre or she'd never get a ride.

Clay answered the Bradleys' door in an unbuttoned blue Oxford, his eyes puffy.

Deirdre peered past him. "Hello, dear. Is your mother about?"

"I'll see." He disappeared.

"This house is so chic." Deirdre sighed, stepping into the front hall. A floating staircase was enclosed in a cylinder of glass brick, and a metal walkway spanned the living room.

In the front hall hung a small pencil sketch in a frame. Eve looked closer; it was obviously a Sforza of St. John the Baptist, in ragged fur with his shepherd's staff. In the corner it said *For Philip*.

"Deirdre, forgive me, I didn't hear your car." Barbara walked in, tying her hair into a knot. Clay was close behind, holding his bathing suit.

Deirdre's cheek grazed Barbara's.

Barbara eyed Deirdre's skimpy tennis outfit.

"Singles with Bitsy Titman," Deirdre explained, "and I was supposed to lunch with Keith, but he's still ill."

"Barbara, is this a Sforza?" Eve asked, pointing to the drawing.

"It is," Barbara said, walking over to her.

"It's not hers," Clay said in a bitter voice.

Eve could feel her mother watching her.

"I was going to swing by his studio today," Barbara said.

Eve had not known Barbara and Massimo were friends.

"Is the Susanna there?"

"Is he doing one? I'll see when I arrive," Barbara replied.

Barbara slung her purse over her shoulder. "Deirdre, thanks for chauffeuring." Eve knew luring her to Margot's gallery was way above her abilities, but she still felt she needed to succeed. She had failed at Griswold but had been given another chance. She was stronger now, more directed.

"Will you pick Clayton up?" Deirdre asked.

"He has a thumb. Cheers!" And Barbara swept from the house.

EIGHT

JUSTINE GAZED AROUND THE GUEST ROOM AT THE PINK reading chair and the bamboo dresser. The wallpaper had a design of tiny curling carnations. Morning sun streamed in through the curtains.

It had taken her hours to clean up last night, not just the dishes but the kitchen and stove. Had India's father left the house that way? Even if Cressida and Miles drove her mad with their naïve optimism, at least they took out the garbage.

Justine got up and walked down the hall to India's room. The bed was empty, neatly made. Justine paused in front of the black-and-white photograph at the top of the stairs. Aside from the 1960s hairstyle and white go-go boots, the picture could have been India. Same slightly upturned nose and faraway expression.

Downstairs, Justine tiptoed across a crewel carpet with flowers and leaves that matched the green lacquered hallway. She imagined hundreds of people sipping wine in the large rooms that spread out on both sides. Laughter and lighted cigarettes, the low hum of conversation. It wouldn't even feel crowded.

In the living room, Justine ran her finger over a carved lobster on a glass table, realizing it was ivory. She bent to examine a framed photograph of a man wearing sunglasses behind a captain's wheel, another picture of India in riding habit on a magnificent chestnut horse. Then a third of a few elegant older people who looked like they were dressed for the opera. Grandparents, great-aunts, and great-uncles. The library, a deep red, had a bay window that swelled between fitted bookshelves, full of books on decorated houses and gardening, the kind her parents sneered at. And in the cavernous aubergine dining room hung a massive violet glass chandelier.

The kitchen still had a faint tinge of rancid garbage. An answering machine beeped angrily on the counter.

India was sitting on the sofa, staring out at the patio.

"Look," she said, pointing.

Justine followed her gaze. The swimming pool was a spinachy mass of algae.

"What happened?"

"Nothing. The bastard forgot to pay the pool guy."

"Who was on the phone?"

"What phone?" India asked.

"The one that was ringing. They might have left a message." She tried not to sound anxious, but it might have been Clay.

"Machine's been full for eons."

India had managed to make fresh coffee, and Justine poured herself a cup before examining her friend. There was a dark stain spreading beneath India on the sofa, and water pooled beneath her boots.

"Are you wet?"

"Went riding."

"How did you get wet riding?"

"We went swimming."

Justine sat on a dry part of the sofa. Beyond the slate patio a flat, sunny field stretched off toward dunes. Faint mist hung over the sea.

"Want to get high?" India asked.

"No, thanks."

The doorbell rang.

"It's awfully early," India grumbled, getting up.

Justine followed her into the hall. India's boots made squelching sounds on the floor.

It was Eve, looking neat in white terry cloth and silver sandals.

"Don't answer the phone or anything," she said. "Jesus, why are you all wet?"

"I went swimming with Mr. Ed."

Justine could see Clay outside, holding the car door open for Mrs. Straus.

He came in with Deirdre, who was clad in a tennis skirt that barely covered her ass. The older, tanner version of Eve's legs.

"India, dear, don't you look lovely," said Deirdre. "Is your father here?"

"No, in Palm Beach."

"What a shame," Deirdre said lightly. "He always was such a creature of habit." Justine examined Mrs. Straus to see if she was making a jab at his addictions, but Deirdre's face was a smiling mask.

India shook her head, her face equally opaque.

"We can't swim," India said. "Algae from hell."

They all stared at her.

Why did they need to swim here, Justine wondered, when there was an entire ocean right outside?

"My house?" Clay suggested.

"Can't we just walk to the beach?" Justine asked.

"Nobody goes to the beach," Eve said.

Justine felt her face flush.

After some discussion, they decided to go to Clay's.

India ran upstairs to change.

Mrs. Straus asked for the loo.

Clay pointed at a door through the library.

Of course, Justine thought, he's been here a million times, he and India and everyone else, growing up side by side.

"I'll wait in the car," Eve said.

Now that they were alone, Clay kissed her. A polite kiss—someone might come in at any moment.

Suddenly she remembered. "I had a dream about you."

"That's weird, I dreamed about you too. We were in a classroom at Griswold," he said, "one of the old ones in Meade. You were at the front, maybe you were the teacher or something, and you were wearing a long blue dress. I was taking an exam, but I couldn't remember anything, even though I studied."

"A long blue dress?"

"You know, flowy." Clay flapped his arms.

If he was dreaming about her, then she was still on his mind. As he was on hers.

"We were in the prop warehouse. It was dark, and this statue thing was breathing in a raggedy kind of way." Justine realized that had to do with putting India to bed and thinking of how Edie Sedgwick had died. And a phone had been ringing, she recalled, but then she realized it was probably the phone here.

They were silent, Clay looking down at the carpet.

"Hey, why don't people go to the beach?" Justine asked.

"Salt and sand?"

Justine imagined licking dried salt off his neck and took a step closer. They were just about to kiss again when Deirdre strode in from the library.

"I'll get my bag," Justine said, backing away and running up the stairs. She grabbed her swimsuit and tore back down.

In the two minutes she had been gone, India had transformed. She wore small turquoise shorts, a canvas tote hung on one arm. Her hair was combed into a ponytail, and she smelled faintly of perfume.

She handed Deirdre a small slip of paper. "Maybe another adult can convince him to do something about the pool. I've given up."

"It seems awfully early to give up on your own father," Deirdre said as they walked outside. "Just wait till you kids are parents yourselves."

The air-conditioning hummed in the Mercedes. Every now and then Justine would catch a shellacky waft of Mrs. Straus's hairspray.

Justine gazed out the window at the furrows of plowed and planted fields, the tall hedges, the weathered shingle houses fringed with blue hydrangeas. Every blade of grass looked as if it had been cut with nail clippers.

They slowed behind some traffic in front of a general store.

"Hey, look!" Eve said, rolling down the window.

On the shoulder was a beautiful and bare-chested hitchhiker.

Justine felt a wave of attraction, despite herself.

"Hey, Bruce!" Eve called.

Clay stared out the window in the opposite direction.

This was all Justine's fault. If only she had told Eve what Bruce had done to her, Eve would never want to see him.

Bruce waved and jogged toward them.

"Who is that?" India asked.

"A fucking *asshole*," Justine said.

"Watch your language in my car," Deirdre snapped.

The convertible behind them honked angrily. Deirdre pulled over a few inches. Bruce leaned in Eve's open window.

"Mom, India, this is Bruce Underwood," Eve said.

"Hi, guys. Any chance you're headed to East Hampton?"

"No, I have a tennis date in South."

"That's cool," said Bruce, tan and gleaming. "I'll just tag along."

"It's getting awfully lonely up here," Deirdre said, patting the seat. Bruce slid in and closed the door. "Where's your shirt?" Deirdre asked.

"Right here," Bruce said, pointing at something tucked under his belt. "Helps hitchhiking."

"Your parents know?" Deirdre asked, pulling a few inches forward.

"Nah, they're in Woodside, California."

"Do you know the Byerlys?" Deirdre asked.

"Sienna's parents?"

"Yes!" Mrs. Straus beamed, telling Bruce how Mr. Byerly and Eve's father went to business school together.

That's another thing about being rich, Justine thought. You had a buddy in every port.

"Know what we call her?" Bruce continued, looking right at Justine.

"Sounds like he'll tell us anyway," India murmured.

"Bruce Underwood, meet India Clarkson," Eve said.

"Charmed," Bruce said, looking anything but. "I'll tell you about Sienna later. A real team player, if you know what I mean."

"Mom, pull over and boot him out," Eve said. Justine hoped she wasn't joking.

"I don't take orders," Deirdre said, "and he's no worse than the rest of you."

"Thanks, Mrs. Straus." Bruce grinned. "Clay, should we pick up a case of brewskis?"

Clay shrugged.

"Last time I checked, all of you were underage," Deirdre said.

"We all have fake ID, Mrs. Straus," Bruce said, flashing her his most charming smile.

"As Dino says, it's always five o'clock somewhere," Eve said.

NINE

"HOME SWEET HOME," CLAY SAID, AS THEY ENTERED HIS house.

Cressida would go apeshit with joy over this place, Justine thought, looking at the bleached floors and track lighting. With its curved flanks of gray wood and bubble-shaped windows, it reminded her of *Yellow Submarine.*

"This way," Clay said to Bruce. "Eve, you guys can use the guest room."

The boys headed upstairs.

"Where's the bathroom?" Justine asked. She could smell Barbara's patchouli.

"Follow me." India led them down a hall past a few framed ink drawings.

The guest room was empty. Twin beds stretched their narrow frames under a portrait of Clay as a young boy, clearly by Barbara. He was shirtless, in a pair of shorts, his dark hair long, and he was holding a stuffed white rabbit. Behind him was a window with a view of distant hills, a Tuscan landscape. He must have been about ten.

Eve came in wearing a tiny black bikini.

They stood and looked at the portrait.

"I feel like it was just a few seconds ago that Barbara painted that," Eve said.

Justine longed to have known him then.

Clay was swimming underwater, his shadow reflected on the bottom. He surfaced and tossed a flip of black hair out of his face. They looked at each other, and Justine wondered when she would get him alone. Bruce came through the sliding doors in madras trunks slung low on his hips.

"Don't tell me those are yours," Eve said to Clay.

"Philip's," Clay said, still looking at Justine. She realized he had never seen her in a bathing suit and wondered what he was thinking; Clay often looked at her with admiration, but never with lust. She knew the hungry look well, and it was not on Clay's face.

"He still has clothes here?" Eve asked.

"His crap is everywhere," Clay said, frowning and pushing off the side.

Even though no parents were present, they were always lurking around in spirit.

Justine could feel Bruce checking her out and avoided meeting his eye.

Bruce dove, arcing up, then plunging down into the pool. He swam up behind Clay and splashed him with a muscled arm. Clay whipped around and splashed him back.

Bruce lurched.

Clay ducked.

Bruce tried to dunk him, but Clay grabbed his wrist. Bruce swung with his free arm, but Clay spat a spout of water in his face.

"You're getting me wet!" India complained.

"It would take a lot more than that," said Bruce.

India looked unperturbed, rolling a joint.

"But you're not my type," Bruce continued. "I like mine with meat on their bones." He glanced at Justine.

How she loathed him, she thought, feeling the straps of the lounge chair cutting into her thighs.

Bruce hoisted himself out of the water. He pushed his hair out of his eyes and stood up. "Where's the beer?"

"In the kitchen," Clay said, "but don't drip all over the floor."

When Bruce had gone, Eve said, "We have to get rid of that jerk."

"What is he even doing here?" Justine spoke for the first time.

India waved a hand in disgust, indicating that the cretin did not merit words.

Clay climbed out of the pool and perched on the side with his legs dangling in the water.

"Why on earth do you put up with that fuckhead?" Eve persisted, over her sunglasses.

Clay stared into the chlorine. "It's not his fault he has massive parental damage."

"Oh bullshit, we all have that," Eve retorted.

They all laughed, except for India, who was taking a deep toke from her joint. She stood up and handed it to Clay. He took some and passed it back.

"Anybody home?" a man's voice called from the driveway.

Clay held his finger to his lips. Justine froze. India stubbed out the joint.

"Helloooo? Clayton?" A man with neat gray hair and Italian loafers slid through an opening in the hedge. "I knew I heard voices," he said.

India and Eve got to their feet.

"Hi, Mr. Bradley," Eve said, kissing him on both cheeks. Justine stood up, squinting at Clay's father, trying to recognize him from the taffeta-clad man she had seen at the Pyramid.

"What are you doing here?" Clay growled, getting up from the edge of the pool.

"Hello, India," Mr. Bradley ignored him. He held his hand out to Justine. "Philip Bradley."

"Justine Rubin," she said. His skin was smooth as he gripped her hand. He had Clay's green eyes, but his nose was more prominent, his lips thinner.

"I said, what are you doing here?" Clay repeated, tucking the end of a towel around his waist.

"I just have to pick a few things up. Your mother said she'd be gone."

"You're not supposed to be here. I read the agreement."

"Funny thing to call it." Philip laughed. He began to walk toward the house.

Clay's voice rose. "You can't sneak in and grab shit." He followed his father.

The sliding door opened. "Heineken or Bud?" Bruce asked, holding two beers. "Oh, hi."

"I'm Philip, Clayton's father. Owner of those trunks. Heineken, please."

Bruce handed Philip a beer. Mr. Bradley opened it and took a sip. He wiped his mouth.

"Go and get whatever you came for and leave," Clay said, his jaw tense.

But Philip was still admiring Bruce. Justine and Eve exchanged a worried glance.

"Cheers," Bruce said to Mr. Bradley. He took a big swig, letting the foam run down his chin onto his chest.

Philip stared, transfixed.

"Get out!" Clay took a step toward his father, his fists clenched.

"Relax," Bruce replied, grinning at Philip. "Your old man's gotta finish his beer."

"I told you to get out." Clay's face was flushed.

Clay moved, but Bruce moved faster, blocking Clay's blow. Clay staggered, and for a moment his arms pinwheeled, then the back of his skull hit the edge of the pool with a loud, hollow *thunk*.

Time stood still as they watched blood pouring from Clay's head into the pool, billowing into a purple plume.

"Ambulance!" Justine cried, her voice sliding into a higher, panicked key. She ran into the house and grabbed the phone.

"Nine-one-one. Where's the emergency?"

"Hang on," she said, panting, as Eve came up behind her. Justine handed her the receiver.

"Twenty-three Hedges Lane. Yes, of course." Eve hung up.

They stared at each other in terror.

"Fuck, what do we do?" Eve said. "Fuck! I'll get ice. You go help."

Justine had no idea what kind of help to give. She ran back to the pool.

Philip was sobbing and cradling Clay's pale head in his arms. His khaki shorts and shirt were covered in blood.

"Is he okay?" Justine asked stupidly.

Philip wailed. "Oh my God! There's so much blood."

Eve appeared with a plastic bag of ice for Clay's head. She touched his wrist.

"His pulse is really fast."

India was hugging herself with her arms, her brown eyes huge, frightened.

Bruce was sitting farther off, still holding his beer, face blank.

They were all frozen in a film still, the only sounds Philip's sobs and the sucking of the pool filter. After an eternity Justine heard sirens, the ambulance screeching to a stop in the driveway. Two brawny paramedics brought in a stretcher.

As they took Clay away, the last thing Justine saw was the red of his blood on the fresh sheet, spreading like a halo.

TEN

THE HOSPITAL SMELLED LIKE CLEANING FLUID AND ANTI-septic mouthwash. Justine stared at the red, yellow, and blue taped arrows on the floor and wondered where they led. Some to the morgue, probably, with those steel drawers full of cadavers. That severed head on Barbara's wall. The staring eyes. Sweet Clay, so pale as the blood seeped from his body.

Philip opened the door, looking authoritative. "He's going to be okay."

Justine felt her shoulders unclench.

Philip sat next to them. The blood on his clothes had dried to brown. "He needed a transfusion so I donated my blood. You can visit him now, but one at a time."

"You first," Eve said, placing her hand on Justine's arm.

Justine stood up, trembling with exhaustion as she walked into Clay's room. Barbara was leaning over him, kissing his bandaged head. He was hooked up to an IV, his pale naked shoulders resting against the pillow.

Barbara gave Justine a teary nod and left.

Justine sat beside the bed and grasped his hand. She leaned forward and kissed him. His lips were soft, and he closed his eyes like a child. When he opened them, they were wet. He wiped at the tears with his bandaged IV arm and blinked.

"How're you feeling?" she managed.

"Tired," he said, almost inaudibly. "You?"

"Fine." *I only thought you were going to die.*

"I'm so sorry."

"About what? It wasn't your fault. It was Bruce!"

It was always Bruce, she felt like saying.

"Bruce didn't ask Philip to barge into Mom's house."

But that wasn't the point. Every time Bruce showed up something terrible happened. Justine wanted to tell Clay that, but she didn't want to argue, not when he seemed so defeated. She just squeezed his hand. He gazed at her, and she gazed back. Were they communing or just realizing how separate they were from each other? Justine turned away and looked out the window. An old man in a hospital gown was taking jerky steps down the path, accompanied by a nurse in an old-fashioned uniform, big white shoes, puffy cap.

"Justine? I need you to be honest about something."

She turned back and nodded.

"When did Barbara get here?"

Clay's face was full of apprehension. For a moment, Justine didn't know how he wanted her to respond.

"She's been here all night."

"Are you sure? She smelled like she'd taken a shower, and if she'd been here all night . . ."

Justine moved closer, speaking softly. "She went home around six this morning to change. She had been in the same clothes all night. You know how much she loves you." *How much I love you.*

He shrugged and fiddled with the tube in the back of his hand.

"I can't live with Barbara anymore."

"It's only another month or so," Justine said. Even so, if she had had to live with Miles and Cressida this summer she'd have gone completely mental.

She wished Clay would come and live with her.

"Listen to me. I need to sleep, so please don't take this the wrong way . . ." he continued. "Bruce has a room in his apartment. I was thinking of camping out there for the rest of the summer."

Justine stood up and walked to the window. The old man and his nurse were gone, the bench empty. A lump rose in her throat and she willed herself not to cry. But she couldn't help it, she'd been up all night and didn't have the strength to fight it.

"Please don't cry," Clay begged. "You just said it's only another month or so. You never have to come over there. I'll come to your place, I promise."

She turned around. "Why don't you care about what he did to me?"

"I do." He sank into the pillow, looking exhausted. "But living with him is better than watching my mother get stoned and paint decapitated men."

Justine wiped her face. She wished he could live with her, but she knew it was India's apartment and not hers to offer. She thought about Barbara and the hookah and her glazed expression.

"It's just a few weeks. It'll be fine."

....

Eve glanced over at the former Mr. and Mrs. Bradley, both staring at the wall of the waiting room in tense silence. How had those two ever gotten married? Philip didn't have a hair out of place, he was plucked, primped, and buffed. Barbara, by contrast, was ragged and frayed. They'd met when they were hardly older than her and David.

Philip stood up. "I'm going for coffee. Get either of you some?"

"Please," Barbara said. "The usual."

"Fine. Eve?"

"Tea, please."

"How do you take it?"

"Milk and sugar."

Philip walked away.

Barbara grunted something unintelligible.

"Working on anything special?" Eve asked brightly.

"Oh, this and that. I've made a recent foray into sculpture."

"Cool! What medium?"

"Stone. Behold." Barbara held out her right hand, the dry skin mutilated by several deep cuts.

"Wow, is that infected?" Eve asked, stubbing out her cigarette.

"Nothing can be learned without pain." Barbara placed her ungouged hand firmly over Eve's. "I wanted to thank you."

Eve had no idea what she was talking about.

"You've been such a dear friend to Clayton," Barbara continued. "When I think back, you've always been there." Barbara's eyes filled with tears. "I really thought I might lose him." Tears ran down her wrinkled cheeks.

Eve shifted uncomfortably.

"You'll understand when you have children." Barbara sniffed.

"Not planning on it. I'll be running a gallery. Having kids will get in the way."

"Ah, you want to emulate Margot?"

"I'll be nicer," Eve said, then added, "but hopefully just as much of a force."

"She's a force all right," Barbara said.

A sudden plan occurred to Eve.

"Speaking of, well, art and so on, I've been meaning to ask you if you'd ever consider selling your Salome?"

Barbara pulled a handkerchief from her pocket and blew her nose. "It's an awfully good painting," she said.

"It is. And I could get you a *very* good price for it," Eve said, trying to keep her voice confident.

Barbara sighed. "I don't know. I've gotten so used to seeing it every morning. Anyway, sweetheart, Holly handles all my sales. I have to admit I take very little part in that."

Eve tried to imagine how the dead staring eyes would strike her on a daily basis. She had to see the Avedon of the man covered in bees, it couldn't be worse than that.

"It would be for my mom and dad," Eve admitted.

This seemed to charm her. Barbara smiled and patted Eve's knee.

"Barbara, please don't be offended, but Holly is kind of fading into the woodwork." Eve leaned closer. Barbara's mascara was smeared. Eve looked around to see if anyone might be nearby, but they were alone. "You're a great, great artist, and you deserve more exposure, especially now that you are doing sculpture. Think about it, you could switch galleries and open this spring with all this amazing new work!"

Barbara raised an eyebrow. "Well, well," she said after a moment, "you may be the next Margot, after all. Did she put you up to this?"

"No!" Eve said. "This is my idea. Margot worships you, and if I brought you in she'd have an orgasm."

"A first!"

They laughed.

Philip was back. "There was a line," he said, handing a coffee cup to his ex-wife. "Your tea," he added, handing the other cup to Eve.

"Thanks, Mr. Bradley. I'll pop in on Clay," she said and walked toward his room.

"Come in!" Clay called.

"Sorry to break up the lovefest," Eve said. "It's real fun out there with Punch and Judy."

Despite her parents' strictness and social climbing, at least they didn't want to tear each other limb from limb.

"Why are you crying?" she asked Justine lightly. "Your boyfriend's alive."

ELEVEN

EVE PICKED UP THE PHONE ON THE GALLERY DESK.

Barbara answered on the tenth ring.

"Mrs. Bradley? I mean, Barbara? It's Eve Straus." Eve could hear Leonard Cohen in the background, and people talking.

"I was wondering, could I come talk to you about the Salome?"

"If you don't mind that I have company."

Eve stood up and slung her purse over her shoulder. Without a word to Raymond she swept out of the gallery.

A few blocks later, she rang Barbara's bell.

When Eve stepped from the elevator, she found Barbara sitting in a rattan peacock chair, naked, except for a few slave bracelets and an enormous evil-eye pendant between her soft, pointed breasts.

Of course Barbara was entertaining friends in the nude. Had everyone gone crazy in some bacchanalian way? Nothing made sense anymore.

Several other people slouched on the sofa around the hookah, a bearded man, a bald guy in a black turtleneck, and a frizzy-haired woman in a long afghan, strumming a guitar.

Barbara stood up. "Darling!" she said. "We've got great hashish. Care for a hit?"

Eve shook her head, keeping her eyes resolutely on Barbara's face. "Help yourself to a drink, then."

Eve headed into the kitchen and opened the fridge, trying to compose herself by concentrating on its contents. How was she going to make a deal with a naked person? A few kinds of seaweed, a jar of wheat germ, a tub of tofu, some exotic-looking vegetable in the cabbage family, Mountain Dew. She took one and opened it.

Eve walked back into the living room, eyeing the Salome, which hung on the wall in a ray of sunlight. Exquisite as ever. She perched on the sofa next to the bearded man, whose shirt was open to his navel.

He exhaled a deep cloud of smoke from the hookah, and it smelled earthy with a bitter edge, like burning dung.

"Vince," he said, holding out his hand.

"Eve."

He offered her the hose.

"No, thank you."

She looked at Barbara refilling wineglasses, her evil eye swinging over the table. The woman playing the guitar smiled at Eve, revealing a gold tooth.

"You know Hatshepsut entertained in the nude," Vince commented. "I've always believed that Barbara was an Egyptian princess in another life."

"Queen," Barbara corrected him.

"Can't you feel how powerful she is?" Vince gestured with the hookah hose. "The human force flowing through her is so intense, that's gotta be some royal karma."

Eve stood up. This was never going to work. Rummaging in her bag, she pulled out a cigarette, lit it, and walked closer to the painting.

Daylight illuminated the silver of the plate, the blue-gray tinge of the severed head. Salome stood holding the platter in front of a red velvet curtain, which an invisible hand had drawn aside. Behind was a room submerged in shadow.

Her ash had become perilously long.

Eve didn't have the faintest idea what Barbara's paintings were worth. She ran through the prices of the Sforza show. Barbara's were probably worth half, she guessed. The best of Massimo's were selling for fifty thousand dollars. What if she could get that for the Salome? It was a shitload of money, but if Eve could pull it off, Barbara might switch to Margot's gallery. The sale would set a record.

"How much?" came Barbara's voice, startling Eve, as her ash fell to the floor. Eve straightened and turned around.

"I know you're not here on a social visit," Barbara said, "so let's just cut to the chase."

....

India rang Massimo's buzzer and waited. After ringing a second time she pushed the door. It swung open onto a steep flight of steps. A piano melody drifted through the hallway. As she climbed, the music grew louder. A Chopin ballade? The arpeggios descended and the piece ended in a few thunderous chords as India reached the landing. Had he played piano for her mother?

She knocked.

Massimo opened the door in paint-stained overalls. He did not seem at all surprised to see her, and pressed her hand to his lips.

"Was that you playing?" India asked.

"It was. It calms me."

"I love Chopin."

"Anch'io."

The loft had a wall of high windows and arched brick ceilings. There were several canvas-draped easels, and a huge carved wooden table with books piled on one end. A grand piano yawned in front of the windows. It was like being in a Velasquez.

"Something to drink?"

"Yes, please."

"Momento," he said, and lumbered off.

India sat at the piano and played the few bars of *Clair de Lune* she could remember. She moved to the window, pressing her forehead against the glass. Night was falling, not a soul knew she was here.

Massimo returned with champagne and two glasses. He popped the cork and handed her one.

"Salute."

The liquid slid down her throat. It was the first thing she'd had all day.

"Is that the Susanna?" India pointed to an easel with a figure of a girl, as voluptuous as a Rubens, sketched in rough strokes. Sunlight sparkled on a forest pool and two bearded men peeked out from behind a tree. Several photographs were scattered on a chair next to the easel.

"I don't look like that girl at all."

Massimo spread his hands, champagne bottle in one, glass in the other. "It is she who will look like you, *cara* Mimi. You can change over there—" He pointed to a curtain in a corner. Massimo took India's empty glass.

India ducked behind the curtain, feeling the effects of the drink already. Making sure she had complete privacy, she took off her clothes and wrapped herself in the robe that hung from a hook. It was soft and warm. Slipping out of her sandals, India padded across the floor and perched on the edge of a burgundy velvet armchair. Massimo knelt beside her on enormous knees and handed her a refilled glass. His brown eyes held golden flecks.

"Tell me about my mother."

"Ah, Kiki," he said, with reverence. "She was an exquisite creature, with a very old soul. Beautiful hair, like yours," Massimo said, reaching out to twirl a lock in his finger. "No. Yours is softer." He gently pushed the robe from India's shoulders. "I loved her, perhaps more than I have ever loved any woman." Massimo traced India's collarbone with a soft touch. She couldn't move. "But Kiki did not love me." Massimo stood and picked up a paintbrush.

India suddenly felt cold. "How did you know?"

He turned. "In the way a man always knows. Kiki was so sad, so remote. I tried. Oh, how I tried to reach her. Have you ever loved without being loved in return?" He shook his large head, reminding India of a big, sad lion. "No, of course not. I hope you never do."

Tears were close. Yes, India did remember trying to reach her mother, trying to help her, and failing. Massimo had loved her mother, and so had she, but Kiki had killed herself even so. Neither of them had mattered enough to change her mind.

"Would you mind taking off the robe?" Massimo was respectful, India realized, and while painting he did not see her as a beautiful girl, nor even as the daughter of the beloved dead Kiki. India was inspiration for Massimo's art. India downed her drink, set the glass on the floor, pulled off the robe, and let it fall. She put her arm across her breasts and sat down, staring at the paint splatters on the wood floor.

Massimo began to paint.

"Are you sure you want me as your model?"

"Hmmm?"

"That girl, she's so voluptuous, and I'm so . . ."

Massimo came closer and refilled her glass.

"May I?" he asked, resting his hand on her knee. He gently parted her legs. *"Prego."* He smiled, taking her hand gently from her breast and placing it on the arm of the chair.

He returned to his easel.

Despite the summer heat, India felt goose bumps spread across her skin. The light had faded to black outside. Traffic surged below on Broadway.

The world didn't matter.

"I hope you're making me look better than in real life," she said after a few minutes.

"Mimi, look at me." He pointed to his massive chest. "Is this what Massimo is? Of course not. This is the flesh in which my soul is trapped. You, Mimi, you are a beautiful bird in a delicate cage and I am a wild animal in a grotesque one. I am painting the bird, not the cage."

He started painting again. Tears ran down India's face. Her mother, passionately loved by this romantic man, dearly loved by her only daughter, and still she had wanted to die.

Massimo put his brush down and came to India. He knelt before her and pushed her hair off her face.

"You are lovelier than you can ever know," he said, "a beautiful and exquisite girl." She took his hand and pressed it to her wet cheek. His touch was soothing, she could feel the tenderness in it. He pulled her body toward his, and she wrapped her arms around his huge shoulders. Massimo leaned in and kissed her. His warm mouth covered her whole face. He lifted her tiny body off the chair and carried her to the table. He laid her down gently, his bulk pressing the air from her lungs.

India closed her eyes in bliss as she sank below the surface of the waves.

TWELVE

CLAY MOVED IN WITH BRUCE. JUSTINE SWORE SHE WOULD never go over there, not even when Bruce was out. A week went by.

The irony was that if she went over to their apartment, she might finally get to tear the boy's clothes off. Imagining their two sweaty bodies sliding over each other's was a fantasy she indulged in as she trekked up and down the aisles at the prop warehouse. With Bruce she had been blinded by his beauty, flattered. That hadn't been love, this was.

On a Thursday night, Justine lay on the floor of India's apartment. She could hardly move for the blaze of heat throbbing through the apartment. It hadn't rained in ages, and the reek of garbage wafted up the four flights. Tonight Dino had lit flowery incense, but it was almost worse, making the apartment smell like kitty litter. The Cat Club.

That first day at the smoker; how long ago it felt now.

Dino was primping in front of the mirror. Justine lay there, smoking and watching him. She heard the front door open and close.

"You look *gorgeous*," said Raymond, wearing shorts and a seersucker shirt. Dino admired his own reflection and went back to adjusting the veil on the pillbox hat. He had made it so greasy that India had given it to him.

"Going somewhere?" Justine said.

"Dancing," Raymond replied, "after a little pick-me-up." He waved a small bag of coke.

Justine imagined them, lights sweeping across their chests, bass pounding out their pulse.

She stood up and moved to the garment rack, fingering a brocade gown. It would be so fun to dress up and go dancing, but Dino and Raymond were probably going somewhere that was boys only. She tried on a floppy felt hat. It fell over her eyes and cheekbones. She would stay under there forever.

Replacing the hat on the shelf, Justine turned around.

Dino had gone back to fixing his coiffure and Raymond was bent over the coffee table cutting lines.

Raymond offered her the rolled bill.

She shook her head. Justine wished India were here. India had been out most evenings lately, without explanation, and she'd stopped smoking pot for some reason. Nonetheless she seemed as calmly beatific as ever.

Justine went into the kitchen and stared at the phone. Even if she didn't go over to Bruce's apartment, she could call just to check. If someone answered, she could always hang up. Taking a breath, she dialed. It rang, but there was no reply.

Dino and Raymond were noisily sucking cocaine up their nostrils in the living room.

Justine waited a minute and dialed again. Still no answer. Where was he? It was almost midnight and Clay had work tomorrow.

"Ciao." Dino waved as he and Raymond left, slamming the front door.

A car alarm bleated outside.

Justine's head filled with nightmarish images, Clay's wound infected, his body tossing with fever. Or he had lost his keys and was sleeping on the stoop. She grabbed her cigarettes, a few bills, and left.

It was still oppressively humid and threatening to storm. Justine looked up at the olive green of the gathering clouds. Maybe Bruce had answered the phone and had been playing with her?

The whole city reeked like one huge human urinal. As a child Justine had been fascinated by glimpses into public men's rooms, the line of men with their backs to the door, trousers loose, heads bent as though they were in prayer. This stench was the piss of men, dogs, and countless vermin.

Thunder rumbled as she reached Tenth Street. The sidewalks of the East Village were full of people. Punks huddled in groups, reminding her of the kids at the smoker. A drunken couple burst from a restaurant, the man guffawing. The woman's head kicked back into a laugh, a flash of lightning illuminating her fillings.

Justine climbed the steps of the brownstone and rang the buzzer.

After a minute, Bruce opened the door, bare-chested with a can in his hand.

"Look who the cat dragged in," he said, blocking the entrance. He smelled beery with a slight tang of sweat.

"Can I come up?"

May I, she could hear Cressida say.

"He's out."

She frowned at him in disbelief.

"Don't worry, momma bear, he'll be back." Bruce stood aside, but just. She squeezed past him, trying not to brush against his skin.

"What floor?"

"You've never been here?" He laughed.

She climbed the stairs, imagining finding a kitchen knife and plunging it into his chest.

"Your ass actually looks good in those jeans," he said.

Actually.

The door opened directly into the kitchen. In the center of the table lay a half-eaten pizza, cigarette butts studding its surface.

"Got any beer?"

"Just drank the last one."

She followed him into the narrow living room. Between the windows hung Barbara's painting of the naked man pierced by arrows. There was a wooden coffee table and a torn plaid sofa.

Kicking off his flip-flops, Bruce reclined on the sofa, taking up the whole thing.

They regarded each other.

"Could you please move your feet?"

Bruce bent his knees very slightly so that she could wedge herself in. Justine tried not to be aware of his toes touching her thigh.

The door to a bedroom opened and a girl with reddish hair poked her head out. She had a pug nose and slitty eyes.

"Give me a sec!" Bruce ordered.

The girl closed the door.

They sat in silence. Justine wanted a cigarette but she didn't want to move.

"You're wasting your time," Bruce said.

"Fuck off."

Bruce jabbed his toe into her thigh, hard.

"OW!" She stood up, rubbing her leg.

"I have a guest."

315

"Don't let me keep you." Justine stood, walked to the wall, and pretended to examine Barbara's painting.

Bruce came up close behind her, so close she could feel the heat of his body, his breath on her neck. She trembled without wanting to. He put an arm around her and pulled her close. She could feel every part of him, could smell him, and felt a sickening wave of desire. Her body caved into his. His lips were on her sweaty neck . . .

"What's going on?" Clay said. Bruce let her go. She turned around.

"Just having a little fun with your girlfriend. She's so hot tonight." Bruce headed into his bedroom and closed the door.

"What are you doing here?" Clay asked. "Is everything okay?"

There was a cry from the bedroom.

"I wanted to find out what was going on."

Clay flopped onto the sofa. "Sorry, I've been so busy." He patted a patch of stained fabric.

There was a smack and a grunt from the bedroom.

Justine imagined what Bruce was doing to that girl.

"I don't get it." She gestured around. "How can you live with him?" She tried to erase the feeling of Bruce against her. She sat beside Clay and put her hand on his knee.

Clay fiddled with the hem of his shirt.

A moan drifted up from behind the wall. Clay looked at Bruce's door.

What was she doing here? Clay had moved in and moved on. It was over, no question. But she couldn't stop. It was like picking at a scab. She moved her hand farther up his thigh.

"Do you actually like me anymore?" *Actually.*

"You know I do. And you also know better than to worry about Bruce." Clay looked terribly tired.

Justine glanced around the apartment, searching for something to change the subject.

"Can I check out your room?"

"Yeah. It's not much."

She stood up and stepped over his outstretched legs, moving toward the door. A simple futon, an open window, bare floors. She lay down and gazed up at the ceiling. A contractor's light bulb hung from a ring on the ceiling where a chandelier might have been, a long orange cord snaked into an outlet. It was cool, in an unfinished, industrial kind of way. *This is where I should have spent every night this summer.*

"Like it?" Clay called.

"Not all alone," she said.

He leaned against the door frame. She beckoned with her finger.

A giggle came from next door. The walls must be made of cardboard.

Clay lay down beside her and looked up at the ceiling, his pinkie just touching hers. Like brother and sister, she thought, as hot tears started. She forced them to recede.

Justine propped herself up and leaned over Clay. Lightning lit up his pale face. One Mississippi. She started kissing him. Two Mississippi. She moved her hand to his belt. Three Mississippi. He tasted like beer, and she thought she could detect cigarettes lingering on the back of his tongue. She unbuckled his belt. He pushed her hand away.

"I'll be right back," he said, jumping up.

She waited a moment, wondering if he was telling Bruce to be quiet. The toilet flushed and Clay was back, wiping his hands on his jeans. Now she could hear both Bruce and the girl. Clay lay down beside her and they started to kiss, and there was something more purposeful in it this time. He pushed her shirt up, she unbuckled his pants.

Within moments they were both undressed. Clay's eyes were closed, kissing her. He was on top, and she could tell that he needed some guidance. She helped, and after a few awkward fumblings, things were working. Finally, Justine kept thinking, watching him moving, finally this was happening. Justine wanted this to last forever, after all this time they had real potential.

Bruce gave a victorious holler and all went quiet at last.

The ceiling cracks smiled over Clay's shoulder. Justine closed her eyes and held on to him. His skin was warm on hers, her hands were in his hair. She had waited so long for this, she wrapped her legs tighter around him, moved with him. When it was over, she asked, "Are you a virgin?"

"I was."

They laughed.

He hopped up and pulled on his pants to get some tissues.

When he came back they kissed for a long time. Clay sat up on one arm and looked at her body. He ran a finger down her chest. "There's something I need to tell you."

She thought she already knew. This was the moment I will remember forever, the one where he says . . .

"I'm not going back to Griswold."

"What?" she cried. "Where are you going?"

"Dalton. It's a school in the . . ."

"I know! When were you going to tell me?" Tears of shock erupted, and she could not force them back.

"I just got in. Please don't cry!"

As if on cue, the sky released its pent-up rain in a clatter, like stones pounding onto the street.

"I don't even have the money to visit!" she sobbed into his shoulder. "How'd you get into Dalton at the end of August?"

"India's grandfather was a trustee . . ." Calendars didn't apply to Clay and India, Justine supposed.

India had helped him leave her? Did Eve know? Of course she did. Justine sat up.

"Sweetie, this has nothing to do with you." Clay had never called her sweetie before.

He stood up and leaned on the windowsill, looking out at the deluge. She wanted to claw his back, tear him to shreds. She had thought Clay was different from Gerald, but no, he was just another guy she followed around. Losing his virginity . . . had it even been special for him?

Justine got up, pulled on her shirt and underwear, and took a step toward Clay. She imagined diving out of the window, ending it all. Looking down at her crumpled body, maybe he'd feel remorse. She could see raindrops bouncing off the open window's sill, onto his bare arms, his bare chest.

"I've disappointed you, disappointed everyone," he said, his voice breaking. "I'm useless."

Everyone had betrayed her, even Bruce behind the wall.

"You're in love with him," she cried. "You've always been!"

He turned to her, stricken. "Oh God, Justine. How can you say that when you and I just . . ."

Just did it, she wanted to say, when you couldn't avoid it any longer.

"He's more to you than I am."

"No, he isn't. You don't understand, you never have!" Clay collapsed on the futon, sobbing.

Justine sat beside him, stroking his back. Just like his summer job, just like his friendship with Bruce, like everything else in his life, he had had sex with her out of a sense of duty. Did he have real feelings at all? He was a stranger.

After a while Clay's sobs subsided and his chest stopped heaving. He opened his eyes and sat up, shaking his head. "Everything's so totally messed up."

"I'd better go."

He kept shaking his head. "Justine, please. I'm sorry. Forgive me."

She turned and left, and this time Clay didn't run after her.

Justine walked to the corner. She couldn't bear to go home and lie in bed alone. Not yet.

It was a balmy night and she walked a few blocks east. On the sidewalk a discarded sofa was occupied by two punk girls smoking clove cigarettes.

She glanced at her watch. One a.m. Justine wished Eve were with her. But her friend had been tucked in her soft bed for hours. How could so many different worlds exist in the same city?

Shoving her hands in her jeans pockets, she felt a crumpled piece of paper and pulled it out.

Stanley. 541 E. 13th Street.

Stanley! He might be willing to talk.

Stuffing the note back in her pocket, Justine headed up Avenue A, staying across the street from the gnarled jungle of Tompkins Square. The Pyramid was down the block, but that night with Clay seemed like ages ago. Now Philip was a father in a pink Oxford covered in his son's blood.

On the corner of Thirteenth a guy in striped hot pants adjusted leg warmers around hairy calves. Funny, Tierney had the same leg warmers, she thought as she walked by. Even now, Justine envied them.

Justine passed tenements with overstuffed garbage cans, the scuttle of rats behind them.

At last she found the building. Windowless holes gaped from the façade, behind fire escapes laden with plants in milk cartons. Vines and wires intertwined across the front. A large, dripping *A* in a rough circle was painted on the brick, and a man with a bandanna on his head leaned in the doorway like a doorman at a club. As she approached, two Dobermans lurched at her, barking furiously.

"Quiet!" the man snarled at them. The dogs strained on their chains.

"Welcome to the Hotel California." He grinned, showing several missing teeth.

"I'm looking for Stanley Glasgow."

"You a friend?"

Justine nodded, wondering if there was a password.

"Second floor, room three." He stood aside, holding back the Dobermans.

"Candles are twenty-five," he added, gesturing to a pile of half-burned stubs on the floor.

"Huh?"

"Pretty dark up there."

She looked at the unlit front hall and realized the building did not have electricity.

"I don't have twenty-five dollars."

"Twenty-five cents, baby face."

Justine handed him a quarter, took a lit candle, and started to climb. The wick flickered over graffitied murals. Human figures, some with animal heads, and crazy writing. She felt like an archaeologist discovering a lost temple of an ancient civilization. Dodging a spot where an entire tread was missing, she continued to climb.

On the landing, a girl was sitting on the floor holding a doll, a candle burning beside her. As Justine's eyes adjusted, she realized it was the bald head of an infant, a pale flap of breast swelling in its mouth.

"Do you know which is number three?"

"One with the eye," the girl said, gesturing with her head.

The door was ajar. Justine pushed it open, revealing a small shadowy room. Ragged curtains fluttered in the open window like summer dresses. The candle illuminated a figure on a mattress.

"Stanley?"

"Hmm?"

"It's Justine." She approached the bed.

He sat up, rubbing his eyes. "Sorry, what time is it?" Right, he probably had to work early.

"Past one. Sorry, I really need to talk to you." His T-shirt was stained and the room smelled rank. "Have you been living here all summer?"

"Yes. It's been an experience." Stanley peered at her. "What's the matter?"

Perching on the mattress, Justine lit a cigarette. Smoking, she told Stanley what had happened.

"I highly doubt Clay's in love with Bruce," Stanley said. "I just think sometimes these hetero guy friendships are weirdly codependent."

Why couldn't Clay have depended on her instead?

Justine thought about going back to Griswold without Clay, without Eve, and having to see Bruce. At least Stanley would be there. Maybe some of his wisdom would finally rub off on her.

THIRTEEN

A FEW MINUTES BEFORE THE GALLERY OPENING, EVE DUCKED
into the bathroom. She glimpsed red suede pumps under one door.
Trying to pee quietly, she heard sniffling. Was Margot Moore actually crying? Could she be nervous about the event? Impossible.
Eve flushed, rinsed her hands, and hurried out.

A brawny caterer bustled by with a crate of champagne glasses,
whistling "Oklahoma." The paintings were hung perfectly, the scent
of linseed oil filling the air. It was the smell of creation.

"Eve! Sorry we couldn't get here earlier!" Deirdre's voice rang
across the tiled floor.

A waiter offered goblets of champagne on a tray.

Deirdre took one. Waving her arm, she strode toward a painting. "Teach me! What about this?" Her mother pointed at a picture
of a naked young boy with outspread wings.

"Cupid with his finger up his ass," Eve muttered.

"Looks a bit like that Caravaggio," her mother mused, frowning
at it.

Was she implying that Massimo was derivative? Well, so was
Barbara, then. The whole New Masters movement was, but to Eve's
mind, brilliantly so, reshaping the old by casting it in a modern light.

"What's the one there with the cloth over it?" Frederick pointed.

"The Susanna, at last! Nobody has seen it. Margot's going to unveil it when everyone's here," Eve explained.

Just then Eve caught sight of Clay taking a glass from a waiter. He downed it and grabbed another.

"Excuse me," she said, and squirmed away, making a beeline across the gallery. "Holy shit!" she said when she got to him. "Isn't this so cool?"

"Hunh?" He smelled like alcohol.

"Are you drunk?"

"Getting there."

The gallery was rapidly filling with guests.

Eve took a glass from a passing waiter. "Aren't you supposed to be back at Griswold?"

"Not going."

Eve gave him a look of disbelief. Maybe he could afford to be a day or so late considering his family connection.

"What about Justine?" she asked.

"We broke up." He drew his finger across his neck.

Why hadn't Justine told her?

"It was mutual," Clay added. "Just wasn't meant to be."

Oh bullshit, Eve thought. There was no way it was mutual. Eve wondered if she could call Justine from the back office. Had that been what Clay meant when he said he wasn't going back to Griswold? What on earth was he doing about school instead?

Taking a few sips of her champagne, Eve made a decision. "Do you ever think about what it would be like to be gay?"

Clay's glass tipped forward. She grabbed it just in time, handing it to an obliging waiter.

"Did Justine say something about that?"

"Nope."

Clay took another glass from a passing tray. "Sure, I have. With Philip how could I not?"

"And?"

"I feel sorry for him."

"Yes, but that is him, this is you. We have to define our lives separately from our parents. We can't let them crush us."

"Oh Jesus! They crush us anyway. Just because I'm just a shitty boyfriend doesn't make me gay. I've finally accepted that I'm doomed to solitude."

"The human condition," India said, joining them. She was in a fitted gray cocktail dress and pumps.

Clay emptied his glass, sloshing champagne onto his front.

Eve and India exchanged looks. India rummaged in her purse and handed Clay a handkerchief. Eve looked around to see if her parents were in the crowd. She glimpsed them, admiring the Magdalene.

India pulled something else out of her bag. Eve looked down. It was an airplane ticket. India Clarkson, New York to Rome.

Suddenly they heard a stir near the front and Massimo strode in, alone.

The crowd parted. A few flashbulbs went off. Massimo bowed and the crowd burst into applause. She and India pushed their way a bit closer.

"Where's his wife?" Eve whispered. India put a finger to her lips.

Margot marched into the room in a red sleeveless dress, her teeth bared in a shiny grin. Eve could not see any evidence that her boss had been crying in the bathroom. Standing before the covered canvas on the wall, Margot put an arm around Massimo. She turned to the cameras and raised a champagne glass, revealing her signature tuft of underarm hair.

"Ladies and gentlemen!" Margot boomed. "I'm proud to present the new work of Massimo Sforza. This is one of the most important and highly anticipated shows of the year, and by far Massimo's most personal and profound. I have labored over it all summer long; no, in many ways, for several years. I know you'll agree my efforts have paid off."

Applause. Eve caught Raymond's eye. Margot would never think to thank her gallery staff, the ungrateful vampire.

"This show is a fitting opening to the 1984 season," Margot continued. "Which promises to be one of the most exciting ever!" She waited for the applause to die down. "Massimo Sforza is himself one of the most influential painters of our time." She waved an arm around. "I am honored to show this triumphant new work, elevating the New Masters movement to a higher echelon." There was loud, enthusiastic clapping. Eve saw her mother nearby, looking elated. "These biblical stories contain lessons for each and every one of us." Margot scanned the crowd. "Lessons that transcend time. Massimo has gone one step further and has taken an autobiographical attitude toward these universal themes." Everyone was silent. "Art asks the difficult questions about the human journey. By plumbing the depths of his own experience, Massimo has taken a daring risk, and you"— she paused—"will be the first to see it." Applause rippled through the crowd. "Massimo, would you do the honors?"

Massimo loomed over everyone. He looked around, smiling, and raised a champagne glass. "To rebirth!" the artist cried, and swept the cloth from the Susanna.

Gasps erupted from the crowd. It was India, her belly hugely distended in pregnancy. Eve glanced toward her friend, but India was still holding the ticket to Rome, her face radiant with happiness.

· · · · · · · ·

Stanley sat across from Justine as the train sped toward New Haven. She gazed out the window over the Long Island Sound, where a few small powerboats were headed out to sea, plumes of water spreading behind them like frothy peacock tails.

Eve and India were probably out there with Clay doing something fun. Then Justine remembered they would all be attending Massimo's opening. The momentous event, and here she was, returning to Griswold while her friends drank champagne without her.

Justine lit a cigarette, and exhaled. Why had she imagined she'd be transformed by a summer in the city, somehow reborn? It was over, and she felt diminished. She thought bitterly about Clay sobbing on his futon, his tear-streaked face. Even his life was moving forward, while she and Stanley were going back.

"Tickets, please."

Justine handed hers over. As the conductor punched them, she felt tears coming.

Stanley leaned forward. "Is Eve really so much better off?"

Justine couldn't help but smile at his telepathy. And compared to Stanley's life, her existence was full of good fortune. She wiped her eyes with the back of her sleeve and stubbed out her cigarette.

Cressida was waiting for them at the station. Justine fell into her mother's soft hug.

"You must be Stanley."

Stanley shook Cressida's hand as Justine climbed into the back.

"Your father's home early and I'm making your favorite roast chicken!"

Justine gave her mother the thumbs-up in the rearview mirror. Cressida smiled and turned her high beams on Stanley.

"Can you join us? I'll get you both to school by nine."

Stanley looked hopefully at Justine, who nodded.

"Yes, ma'am. Thank you."

"Call me Cressida."

Justine wondered how long it had been since her friend had had a home-cooked meal. Cressida made a delicious gravy too.

Her mother turned on the radio, but, as usual, all she got was static. She switched it off. "How was your summer, Stanley? Were you working?"

Justine rolled down the window. The air-conditioning was still broken. Same old scene. As the breeze swept her hair off her face, Justine remembered that terrifying drive to the Hamptons with Barbara—the cocaine, India on the back seat, Clay's unhappiness. It felt like a lifetime ago, and someone else's life. The whole summer had felt like playing dress-up in someone else's clothes. Now she was back in her ripped jeans.

Wasn't Eve so much better off? Weren't they all? They had choices. And money. But she knew she couldn't dissect their lives, keeping the good parts and discarding the bad. Justine watched her mother's plump hands on the worn steering wheel, listened to the familiar lilt of her voice as she chatted with Stanley. Settling back into the worn car seat, Justine tried to imagine swapping Cressida for Barbara, for Deirdre. What was that saying about the devil you know? Justine hugged her arms around her body and faced into the wind.

ACKNOWLEDGMENTS

I am grateful to many: Cynthia Kling, brilliant teacher, confidante, lighthouse in a storm, and dear friend. Fran Lebowitz, who coaxed this novel out of the closet. Elisabeth Schmitz, who saved me from the slough of despond. Lorin Stein: to learn from you is like taking a piano lesson with Chopin. Patricia Marx, a most loyal, creative, and hilarious brainstormer.

Thank you to my early readers and friends Jane Mendelsohn, Aline Brosh McKenna, Alexis Gelber, Katie Roiphe, Stephanie Cabot, Genevieve Toles, Christina Clifford, Norman von Holtzendorff, Alissa McCreary, Sophia McCreary, Warren St. John, and Hanna von Goeler.

For inspiration and forbearance, my lifelong partner in crime, Jessica Rosenblum.

Thank you to my energetic and brilliant agent, Alice Whitwham, and to everyone at the Cheney Agency. To my patient and incisive editor, Allison Lorentzen, not only for her intelligence but also for her optimism and good cheer—qualities that are in woefully short supply these days. And to the team at Viking: Brianna Harden for her gorgeous cover design, Jason Ramirez for elegant art direction, Brian

Acknowledgments

Tart, Andrea Schulz, Kate Stark, Lindsay Prevette, Brianna Linden, Lydia Hirt, and Mary Stone. And thank you to Nancy Palmquist for her thorough and considerate copyediting.

Thank you to my family, and particularly my husband, Chip Brainerd, for cooking, cleaning, and parenting without complaint so that I could write.